# Smith's
## MONTHLY

*Every Month Original
Novels, Stories, and Articles*

*USA Today Bestselling Writer*
**Dean Wesley Smith**

# TABLE OF CONTENTS

# Smith's Monthly Issue #2

All Contents copyright © 2013 Dean Wesley Smith
Published by WMG Publishing
Cover and interior design copyright © 2013 WMG Publishing
Cover art copyright © by Philcold/Dreamstime.com

*Thanks for Supporting This Project!*

*Dean Wesley Smith*

## Introduction

# THE CRAZINESS CONTINUES

**ISSUE #1 OF SMITH'S MONTHLY** is live on electronic sites and spreading out to regular paper bookstores as I type this. And subscribers are being sent their copies.

It is launched. The ship has taken to flight. We haven't jumped to warp drive yet, but we're moving.

I find it simply amazing that a magazine devoted to only my stories and novels and articles is actually going to more than one issue now and seemingly heading off into many, many issues to come.

In fact, Issue #3 content is almost ready and by the time you get this I will be writing hard for the stories and novels that will be in #4. So this grand experiment is continuing on solidly.

I want to take a moment and thank those of you who subscribed to this crazy project. Your support means a great deal to me. So thank you.

## Now on to some new and fun stuff.

Between the first issue and this issue, at smithsmonthly.com we have started a new feature called "Free Story of the Week." Every week we will put up a new short story that you can go to the site and read for free.

Yeah, I said that. Every week.

I suppose I need to be careful with the word "new" in that announcement. The story will be new to you and the site, but will be an older story of mine, often one I sold to a magazine or an anthology at some point in the past. I have hundreds and hundreds of published short stories, so the weekly feature has more than enough content to continue on for some time.

But just to be very clear, unlike most of the stories in *Smith's Monthly*, which will be original and published first in the magazine, the stories on the website will be from all of my years of professional writing.

So you can follow *Smith's Monthly Weekly Free Fiction* on the website. Just another new feature to say thank you to those supporting my writing.

## Writing in Public

If you want to follow the writing process of each story and novel in every issue of this magazine, you can follow my blog at deanwesleysmith.com and read the "Writing in Public" posts.

I feel those posts are part of the fun of this magazine.

Harlan Ellison used to sit in a bookstore window and write a story on a manual typewriter. As he finished each page, he taped the page on the window for those following along outside the store to read. If you weren't lucky enough to be around the store that day, you would find the stories in major magazines or books later on.

Many, many of those stories won major awards.

As the publisher of Pulphouse Publishing, we were going to gather up all of his stories he wrote in that fashion and publish them together in a large, three-volume set called *Ellison Under Glass*. But we never got the book out because Harlan kept doing more and more of the stories.

I hope some publisher picks up that idea at some point and finishes it. There were some amazing stories in those three volumes.

So this magazine is my way of helping everyone who is following my "Writing in Public" blog find the stories quickly and easily, like pasting the pages to a window. At least you will be able to see them within a month or so of me writing the stories or novels.

And if you have no interest at all in how a writer works, ignore that part of my blog and just enjoy the stories and novels. And drop by smithsmonthly.com every week for a free story.

So now this issue continues the voyage into a new world of publishing. We are past the start. We are launched out into the wilds. Now, as the opening of the *Star Trek* television shows often said, *"... the continuing voyage..."* (Cue the voice-over music.)

I can only hope for a five-year mission with this magazine. But right now, I'm very, very happy it's a new month with all brand-new fiction.

As with the first issue, there is a new novel, four new stories, and some new chapters in ongoing stories in this issue.

I hope you'll stay with me on this journey into the unknown worlds of publishing.

As I said last month, I can promise entertaining fiction every month.

A lot of it, actually.

*Dean Wesley Smith*
*October 7, 2013,*
*Lincoln City, Oregon*

# Available in November
## from all your favorite booksellers

DEAD MONEY *could be the start of a new thriller genre—
the political poker thriller.*

—*Sheldon McArthur,
former owner of
Mysterious Books in Los Angeles*

# DEAN WESLEY SMITH

Can a simple poker player
give a ghost a reason to live?

# A NIGHT with a FORGOTTEN GOD

## A Poker Boy Story

**USA TODAY BESTSELLING WRITER** *Dean Wesley Smith returns to his most popular series that features the superhero Poker Boy and all his sidekicks.*

*Poker Boy once again finds himself facing the task of saving someone. But this person seems to be a ghost.*

*Can a simple poker player give a ghost a reason to live? If anyone can do it, Poker Boy can, all between hands of cards on a great Saturday night.*

# A NIGHT WITH A FORGOTTEN GOD
## A POKER BOY STORY

# ONE

**YOU WOULD THINK** that with all my varied superpowers, I would have one that would warn me when a really good night was about to turn into something else. Just a tingling, maybe a little buzz behind one ear, something.

But nope.

This Saturday night started off as normal as a Saturday night gets for a superhero working for the gods of gambling.

I was playing in a great no-limit game in the poker room at Spirit Winds casino. Since I was Poker Boy, and playing poker was what I also did for a living between rescuing people and saving the world, finding a good game with decent players on a Saturday night was about as good as it came.

The noise from the nearby casino was a steady background sound of people excited at the craps table and bells and alarms of slot machines.

A faint smoke smell drifted in from the casino floor where smoking was still allowed. At times I figured it was almost demanded that a person had to smoke to play a slot machine. Smoking in poker rooms had been banned a decade ago, and for that I will be forever grateful.

I had just had a snack at the free buffet that they set up in the poker room. The entire five-foot buffet was basically some crackers and cheeses and curled up vegetables of one sort or another. I stuck with the crackers and some cheese and a bottle of water. I figured that would get me to a late dinner.

The Spirit Winds poker room had fourteen tables and right now there were seven games going, with another table about to start up. The game I was in was the major game in the room, and we were tucked to one side of the big room so that people could stand and watch from the edges of the room.

Right now we had about ten people watching the play.

I loved this casino and considered it my home casino even though I spent most of my time in Las Vegas and had an invisible office floating a thousand feet over the MGM Grand Hotel and Casino. This little casino tucked off in the Oregon mountains felt like home.

I had played here before I met Stan, the God of Poker and my boss, and before I found out I was a superhero. So my roots were here.

And no one in this casino really knew anything about my alter identity as Poker Boy. They just all called me "Hat" because of the black fedora-like hat I always wore and the black leather coat. No one in Oregon knew that hat and coat was my superhero uniform that helped strengthen my superpowers.

I loved the area of the Oregon Coast Mountains so much, I was building a huge home about a mile away from here on some land I owned. Actually, Patty

Ledgerwood, aka Front Desk Girl, and I were building the home, paying a guy I had helped rescue a year or so ago.

We weren't married, but we had been an item now for years and I had a hunch the marriage thing would come at some point. We had talked about it, but since we were both superheroes, we figured taking our time wouldn't hurt. Especially since we were both basically immortal now. I still looked like I was thirty, as did all gods and superheroes. I was going on fifty in real years.

Patty wouldn't tell me her real age, but I had a hunch from some of the things she had said, she was well past one hundred years old. Thankfully, she just looked thirty as well.

The home we were building was tucked back in the trees on forty acres. When done, it would have a huge indoor pool and game room. It was being built partially out of local logs. It was costing me over two million to build and wouldn't be done for almost another year, but Patty and I loved to visit it every week or so and see the progress and just sit and stare out over the valley. The view from the new house could take your breath away at sunset and at sunrise.

Patty had been surprised I had so much money that I could afford a two-million-dollar home, and honestly I was surprised as well. I had just never really counted it up. Since I learned how to teleport, I no longer had to fly anywhere, so about all I spent my winnings on was food.

And other investments, which, it seemed, often turned out to pretty good investments.

Patty helped me figure it all out once before we started construction and the total had shocked both of us. Two million for the home wasn't going to dent how much money I had.

I had bought into the no-limit game for two hundred and in over two hours I had built that up to over a thousand. And had fun doing it, and it seemed the players around me were enjoying the game as well, which made it even better, even though they were losing.

It was still just a little before eleven in the evening. Patty worked the front desk at the MGM Grand Hotel in Vegas and I didn't have to meet her until two in the morning. So I had three more hours of play left before I had to cash out, teleport to Vegas, and go out for a late dinner with the woman of my dreams.

The noise from the nearby casino floor for a moment seemed to suddenly fade, then came back again strong.

I glanced around, but no else had noticed and I could see or feel no reason for anything like that to happen.

And none of my warning senses were going off at all.

Weird, just weird.

Then, out of the corner of my eye I caught a glimpse of a guy standing to one side of the room, just watching the game.

But he wasn't really there. More like a ghost.

I could see the wall right through him without a problem.

My wonderful Saturday night had just taken a turn onto a new road. Which road would depend on what the ghost wanted.

# TWO

NOW, I HAD come to believe in a lot of things since becoming a superhero, such as aliens, old races of Titans, and powerful gods of math. But I still hadn't heard a word that ghosts were real, and I kind of still doubted they were.

With one eye on the ghost, I took myself out of time.

Around me the noise of the casino shut off, leaving the entire place instantly silent.

And everyone froze in the instant.

People's faces do not belong frozen in an instant. It twists them all up into something not natural or attractive.

Jumping into an instant of time felt like I was actually stopping time, but all I was doing was moving into an instant.

Time was still going on just fine and I hadn't stopped anything. I just existed outside of the flow of time.

I stood and headed toward the ghost.

He was frozen as well, his attention focused on the table I had been playing at. He wore an old-fashioned dark cloth shirt, dark cloth pants, and a wide rope belt. Over that he had what looked like an 1800s dress jacket. He had short dark hair and no beard at all.

He stood not more than five foot tall and he looked around thirty or so.

I studied him for a moment, not having a clue what to do next.

I could see right through him, of that there was no doubt. And from the looks of a woman's face standing about five feet away, she had noticed him as well just as I froze time.

So it wasn't just my powers that saw him.

I had no idea what to do, so when that happened, I did the most logical thing.

"Stan!" I shouted at the ceiling.

I have no idea why I always shouted his name and why it was at the ceiling. Just an old habit from my first days as a superhero when I was calling for him all the time it seemed.

He appeared between me and the ghost looking like the God of Poker always looked. He had on tan slacks, a tan shirt, a slightly darker sweater without an identifying mark on any of it. His hair was cut perfectly and his face always neutral. He stood exactly five-ten, not too short and not too tall. And he seldom smiled, although over the years I had seen him shocked a few times and smile a few other times.

In other words, he was the kind of guy who could walk by you in a hallway and most people would never remember anyone walked past them.

"Winning?" he asked.

"Of course," I said.

"So what's the problem?"

I pointed to the short ghost standing behind him.

Stan turned and then just shook his head.

"What is it?" I asked.

"Not what, who. That's Ben."

"So he's not a ghost?"

Stan shook his head and I felt relieved.

"Nope, he's a god."

## THREE

**OF ALL THE THINGS** Stan could have told me about the nearly invisible guy wearing rumpled old-style clothing, the fact that he was a god stunned me.

And as a god, he had let me get out of time and approach him. All the gods I had met, and that was no small number, were able to sense when someone slipped out of time around them.

"So what's he the god of?" I asked.

"Lamplighters," Stan said, his voice sad.

"Lamplighters? What's that?"

"And thus the reason for his condition," Stan said. "His entire area is being forgotten. Lamplighters used to be a huge number of men, and a few women, who went around city or town streets all over the world and lit the lamps. They reached the height of their profession in the gas-lamp era."

"There was a god for that?" I asked.

Stan gave me a dirty look. "I'm the God of Poker. There's a god for everything."

I looked at Ben the god ghost and finally caught a clue. When a god's area went away, eventually the god did as well.

"How come he couldn't shift to another area?" I asked.

"Some are able to," Stan said. "Some would rather just fade away as their area of expertise does with time."

"So what's he doing here?" I asked.

Stan shrugged. "Let's ask him."

A moment later Ben realized he had been taken out of time and that Stan and I stood there staring at him.

"Stan," Ben said, his voice not much more than a distant whisper even though he seemed to be talking normally. If we hadn't been out of time and the casino completely silent, I never would have been able to hear him.

"Ben, great seeing you again," Stan said. "Haven't found a new area that interests you yet, I am gathering?"

Ben held up his nearly see-through arms and laughed. "Yeah, pretty obvious. You know there are less than one hundred professional lamplighters left in the world?"

I almost said I was surprised there were that many, but I managed to keep my mouth shut and let Stan do the talking to someone he clearly knew out of the past.

"So what are you doing here?" Stan asked.

Ben sort of half-pointed at me. "Since I have a lot of time on my hands, I've been following Poker Boy and his team and all the good work all of you are doing. And how many times the team has saved all of us."

I nodded my thanks and again kept my mouth shut.

Stan did the same thing, so Ben went on in his whisper-sounding voice.

"So I wanted to come and see if I could get a chance to ask Poker Boy what area of expertise his team was missing and I would move in that direction with the hope that in a few hundred years or so I might have enough of my powers back to be able to help out in a crisis or two."

Areas we lacked?

I honestly hadn't given that any thought.

Not one.

The team consisted of Patty, aka Front Desk Girl who had the ability to calm anyone into a smile, including me in the most stressful of times.

Screamer was an original member. He could link people's minds together and read thoughts.

We had Smoke, part wolf, part human, who could walk through walls and sense and smell things from great distances.

Madge, a superhero in the area of food service, added in her keen eye and ability to cut right to the point of something. Plus she made the best milkshakes ever made on the planet.

And then there was Stan, my boss, a god who seemed to know almost everyone, kept us all balanced, and knew were to go for help when we needed it.

We had a few others who had helped on certain missions, but that was the core. What were we missing?

A very good question.

And clearly a question that just might save Ben's life. But, one thing I didn't know about Ben. Did the powers-that-be want him saved? I had met my share of gods and not all of them were liked.

Maybe Ben's demise was something no one wanted to stop.

"That's very flattering," I said to Ben. "And let me think for a minute. And I'm going to need to talk with Stan, if you don't mind, since he's my boss in all this."

Ben smiled and meekly waved. "Oh, sure, no problem. Thanks for even considering my crazy question."

With that Stan put Ben back frozen, and we turned and walked away, weaving between the people stuck in real time in varied poses.

The silence was intense and I wanted to make sure Ben couldn't hear my next question to Stan.

Finally Stan stopped near the tiny buffet of crackers and cheese and browning lettuce, frowned at it in clear disgust, and then turned to me.

"What's he like and can he hear us?" I asked.

"He barely has enough power to maintain his essence in the world," Stan said. "He can't hear us. And he's a very, very nice man, from everything I heard and know about him."

"So people would welcome him being saved?"

Stan nodded. "I don't think he has an enemy anywhere, and that's saying something with gods."

I agreed with that. I had seen more bickering and feuding among the gods than I would have seen watching kids play on a playground during recess. With great power and years of age comes great pettiness, it seemed.

"Why didn't he just move around into other areas of city government?" I asked Stan, glancing back at the ghost.

"He doesn't interact well with people," Stan said. "He's very shy and not strong enough for management, not physically able to handle something like garbage, and besides, there just aren't a lot of slots sometimes for a god to move to."

"So he just stayed where he was and the world went past," I said.

"Exactly," Stan said.

"I wonder what he's been doing with his time for the last hundred years?"

Stan just shrugged.

My little voice, which was part of my superpowers, kind of dinged me. The answer to Ben's problem had something to do with what he had been doing since electricity started lighting city streets.

"Let's go ask him," I said.

Stan looked puzzled, but just shrugged why not.

I turned back and weaved my way in and around the frozen people.

As we got close, Stan brought Ben out of time and into the silence of our little bubble.

Before Ben could say anything, I asked him point blank. "What have you been doing to fill your time over the last one hundred years?"

He looked down at the floor, clearly embarrassed. Then he said even softer than normal, "I read."

"Read?" I asked. "Read what?"

"Everything," he said, clearly a glow filling him slightly. "I love books, all sorts of books. I love bookstores, libraries, everything about any form of books. I even love the new electronic books."

He reached into a pocket of his loose old jacket and pulled out an electronic reader.

I glanced at Stan who seemed as shocked as I felt, but it was hard to get a read on the emotions of the God of Poker.

"How much do you remember about what you read?" I asked.

"Everything," he said. "My memory is photographic, even slipping away like this. I know which book I read what in and when and who the author was and everything. I own a large castle outside of London and it's completely full of books. I guess you would say I'm a hoarder."

I flat didn't want to think about an entire castle full of ancient books. I could easily see his passion was everything books and reading. Everything.

"When did you start this reading?"

"Gutenberg invented the press and it wasn't long after that. But I also have collected and read a lot of old scrolls and have spent many a wonderful day in the Library of Alexandria."

"That still exists?" I asked, stunned.

Beside me Stan said, "Oh, sure."

Ben nodded.

Damn I had a lot to learn about history and the gods and everything else. I really hated always being the young and stupid one in a conversation among old gods and superheroes.

Then it dawned on me what I had just thought.

Knowledge. If my team had the knowledge of history stored in Ben's head, we would be a ton stronger.

A million times stronger, actually.

I turned to Stan. "Is there a god of books, a god of libraries, a god of bookstores?"

"Yes, yes, and yes," Stan said.

"Can a god go back to being a superhero if there are no spots open?"

"Sure," Stan said, nodding and thinking.

"Good," I said. "We need to find a spot somewhere in the book world for Ben, because we need him now on the team."

Ben looked stunned and Stan just smiled.

I looked at Ben feeling how lucky we all were that all the knowledge that Ben had gathered had not just faded away with him.

"I'll be right back," Stan said.

He vanished and I smiled at Ben, who was looking stunned and very shy. I could see why he hadn't been able to stay in the city government world of gods.

"I don't understand," he said, looking up at me.

"Do you trust me?" I asked.

He nodded.

"Do you love books and reading?"

"More than anything in the world."

"And you can remember everything you've read?"

"Everything."

I nodded. "Then the team needs you now, not a hundred years from now. So we just got to get you out of this fading-away state."

Ben was about to say something when Stan reappeared with a striking woman in a white blouse, long black skirt, and black glasses. Her shiny black hair was pulled back and tied in a bun to the back of her head. She was short, maybe five-two at the most, but she radiated power.

A lot of power, actually.

She saw Ben and instantly put a hand over her mouth in shock. "Oh, my, Ben, what's happened? You didn't move from the lamplighter position, did you?"

He just shook his head and looked down at the ground, ashamed.

"Baalat, I'd like you to meet Poker Boy," Stan said. "Poker Boy, this is Baalat, the god of all reading and books."

She turned to me and smiled. I managed to bow slightly and she extended her hand and I shook it. Her skin felt smooth and firm and her grip firm as well.

"I have heard so much about your team," she said. "We all owe you so much."

"Thank you," I said. Then somehow I managed to focus my attention away from one of the most powerful and stunning gods I had yet to meet and back to the problem at hand.

"Ben has a photographic memory for everything he has ever read since books were invented."

"You do?" Baalat asked Ben directly, looking at the ghost of a man.

Ben nodded and said nothing, still staring at the ground at his feet.

So I kept going, pitching his case. "And Ben has been reading scrolls as well from before books. And he loves electronic books. He tells me he loves all books, no matter what type or shape. He loves reading. Period."

"Is this true?" Baalat asked, looking away from me and back at Ben.

Ben this time looked up and nodded, staring into her eyes. "Completely. It's all I ever do is read. I haven't had much work to do for a very long time."

I went on. "The knowledge he holds of history and facts and lost arts in that photographic mind would be invaluable to my team and some of the major problems we face. But he needs to have a position somewhere that will allow him to regain strength. Stan and I are hoping you might have that spot available, and let him have the time to work with my team as well."

Baalat smiled at me and I darned near melted. "Poker Boy, you are as amazing as everyone says."

Then thankfully, before my knees gave out under the high-wattage smile, she turned to Ben.

"Would you like to work for me as one of the Gods of Reading and Books?"

I thought Ben was going to turn into a ghost child right in front of us, his smile was so big. "I would so much enjoy that?"

"So we need to get you transferred, but I don't think your old boss will much care, do you?"

"He's been pushing me for fifty years to find something," Ben said.

"Good," Baalat said.

Then she turned to me. "As soon as I get Ben squared away and trained in some of his new duties, I'll have him contact you."

"Thank you," I said. "But please not too long. If something big comes up, we're going to need him."

Baalat smiled. "When you need him, he will be there."

She nodded to Stan and then she and Ben vanished.

"Looks like we have a new team member," I said, smiling at Stan.

He just shook his head and patted me on the shoulder, smiling. "Now I understand why you also save stray dogs."

And with that he was gone.

I headed back over to the table, sat back down and released myself back into the flow of time.

The sounds of the casino smashed in around me.

And the wonderful Saturday night went on.

Then, to one side of the table, I caught something out of the corner of my eye.

It was ghost Ben standing there, smiling at me.

And then I saw his lips move as he clearly said, "Thank you."

And then he vanished.

And the very next hand the dealer dealt me pocket aces, so I knew Lady Luck was smiling as well.

---

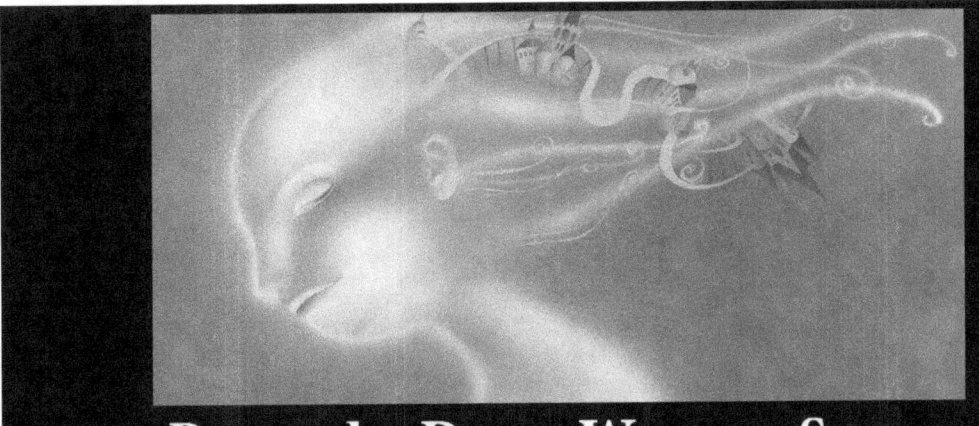

**Poems by DEAN WESLEY SMITH**

# A Comic Collector

On my hands and knees on the concrete floor,
I reach back for the Ziploc-bagged comic book
tucked behind the toy truck,
next to the stack of white china plates.

I have found an antique mall treasure,
a 1940 Dick Tracy comic book,
a 16 page giveaway for a shoe company
that no longer existed when I was born.

I smile at the dealer's stupidity,
the price just seven bucks.
I know the Comic Guide value will be well over
one hundred in the comic's current condition.

My knees hurt, my wife pretends to be happy for me,
I take the comic home, put it in a good bag,
file it with my other comics, and store it in a dark place.
I may look at it again once more before I die.

USA *Today* Bestselling Writer

# DEAN WESLEY
# SMITH

Sometimes
the past
haunts you.

# A PITY ABOUT THE
# DELUSION

*USA TODAY* **BESTSELLING WRITER** *Dean Wesley Smith returns to his acclaimed world of the novel* Dust and Kisses *with a side adventure.*

*Mandi Meyers wants to find her parents' bodies. So she takes a trip to their home outside of Portland, Oregon, only to find impossible, yet familiar things.*

*Sometimes we all must learn that nothing with parents ever changes.*

# A PITY ABOUT THE DELUSION

## ONE

**MANDI MEYERS TURNED** the big, white Ford Explorer SUV onto Bryant Street and drove slowly past all the suburban homes that were damn hard to tell apart. Luckily, most of them had big numbers attached to the wall beside the standard two-car garage door.

She was looking for 1622, which would be on her right side.

All the lawns had once been beautiful, but now were patches of weeds, brown and dead now that it was summer and hot. All the cars left on the street were parked in the driveways or along the curbs. There clearly hadn't been that many people in this neighborhood home when the world ended. She figured that most everyone here had jobs in downtown Portland and had died there, their cars more than likely parked in a transit-station parking lot.

The few that had died here on Bryant Street in that mid-morning were either self-employed or the parent that stayed home with the kids. But school in this town had already started in late August when the world ended, so she doubted there would be many kids' bodies here either, even though this neighborhood was clearly one for young families.

She was used to mummified bodies in cars and along sidewalks, still in the same positions where they had fallen three years before. It felt strange to not see any bodies at all.

And if not for the weeds and brown lawns from the summer heat, she wouldn't have been able to tell anything at all was wrong with this subdivision.

When the world ended, she had been working for the United States Air Force after finishing college. She had been twenty-three that day three years ago and had survived because she was working about thirty feet underground when the electromagnetic pulse hit the Earth and killed everyone who wasn't inside protection.

No one knew the pulse was coming from space. One minute the world had billions of people, the next there were only millions left, most scattered across the planet wondering what had happened.

Many of the survivors killed themselves shortly after the first wave of deaths or went insane, unable to come to grips with everyone they loved being dead. But Mandi had been single and young. When the wave hit, her parents, her only family, had just moved to a small town in the Portland, Oregon metropolitan area.

She actually hadn't seen them for a number of years, so she really didn't miss them that much.

She had stayed with the other survivors in her unit and slowly, over time, a form of national organization started to come back together.

It seemed a lot of people in the military had survived, and a lot of people in subways and in tunnels and so on. And everyone wanted to rebuild before too much was lost.

Now, there was a national plan to restart five cities in the country and Portland had been picked as one of those cities because of its nearness to clean water, its long growing season, and mild winters. She had volunteered to come here and live and work.

Mostly she had picked Portland because she knew she would find the time to finally deal with her parents.

She had arrived last week in the first wave and had been too busy setting up everything for the thousands more that would follow to try to get here, to her parents' home, before now.

So finally, after three years of wondering, it was time for her to face the loss of her family. She had always known they would be dead, but seeing them was another matter. She needed to do that, then at some point get help coming here to bury them.

Her best friend, Donna, had offered to come along to her parents' new home on this first trip, but Mandi had declined, saying she needed to do this herself. She didn't even know if they had been home that morning of the electromagnetic wave.

If not, her parents were somewhere in the city and were going to be tough to find among all the bodies. But since the new government was working to give every body a decent burial and record what information was with the body, she might find them eventually.

Donna had been really, really worried about her coming alone. She said what little Mandi had said about her parents had not been complimentary. But Mandi had insisted she would be fine.

It had taken her almost an hour from downtown Portland to work her way out here into the suburb city called Lake Oswego. Part of the way the big freeway had been cleared by her people.

And part of the way she had been forced to use the police bumper attached to the big SUV front to gently nudge a car or two out of the way.

But now this suburban street was clear.

The winding street turned to her right and then wound back to the left.

She was getting close. Then, as she came around a gentle bend in the street she could see her parents' home.

The lawn was green.

Flowers were growing in the flowerbed along the sidewalk.

*That wasn't possible.*

# TWO

**MANDI STOPPED THE CAR** and closed her eyes, then opened them again.

The lawn was still green among rows of brown lawns and the flowers were clearly being watered.

From military satellites, she knew that only two people had been living in downtown Portland itself, and there were scattered survivors living out in the suburbs, but she hadn't really paid any attention to see if any of those survivors lived close to her parents' address.

Let alone their very address.

She shook her head to try to clear it, but the green grass and flowers remained.

She pulled the big SUV over near the front of the house and sat there, shaking.

Then she took a couple of deep breaths.

She had to think and be clear or this could turn out very ugly.

She had no idea who was in that house or how sane they might be. She leaned over and took out the loaded service pistol she had put in the glove box of the big car.

Donna had insisted on that just in case.

With the pistol in one hand, she slowly climbed out of the big SUV and into the heat of the later afternoon sun. She tucked the pistol in the back of her jeans and ran her hands through her short, brown hair.

She had kept it short for the last three years since it was just easier to keep clean and take care of.

The green lawn was still there in front of her parents' house, as impossible as it was.

She moved slowly up the walk towards the front door, some of her basic training coming back in.

She moved slowly, one hand on the gun, as she scanned the neighborhood, looking for anyone watching her.

Nothing moving at all in the heat.

Except for this one house, the neighborhood was dead.

She reached the front porch and rang the bell, feeling so numb she couldn't believe any of this was possible.

Was she having a hallucination?

Had she gotten sick on the way out here, or was she having some sort of reaction to actually finally seeing her parents dead?

She had no idea who was going to answer that door or what kind of reception she was going to get. For all she knew, one of her parents had survived and had gone completely crazy in three years and wouldn't even recognize her.

After a moment the door handle turned and the door swung open.

Her father stood there, trim and fit and looking younger than she remembered him.

And he was as naked as the day he was born, with a drink in one hand.

She forced herself to look only into his eyes.

Music drifted from the inside of the house and Mandi could smell the wonderful odor of baking cookies.

"Hey, Mandi," her father said, smiling at her. "Glad you could make it. Come on in."

She started to open her mouth, but she knew she could say nothing.

That was not the response she had expected at all.

"Don't let all the cold air out," he said, standing back from the door. "It's hot enough in here as it is."

He laughed at that for some reason.

It was a saying he always had said when she was growing up with them in Southern California.

She nodded to him and stepped through the door.

He shut the door behind her.

The cool, air-conditioned air felt wonderful after the heat outside.

And all the lights were on.

Somehow her father must have set up a generator to run the lights and the air-conditioning.

The home looked standard, right out of the 1990s, just as their home had been when she was growing up. Couches were nice brown cloth and the carpeting tan. A large-screen television sat in a large entertainment center on one wall, and two recliners faced that area.

There was a large dining area off the living room with an oak table with ten matching wooden chairs. A wide, carpeted hallway disappeared off to the right. It must go off to bathrooms and bedrooms.

This was a nice, spacious suburban home, nicely furnished and kept clean.

Then from the kitchen area off the dining room, Mandi's mother shouted, "Who is it, dear?"

"Come see," her father said, smiling at her. "Mandi has decided to join the party."

Mandi recognized that phrase, but darned if she could place it.

Her mother came out of the kitchen, also totally nude and thinner than Mandi remembered.

Her mom smiled at her. "Glad you could make it, dear. Jim, get her a drink before the other guests get out of the pool."

Mandi again just opened her mouth, then closed it.

What the hell could she even say?

It had been three years since the world had ended. Yet her parents seemed to think everything was normal and there were other guests in the pool.

And why were they standing around naked.

And why weren't they excited to see her?

It felt more like she had just stepped back in time, into her own past. There was so much of that past she had pushed away and forgotten. This felt like part of it.

But that wasn't possible.

She could feel the room spinning some, so she moved over to a chair at the kitchen table and dropped into it.

Her mother smiled at her and went back into the kitchen while her father went to the bar in one corner of the family room and started working on a drink for her.

Neither of them made any movement to cover up their nakedness in front of her.

At that moment, the sliding back door to the kitchen area opened and four other naked people walked in, all of them in their late twenties, all of them laughing and dripping wet.

Somewhere, in her distant memory, she recognized them.

All of them.

"This can't be happening," she said to herself, shaking her head.

She closed her eyes, but the laughing and the voices continued.

"Not feeling well, dear?" her father asked. "It's okay if you just go back to your room."

"Sure is," her mom said, coming in and putting a plate of chocolate chip cookies on the kitchen table.

The four other nude people gathered around, each grabbing a cookie.

"You better get a couple of those before they're gone," her father said, winking at her.

Then all of the naked people went into the living room and sat down, laughing

---

*Sometimes a lost gold mine offers up more than just gold. And sometimes a secret should remain a secret.*

*A generational science fiction story from* USA Today *bestselling writer Dean Wesley Smith.*

*A version of this story by Dean Wesley Smith first appeared in* The Secret Prophecies of Nostradamus *edited by Cynthia Sternau and Martin H. Greenberg.*

*Now available in audio, paperback, and electronic editions from your favorite bookseller.*

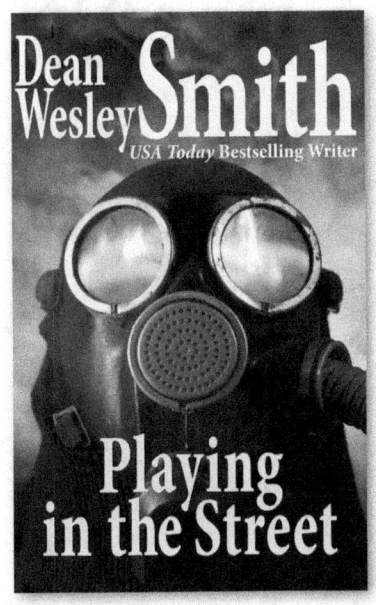

and talking while Mandi sat at the kitchen table, stunned.

She put her head down on the hard wood, jammed her eyes closed as she used to do when she was a young girl and didn't want to see or know something her parents were doing, and just let the voices and the scene of six naked people sitting around fade away.

# THREE

**THE NEXT THING** Mandi knew, a hand was gently touching her shoulder.

"Mandi? Mandi?" the voice whispered. "Are you all right?"

She pushed back from the table, stunned, almost tipping her chair over in the process.

The house was dark and hot and smelled like a tomb. She had dust on her hands and, she was sure, on her face where she had put her head on the dusty tabletop.

Donna stood there with Henry Stevens, one of the main contractors working on getting the airport back up and running. Both of them had flashlights tied to their heads and another in one hand.

"I got worried when you didn't come back," Donna said, "so Henry and I came to see if you were all right."

"How long have I been gone?" Mandi asked, trying to brush herself off.

"Seven hours," Donna said.

Mandi nodded and stood.

Donna handed her a flashlight and Mandi went out into the living room.

Six bodies were there, on the couch and chairs, none of them wearing clothes.

They had basically become mummies in the heat of the house.

Donna recognized her father in a big recliner and her mother sitting next to another man on the couch.

"My mother, my father," Mandi said, shining a light on the two grinning skeletons as a way of introducing them to Donna and Henry.

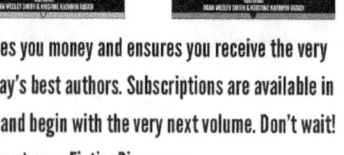

Mandi just shook her head, staring at the scene. It had been just after eight in the morning on a weekday when the electromagnetic wave hit and killed most everyone. And yet her parents, even here in Portland, even at the age of forty, were still up to their old games.

"Do you know these other four?" Henry asked.

"More than likely neighbors," Mandi said. "Over for a morning of sex and mate-swapping, more than likely, considering none of them are dressed."

Donna glanced at her, a very worried look in her eyes.

"Don't worry," Mandi said, smiling at her friend. "I dealt with my parents' behavior a long time ago, when I was very young. I had forgotten it until now."

"Wow," Henry said, shaking his head. "Way beyond my comfort level."

Both Donna and Mandi nodded.

It had always been beyond Mandi's comfort level. She had grown up with naked adults coming and going at all hours and the sounds of sex coming from strange places in the house. It was no wonder she wasn't interested in sex or getting married.

She was really going to need some help getting past that childhood, if she ever could.

Maybe seeing them like this would help.

Maybe.

With one last look at her parents, she said, "Let's get out of here. Let them have their party. For them, it was the perfect way to leave the planet."

She went toward the front door and waited until Henry and Donna were outside ahead of her. Then with one last look at the six naked mummified bodies in the suburban house, she said what she had always said to her parents when they told her they were "getting together with friends."

"Have fun."

As she pulled the door closed, she thought she caught the sound of laughter and ice in a glass making a clicking sound as someone drank for courage.

Or maybe that was just her memory.

~

USA *Today* Bestselling Writer

# DEAN WESLEY SMITH

THE LIFE AND TIMES OF
BUFFALO JIMMY

Chapters 4-6

## WHAT CAME BEFORE...

**NINETEEN-YEAR-OLD** *Boston native Jimmy Gray had been traveling with his parents and older brother, Luke, headed west to find a new home and new riches.*

*Before even reaching Independence, they were attacked and robbed by Jake Benson and his gang. Jimmy's parents were killed, his brother wounded.*

*In one of the wildest towns in all of American history, Jimmy Gray, a sheltered, educated son of a banker from Boston, suddenly finds himself very, very much alone.*

# THE LIFE AND TIMES OF BUFFALO JIMMY

## SOME HISTORICAL BACKGROUND

**IN THE SUMMER OF 1866,** *the country was just starting to recover from the Civil War. Thousands of families were moving west for the promises of free homestead land and the dreams of becoming rich by finding gold or silver. All the men and their families went by wagon company, leaving Independence, Missouri in the spring in hopes of making it over the mountains into California or Oregon before the winter snows.*

*The trip took seven months or longer of crossing deserts, mountains, and rivers, and fighting either the storms or blazing heat. It was a rare family that made it all the way without death touching them in one way or another. Most of the time, those who did make the end of the trail arrived only with what they could carry, since they often had to leave their family possessions along the trail at one point or another.*

*Also, in 1866, thousands of professional soldiers released from the Civil War were headed west, often still in the mood to kill anyone they didn't agree with.*

*Add to that the fact that the different tribes of Native Americans were still scattered in their original homelands and were becoming very resentful of all the white settlers.*

*The Seventh Calvary, released from the war, had been assigned to go west and take care of that "problem."*

*The giant buffalo herds were being killed off for their skins and to starve out the Native American tribes that depended on them to survive.*

*The railroads were starting construction from both ends, but were still years away from meeting up in a transcontinental line. The Butterfield Stage line, for a few short years, tried to serve as a postal and passenger carrier on the mail trails, but the ride was so rough inside the stages that no one ever traveled that way and the stage line soon went out of business.*

*There was no law in the west except inside the larger towns and western cities, and then it was hit or miss. The west was a place of survival of the fittest. The good people did their best to keep order, and when circumstances got too bad, the good people formed vigilante groups and made the law themselves.*

*1866 in the American West was one of the most interesting places and times in all of American history.*

## Part Four
# LUKE'S CONDITION

**THE NEXT DAY,** Doc Davis had said that there was no improvement in Luke's health, and he didn't really know what was wrong.

And he said the same thing the next day as well. "He just needs to rest."

The two days had been filled with rain and cold winds. Jimmy had spent much of the last two days either sitting beside Luke's bed, or searching carefully around town for Benson, walking in the rain with his hat pulled down to hide his face.

Jimmy had decided that he couldn't constantly hide from Benson. It would be better if Jimmy found the killer first, and kept track of him. As long as he was in town, or with the hundreds of wagons camped out on the plain, he would be somewhat safe. But he and Luke would be a lot safer if he knew where Benson was. And if Jimmy did find him, when Luke got better, they would be able to tell the sheriff what Benson had done, and get him arrested.

During the two days, Jimmy had come to know the town of Independence pretty well, including which parts were just too dangerous for him to get near. It seemed even bigger than he had first thought. When he asked one shopkeeper how many people were here, the man had laughed and said, "At what moment? This time of the year, there has to be a hundred thousand people here and out in that sea of wagons."

How was Jimmy ever going to find one man in a city that size? It seemed impossible. And he didn't feel comfortable going into the saloons, at least not without Luke at his side. So finally, he just decided he would stand with his hat low on his forehead where he could see five or six of the biggest saloon's front doors and watch for Benson.

Jimmy knew he had to play this smart if he was going to get the justice his parents deserved and stay alive doing so. It was like a big game, with life and death as the stakes, and he was doing the best he could.

On the morning of the third day, the sun came back out enough to make the air thick and steamy. The muddy streets mixed with horse manure smelled even worse, if that was possible. Somehow, the town's people had gotten used to the smell, but Jimmy had grown up in Boston, where they paved the streets for the most part, and kept them mostly clean.

Jimmy tied up his horse at his normal spot on the side street just down from the doctor's office. With the sun out, laughter echoed everywhere along the main street. And everyone was moving at a more frantic pace, if that was possible.

Dozens of smaller trains had been leaving every day since he had arrived. A couple of the really big trains, with upwards of a hundred wagons each, were getting ready to head out, and that made him even more worried about what he was going to do next.

He had a wagon and five horses he needed to take care of. The Tasker family had been watching them while he was visiting Luke. He didn't have any help after they left.

"Hi, little brother," Luke said, smiling as Jimmy walked into the back room of the Doc's office. Luke was sitting up in bed, and seemed to have some color in his face.

Jimmy felt his mood soar even more. Suddenly, it felt like the weight of the world had lifted from his shoulders. He wanted to rush forward and just hug Luke, but somehow he stopped himself and just stood beside the bed smiling.

"He's doing better," Doc Davis said to Jimmy. "But for now, I want him to stay right here where I can watch him. He's very weak and a long way from being recovered. And with all the cholera going around, I wouldn't want him to get that in his condition."

"Thanks, Doc," Jimmy said.

Luke smiled. "Yes, thank you, for everything. Especially that young nurse you have helping you."

Doc Davis glared at Luke. "That's my daughter."

Luke's face went back to pale.

Then Doc Davis laughed a deep, rich laugh that filled the room, patted Jimmy on the shoulder again, and left, still laughing.

*How was Jimmy ever going to find one man in a city that size? It seemed impossible.*

"He got you with that one," Jimmy said, also laughing.

"Yeah, he did," Luke said. "But she's still cute as a Sunday bonnet."

Jimmy pulled up a chair beside Luke's bed and with Luke leading the questioning, he filled in his big brother on what had happened over the last few days since they got to Independence, what the town was like, what the vast camp for wagons looked like.

The conversation felt wonderful and Jimmy was sure it was the longest the two of them had talked in a long time.

"I've been looking for Benson," Jimmy finally said, worried about what his big brother would say.

Luke looked suddenly serious and worried. "Jimmy, he and that gang of his are cold-blooded killers. I don't want you doing anything until I'm with you."

Jimmy laughed. "You don't have to worry about that. I'm just trying to find him. I won't let him see me if I do."

"Good," Luke said, sighing. "I'll be getting better soon, I promise." He settled down into the bed a little more. He was again looking tired and pale.

Jimmy pushed his chair back. "I'll let you rest and be back later this afternoon." He patted his brother's shoulder. "Glad you decided to stick around."

"Yeah, me too little brother. Me too."

## Part Five
# FINDING FRIENDS

**JIMMY PULLED HIS HAT DOWN** low to hide his face some, then walked out of the doc's office and into the warm, morning air, the spring back in his step. He almost felt like whistling. Pretty soon Luke would be back on his feet and helping him. And that was the best news he had had in a week. He wouldn't be alone.

He moved up the crowded sidewalk to a spot where he could see the front doors of five of the major saloons along the street, all doing a noisy business even this early in the morning. Through the windows of the closest one, he could see two card games going on, and a dozen men standing at a long bar.

He moved to the inside of the sidewalk and leaned against the rough wood wall of a lawyer's office, out of the way of all the hustle and bustle of people filling up their wagons from the dozen general stores along the street. If his mother and father had lived, more than likely he would be one of those people busy filling saddlebags and wagons with provisions.

"Which wagon you working?" a voice asked beside him.

He spun around, ready to run, his heart beating wildly in his chest. A young guy about his age was leaning against the wall. At first, Jimmy thought the blond-headed guy was older, but then his blue eyes told him he was about Jimmy's age. He had his long hair tied back and wore a buckskin jacket that clearly had seen some wear.

"I don't have a wagon here in town," Jimmy said, letting out the air he had been holding and trying to not let the guy see how scared he had been. "Just looking for someone."

The kid laughed. "I told Truitt you weren't competition. But he wanted me to ask."

"Competition for what?" Jimmy asked.

"Working the wagons," the guy said, as if Jimmy should know what that meant. "You got a family?"

"A sick brother in Doc Davis's back room," Jimmy said.

"So you're alone," the guy said, nodding. "So am I. So is my friend Truitt." The guy stuck out his hand. "I'm Zach. Zach Roy."

"Jimmy Tyler," he said, smiling at finally meeting someone besides the doc. "So, what's *working a wagon* mean?"

"Watch," Zach said and pointed at an open-topped wagon being pulled by two horses. The wagon's horses had been tied off just down the street from Hill and Stevens General Store. As Jimmy watched, a young man with chopped up brown hair and pants that were too short for him approached the wagon from along the street side, seeming to wade effortlessly in the mud.

"That's Truitt," Zach said. "Watch him closely. He's a master at working a wagon."

There was no one near the wagon. The owners must have been in the store.

Truitt had clearly timed his arrival near the stopped wagon as another wagon passed close by. As the second wagon went by, Truitt seemed to be knocked against the stopped wagon as if he had been grazed.

He caught himself against the wagon, and then almost faster than Jimmy could follow, Truitt had a bag from the back of the wagon under his arm and was heading across the street and toward a side street as if he'd always had the bag with him, walking as if nothing was different.

"Looks like a bag of beans," Zach said, smiling. "That will keep us eating for a few weeks."

"You're stealing food?" Jimmy said, turning to face Zach.

Zach just smiled and shrugged. "When you have no money, you do what you have to do."

Jimmy started to say something, then stopped. He had come very close to being in Independence without money as well. If Benson had found his father's secret stash, Jimmy would right now be thinking about how to get food and pay Doc Davis for treating Luke.

"You don't have a family?" Jimmy asked Zach as Truitt disappeared safely down the side street with his prize.

"All my family, my parents, my girl died of the cholera in St. Louis a few months back," Zach said, his voice level and cold. "I promised my dad before he died that I'd head west, carry on with the family dream. So far, this is as far as I've got."

"What about Truitt?" Jimmy asked.

Zach shrugged. "He's alone and won't talk much about it. So, since you're not working the wagons, who are you looking for?"

Jimmy decided that he could trust Zach. He didn't really know him, but he felt like he did, and for now, that was enough.

"I'm looking for the man and his gang who killed my parents. Shot my mother in the back. Two days ride back toward St. Louis."

"Oh," Zach said. "What do you plan on doing when you find him?"

"At the moment, nothing," Jimmy said. "But eventually, when my brother gets well, we'll somehow make him pay for what he's done, report him to the sheriff or something."

"Well, it's a plan," was all Zach said.

## Part Six
# BUILDING A GANG

**LUKE'S HEALTH** seemed to level over the next two days. He didn't get better, but he didn't get worse, either. They had talked a lot about different things, including what to do with the wagon and horses when the Tasker family left. So far, they hadn't come up with any solution.

Each day, while looking for Benson, Jimmy had run into Zach and Truitt. He had come to like them both, but refused to help them work a wagon. He didn't much like the idea of stealing, and at the moment he didn't need to in order to eat and take care of Luke.

It was on the afternoon of the second day, when there weren't enough wagons on the street to make it safe to work them, that a new opportunity arose. Two drunks had staggered out of a bar and gone down a narrow alley to either be sick or pass out. To Jimmy's surprise, the moment Zach and Truitt saw the two drunks, they laughed and said almost together, "Time to roll a drum."

Jimmy decided he actually didn't want to know what that meant, so he stayed in his spot watching the saloon doors while Zach and Truitt moved across the muddy street and to the alley that cut between two buildings. It was too narrow for a wagon and it looked like it held nothing but garbage and broken furniture from a nearby bar.

As Jimmy watched, Zach and Truitt approached the two drunks. Zach said something, then reached down to touch the one drunk. The next moment, the man had a gun in his hand faster than Jimmy could ever imagine being possible. And especially amazing for a man who seemed as drunk as that man looked.

Without losing his aim, the man climbed to his feet to face Zach.

The second man grabbed Truitt and held on while Zach backed against the wall, his hands in the air. Clearly, the two drunks knew what *rolling a drum* meant, and didn't much like it.

Jimmy started across the muddy street, not really sure what he was going to do to help, but Zach and Truitt had become his friends, so he had to help them somehow. His stomach twisted into a knot, but he kept walking, trying to think of anything that might set them free.

As he entered the alleyway, the smell of mold and vomit washed over him and made his stomach even tighter. He could hear one of the drunks threatening to shoot Zach. Some men were fun drunks, others got mean. Jimmy had seen them both in Boston. Clearly, this man was one of the mean ones.

The other drunk held Truitt pinned tight against the wood wall. This situation was going to get downright deadly in about ten seconds if Jimmy didn't do something.

And fast.

"Deputy Roy," Jimmy said loudly, pretending nothing was wrong as he walked toward the man with the gun. "Want me to call the sheriff? Seems you're having a little trouble with getting these two drunks out of this alley. But I will say, this will be a might embarrassing letting these two get the drop on you."

Zach, not missing a beat, laughed. "It sure is."

"You're going to be *dead* embarrassed, mister," the drunk holding Zach said, putting the gun under Zach's chin. "You was gonna rob me."

Jimmy decided right at that moment that he was really starting to hate guns, but he managed to laugh. "And why would you want to go and be hanged for killing a deputy on such a wonderful spring day?"

"This guy ain't no deputy," the drunk said. But even as he said that, he pulled his gun back and pointed it slightly upward. Clearly Jimmy had confused him.

"He sure is," another voice said from the back of the alley.

A moment later, a young guy, really short, and Jimmy figured him to be no more than eighteen years old, even though he looked younger, stepped out of the shadows and moved right up to Zach. He grabbed Zach around the middle and hugged him. "He's my dad. You wouldn't want to kill my dad, would you?"

By this point, Jimmy could tell the drunk was getting really confused. And overwhelmed. Actually, Jimmy was confused as well, but he kept playing the hand he had started.

"Deputy Roy, when did you start letting your son play in the alleys?" Jimmy asked.

"He's not supposed to be here," Zach said, following right along.

Then, while the drunk with the gun stared in amazement at Zach and the young kid holding him like he really was his daddy, another man with long black hair braided into a ponytail stepped out of the shadows and hit the second drunk with a chair leg.

The crack echoed through the narrow alley.

The drunk let go of Truitt and slumped to the ground with a loud moan.

The first drunk spun around, for the first time pointing the gun away from Zach.

The young kid, getting almost airborne, kicked the man's gun hand hard.

The gun went flying into the shadows, landing in something that sounded very wet and very sloppy.

"Ow!" the drunk shouted and held his injured hand against his chest. "Mister, I'll kill you for that."

Zach stepped forward and punched the guy once in the stomach.

When the guy doubled over, the kid with the long braided hair hit him with the chair leg.

The younger-looking kid searched one drunk's pockets while Truitt looked through the others, then all five of them headed out of the alley, across the street, and down a side street, laughing as they walked.

"Thanks," Zach said, glancing at Jimmy. "That was some quick thinking."

"I had a hard time not laughing though," said Truitt, shaking his head. "Deputy Roy. What a hoot."

"Yeah, had me laughing too," said the shorter guy who had kicked the gun.

"Thanks for the help," Zach said to the new men with them. "Who are you two?"

"I'm C. J.," the short one said as they reached a side street and turned toward the edge of town.

"Longfellow Runningwind," the other said, his voice deep and slow.

Jimmy wasn't sure, but he sounded like he had a New York accent.

"Call him Long," said C. J.. "Just easier."

"You mind?" Zach asked and Long said no.

Jimmy looked at Long, suddenly realizing that he had just met his first Indian. Or half-Indian, more than likely.

"We better lay low for a few hours," Zach said. "We got beans and some bacon at our camp if you're interested."

Both C. J. and Long looked very interested, both nodding so fast that it was clear to Jimmy that they hadn't eaten today.

Jimmy felt almost embarrassed that he had had a good breakfast at his wagon and had money to buy provisions, at least for a little while. But he didn't say anything. He just felt good having a few friends. That hadn't happened since his last day in school in Boston. He didn't realize until now how much he missed his friends back there.

And how much safer he felt hanging around with them.

> *"Deputy Roy, when did you start letting your son play in the alleys?" Jimmy asked.*

Zach and Truitt's camp was a small tent and a lean-to in a small grove of scrub brush near the edge of a small stream. More than likely, this stream would be dry in the summer, but right now, it was flowing good enough to give them some decent water. And they were upstream from the town and the mass of wagons on the other side, which made the water pretty safe to drink.

Truitt dug out some beans and a large pan and filled it with water while Zach started a fire. With the beans, Truitt put in a few scraps of bacon and a pretty good handful of salt. Then, as the beans were cooking, the five of them sat around the fire and talked.

It turned out C.J. wouldn't say anything about his family or his past, but it was clear to Jimmy that the short, blond-haired man had been to school somewhere. He wore wire-rimmed glasses and was constantly cleaning and adjusting them.

None of them wanted to talk about the war at all. Jimmy had learned early on in the trip that talking about the war was always a bad idea. Jimmy had managed to miss the war because he had been too young, and Luke had gone in, but missed most of the action.

Jimmy had also been right about Long. His mother was Sioux and his father white. Long had spent time in both worlds. He had gone to school just outside of New York and had left his mother to get away from the Indian way of life, but had also managed to stay out of the war.

As the beans were being served, C. J. admitted that it was the first meal that he and Long had had that day. They were basically living in that alley, trying to find a way to head west. They had no money, no horses, nothing to their names but clothes and an extra pair of glasses for C.J.

"Well, Jimmy," Zach said, "isn't it about time you tell us who you've been looking for?"

"Yeah?" C.J. said. "Standing out there against that wall for hours certainly draws attention to you.

*Written in the fast-paced style of James Patterson,* Dead Money *takes readers into all aspects of poker, from high-stakes private games to one of the largest tournaments of the year at the Bellagio Casino in Las Vegas.*

*Considered a sport by the courts and television, the prize money given away in major poker tournaments far exceeds the total of golf and tennis combined.*

*But when one of the greatest poker players of all time dies, the stakes rise even higher.*

Jimmy could feel his stomach twisting. "I didn't know I had been that obvious." He had been trying to stay hidden from Benson, and had actually been as obvious as a wine stain on a Sunday-go-to-church shirt.

"Maybe not to most," Truitt said, "but for those of us who watch for any small detail to help us survive, you're one dang big question mark."

Jimmy took a deep breath and managed to laugh. "All right, I'm looking for a man named Jake Benson." He quickly told them the story.

"So, where's your brother?" Long asked when Jimmy finished.

"Doc Davis's office back room."

"He getting better?" Zach asked, actually looking like he cared.

"Not much," Jimmy said. "He's going to need a lot of rest and care."

Suddenly, Jimmy had an idea. His father's voice rang clearly in his head. *Out west, there is safety in numbers.*

"Look," Jimmy said, "I need to go check in on my brother and talk to him about something. Are you four going to be here in an hour? If so, I've got an idea you might all like."

Zach glanced at Truitt, then at C. J. and Long.

"I am in no driving hurry to return to that alley," C. J. said.

Truitt snorted. "I couldn't agree with you more about that. Just stay here for the night."

Zach nodded. "We'll be here."

"I'll be back after I talk to my brother. And don't worry if you hear a horse approaching. That will be me."

"You have a horse?" C. J. asked, surprise on his dirty face.

"Actually," Jimmy said, smiling as he turned away. "I have five of them."

"Oh," was all he heard Zach say.

*Continued next month…*

---

# DEAN WESLEY SMITH

Saving People Can Get
Really Complicated

# LONG SHADOW

*USA TODAY* **BESTSELLING WRITER** *Dean Wesley Smith once again returns to the world of his acclaimed novel* Dust and Kisses *with a story set a few years ahead of the novel.*

*Buster and Ben, two time travelers from a hundred years in the future harvest what they call "Shadows," people destined to be killed when most of the population of the planet gets wiped out. The future needs those people to help society rebuild.*

*But an alien human might have other ideas.*

# LONG SHADOW

## ONE

**"YOU KNOW** there's no such phrase as "Long Shadow Best Eaten?"

The time was ticking at five and people were already starting to pour out of the tall buildings around us on Forty-First Street. New York was always tough around quitting time because of all the office workers. The sidewalks got packed, everyone had something to carry, and the entire city seemed to be in a hurry to be somewhere else.

I leaned against the stone side of the Grant Building, letting the firmness of it hold me up and keep me out of the way of the passing crowd. The key with living in this city was to just step off to one side of the flow. No one saw you when you did that. New Yorkers were trained to not look at any person who wasn't moving.

Not moving made me feel invisible, and I liked to feel invisible. Invisible was good in my line of work.

My best friend, Ben Longknife Jump, leaned against the building beside me, also standing still. His long black hair was pulled back tight and a floppy cloth hat with decorations on it covered his head. Most of the decorations were parts of old jewelry and buttons he had found in the gutters.

Both of us had on Army jackets with about six billion pockets and old jeans. The evening was a little too warm for the big Army jackets, but neither of us ever took our coats off. The coats were sort of our walking homes. Especially when we were out on a job like we were now.

I had on a tan baseball cap without any baseball team logo on it. Both of us wore tennis shoes, dirty and scuffed-up so that they didn't look out of place.

We both wore our standard issue sunglasses that were not so standard, but they served us fine.

"Sorry, Bub old buddy," Jump said, not even much moving his lips as he talked. "The saying has magic to it."

Jump called me Bub most of the time since my real name, Buster, just made him laugh. I had always gotten that reaction while growing up as well, so Bub suited me just fine.

None of the regular folk streaming past us noticed us in our lack of movement. Not one woman in a business suit or a man in a tie and jacket even glanced our way.

We were nothing more than decoration along the sidewalk to pay no attention to.

Invisible.

Invisible was a ton better than being laughed at or punched aside.

"What kind of magic does it have?"

"The good-eaten kind," he said.

I had to admit I was hungry and had no doubt Jump was as well. We'd been out on the street for too long this time. But I couldn't make the connection between a shadow and food. All I knew was that pretty soon we were going to need to get something to eat.

Pretty darned soon, actually. My stomach was starting to make sounds I could hear over the traffic.

Before I could ask him to explain a little more, he said, "Target. Ten o'clock."

Without moving or turning my head I looked in that direction.

The display on the inside of my glasses gave me all of the target's vitals. Judith Benz, thirty-one, single and in no relationship. She lived alone in a small rent-controlled apartment up near Columbia. She stood five-two, with short red hair and golden-brown eyes.

I had been attracted to her in her picture, but now, seeing her, I was instantly in love.

I thought I was hot in my big jacket before, now I was sweating.

She was amazing.

Completely amazing.

In all my life I had never been attracted to a woman like that so instantly.

She actually was trying to hide her incredible looks. Today she had on a black business suit that seemed a size too large. She wore white tennis shoes, with her working shoes sticking partially out of her black purse over her shoulder.

She walked with an intense stride that told me that she was in charge and didn't like to be messed with.

The information about her kept scrolling past my left eye as I watched her walk in our direction. She was brilliant, far, far too smart for her senior editing job at some publisher. She had two degrees in higher mathematics and had moved to New York to follow some friends on an impulse and just stayed.

Her genetics were pure and she was free of disease.

Targets didn't come any better.

Or any better looking.

No one was going to miss her, and we really, really needed her.

And I really, really wanted to get to know her better. I hoped to if she ever forgave me for what was about to happen.

We were actually saving her, since she would die anyway in just over two-and-a-half years.

Jump moved over about a half a pace in a way that no one noticed. Now there was a Judith-sized hole between us.

I clicked the link between Jump and me as she got closer and the air between us sort of shimmered. That was the gate to the holding cell in our ship in orbit. From there we would jump her back home and if I were lucky, I'd get a chance to show her around her new home and explain what happened.

Jump and I both stood completely still as she got close to us. With targets we just set out a shield that slid the target into the field between us without so much as them missing a step.

They didn't feel anything at all and still thought they were moving forward. They never knew what hit them until they were on the other side.

We never moved and no one around ever noticed that a person had just vanished into a hard wall.

But Judith surprised us both.

One step short of the screen as it extended out in front of her, she just stopped and looked at both of us.

"How stupid do you two think I am? I have a few questions for both of you idiots."

She touched a watch on her wrist and I could suddenly feel myself being transported.

And I had no way of knowing where.

But even with that, I didn't like being called an idiot by a woman I was lusting after.

# TWO

"OKAY," SHE SAID, sitting and facing us across the table. "Where are you two from?"

We were in what looked like the control room of a huge ship. Out the window or view screen that was an entire wall of the room, I could see the Earth floating below us. From the looks of it, this ship was in high orbit.

There was no one else in the control room and Jump and I were both sitting in chairs in front of what looked like a conference table to one side of the control room. There were three plates and silverware on the table, but no food.

Judith sat across from us, still dressed in her black business suit like a normal New Yorker, which she clearly wasn't. She looked a little angry and her golden-flecked brown eyes were pretty intense.

And I still found her amazingly attractive.

I was still half-angry with her for calling me an idiot. But that anger was vanishing quickly considering where I found myself.

The entire place smelled of roast beef and some sort of potatoes and I realized once again how hungry I was. My stomach actually rumbled loud enough to hear.

I glanced at Jump and he just shrugged, saying basically at this point we had no other options but to tell her the truth.

I turned and looked her in the eyes and almost couldn't get a word out. For a second I felt like a teenager facing my first date.

"We're from one hundred years in the future," I finally said. "We're trying to take some likely people to help us jumpstart the energy back into our rebuilding. And in the process we're trying to save their lives, basically."

She frowned, clearly surprised at my answer. "Assuming I believe you can travel in time, what exactly are you saving them from?"

It suddenly dawned on me she wasn't a time traveler. We were actually in an alien spaceship. And more than likely miss red-haired Judith that I was lusting over was an alien as well.

Jump looked at me, just as surprised. He clearly had come to the exact same conclusion.

"Answer for answer," I said, leaning forward toward her. Alien or not, I still wanted to get to know her a ton better. "Where are you from?"

"Originally, two galaxies over from here, but I've been working with the Seeders now for longer than you want to think about. This spiral arm of this galaxy is my sector to watch over all the planets and to help each civilization along in its growth."

"You human?" Jump asked.

"As much as you two," she said.

I liked the sound of that.

And if I hadn't been sitting in a monstrous control room on a big space ship in orbit over Earth a hundred years in my own past, I would have thought her a lunatic. But she had said all that with a completely straight face, like she was reporting it.

"So, my turn," she said, "what are you saving these people from by kidnapping them into your future? Again, not saying you can travel in time, but that ship of yours in orbit below us is certainly for some sort of travel and I sure wouldn't trust it out of orbit."

"You can see our ship through our shields?" Jump asked, sitting forward as well. He had been the one to design those shields and he was very, very proud of them.

"Not really shields by my standards," she said, smiling at him. "But you didn't answer my question."

"In two years and six months and eight days," I said, "a seemingly harmless electromagnetic cloud will sweep over Earth for exactly five seconds."

Her pale skin seemed to be turning even paler. So I went on.

"The wave will short-circuit the human brain and only those inside something metal or a distance underground will be spared."

"About two million out of the billions down there live through it," Jump said, his voice low and clear. "And by the time the survivors start to reorganize three years later, there are only about half that many left."

I went on, continuing the story of my planet. "The number drops even farther in the following fifty years before finally stabilizing. We need help from more humans to really start growing again as a culture. We are technologically advanced in some areas and far, far behind in others."

"And most of the planet of our time is a wasteland," Jump said. "So we are back here in our own history pulling out the shadows of the dead to come forward in time and help us."

"That's what we call the people walking down there," I said. "Shadows."

Jump nodded. "Because to us, in the future, they are all ghosts and shadows is a better term."

Miss Red-Hair and Golden-Eyes sat there, staring at both of us.

I felt like her eyes were boring into my soul and I honestly didn't mind. She could stare at me like that for as long as she wanted.

After a moment of silence, she said, "Shit, you two are telling the truth."

I was stunned that aliens swore in American slang.

She stood. "Dinner is on the way. I'll be right back."

Then talking into the air she said, "Benson, we have a major problem. I'm coming to you."

And then she just flat vanished.

Again the silence filled the big command area like a thick weight on everything.

I just sat there smiling at where she had been. "She's really something, isn't she?"

"Oh, no," Jump said, shaking his head at me.

"I'm still fairly young and have emotions," I said. "So sue me."

He just kept shaking his head.

A moment later some of the best smelling pot roast and potatoes and brown gravy appeared on the table in front of us. There was also corn, slices of wheat bread, and glasses of water.

I glanced at Jump who was smiling at the food.

"Long shadow, good eaten," he said as he reached for the bowl of potatoes. "I told you."

"I'm fairly certain this isn't what you meant," I said as I went after the pot roast.

"Magic is magic," he said.

# THREE

**WE FINISHED EATING** and then both of us went over and stood in front of the image of Earth floating below. It sure looked like some big window, but I had no idea how that could be possible, so I figured it was an image on a screen.

Judith appeared beside us, staring down at the planet below.

"You are correct, we can see the electromagnetic pulse wave. The planet's speed and the speed of the pulse will bring them together at exactly the moment you stated."

"Can you stop it?" Jump asked.

"No," she said. "And we can't protect the planet. This event has been known for some time. I was just not informed. I can tell you that in a more advanced sector of this galaxy we are now frantically mounting a rescue mission to build enough ships to take as many people off planet as possible."

"Rescue mission?" I asked, turning to face her.

She nodded. "We have no way to stop the first wave or rescue enough people from that first wave, but we will rescue about two million people from being killed in a second pulse wave following the first. You are proof of that."

"Because we are still standing here," Jump said.

I realized at once what he meant. If the aliens had been able to stop the first wave or block Earth from it, we would no longer be standing here, since we would have had no reason to come back in time.

And we were still standing here because we instigated the rescue of the survivors.

"Exactly," she said to Jump, nodding, clearly very sad. "I wish we could do more."

I looked over at her with another thought that sent chills through me. "When we get back to our normal time a hundred years in the future, you are going to disable our time-travel capabilities, aren't you?"

"We will," she said, nodding. "It's far, far too dangerous for a young culture like yours to have."

"So our mission concludes?" Jump asked.

"No," she said.

I was surprised at that. Very surprised, actually.

"I will monitor you and your other operatives to make sure you take no one that survives the first wave," she said. "You have done fine so far from what we can tell from your ship's records."

Now I was flat stunned.

She smiled, but the smile was sad.

"We rescued almost two million from being killed by the second wave," she said. "If you and your teams pick up the pace, you could rescue thousands and thousands more into the safety of your future."

"Would you help us?" Jump asked.

She sadly shook her head, staring at the Earth below.

"And we won't remember any of this, will we?" I asked, knowing full well the answer.

"I'm afraid not soon," she said. "But maybe, in a hundred years or so, we'll meet again and I can refresh your memory."

"I'd like that," I said, smiling at her, not wanting to think about how old she would be or how she could live that long. I just didn't care.

She looked at me and smiled as well. "So would I."

I damn near melted right there.

"Long shadow," Jump said, nodding.

# FOUR

**I STOOD WITH MY BACK** against the stone wall of the Grant Building, not moving, letting the crowds of New Yorkers flow past.

---

*Sent to investigate the sudden appearance of the statue of a naked woman in a park, Pilgrim Hugh must first decide if placing a statue without permission constitutes a crime.*

*And why had the statue of the naked woman lost all her personal parts? Are those missing personal parts the answer to the origin of the statue?*

*Another strange Pilgrim Hugh Incident.*

*Now available in paperback and electronic editions from your favorite bookseller.*

Only it seemed the sidewalk wasn't as busy as it had been a moment before.

"Looks like our target isn't showing," I said to Jump. "Let's move to our next target."

I was really, really disappointed. I really hoped we could somehow get Judith. Everything about her attracted me, and I had spent an hour last night just staring at her picture.

"How did we lose the last hour?" Jump asked as we pushed away from the building and headed toward Broadway.

I glanced at the time in the upper corner of my glasses. It had been just before five, now it was almost six.

That wasn't possible.

"Did we both just fall asleep?"

"If we did, we ate while we were sleeping," he said.

I suddenly realized that I was no longer hungry as well.

"Okay, maybe both of us need a day off, some rest back on the ship," I said.

"When we forget we ate, we need rest. I can't even remember what we had for dinner."

"Pot roast," he said. "And it was really good, but damned if I can remember where."

I took one more look at the image of Judith on my screen, then with a sigh flicked her off and brought up the next target. A white kid around twenty living alone four blocks from here. He had an IQ that couldn't be measured.

Maybe tomorrow we could try to rescue Judith again. I would hate to see her turn into just a shadow, a fleeting memory in my life.

She felt special for some reason.

～

# DEAN WESLEY SMITH

## The ADVENTURES OF HAWK

### Chapters 4-6

# WHAT CAME BEFORE...

**NINETEEN-YEAR-OLD** *Danny Hawk, his uncle, and his best friend Craig, were in Cairo to look for his missing father. Danny had witnessed the death of his only contact in Cairo, Professor Davis, because the professor had Danny's father's journals.*

*Danny knows that the men who had killed the professor were now after him and the journals. Danny finds the journals and gets his uncle and friend to safety in an airport hotel where he tells them what happened. They decide to keep searching for Danny's father and try to rescue him.*

# THE ADVENTURES OF HAWK

# CHAPTER FOUR

*August 17, 1970*
*Gizera Hotel, Cairo, Egypt.*

**MAKING SURE THAT** they weren't followed, Danny Hawk, his best friend, Craig, and his uncle Steve left the airport restaurant and hailed a cab to a hotel that Danny had found a small ad for in the airport. It was on the west side of the river on Gizera Avenue. The hotel was spread out around a number of courtyards, each filled with decorative rock and a few palm trees and nothing more. It wasn't an upscale tourist hotel, but it wasn't bad. It looked like it catered more to businessmen from the area.

The area smelled lightly of dirty water and animals. Not at all a smell Danny would have expected in the center of a big city.

Again, they got a room for Uncle Steve while Danny and Craig shared a room with two beds. They registered under false names, booking the room for three days. The night clerk had been so tired, he hadn't even asked to see their identification or passports like the bigger hotel had done.

Craig just passed out, snoring lightly, his six-foot plus frame dangling over the edge of the bed, but Danny didn't sleep much during what was left of the night. But he managed to rest and think. So by breakfast in the small hotel restaurant, he was feeling more in control.

Scared and completely over his head, but in control.

The men who were looking for them would have no way of tracing them through the thousands of hotels in Cairo. More than likely, they were still watching the Continental where they had been staying. And would for a few days at least, since Uncle Steve had paid for three nights and they hadn't checked out when they left.

"What's the plan this morning?" Craig asked Danny.

"We should contact the authorities," Uncle Steve said, using his confident voice. The voice Danny knew he always used when trying to get something from someone.

"And say what?" Danny asked, staring at his uncle. Sitting in the airport restaurant last night, he had told them the entire story of how he managed to escape and get the notebooks.

Uncle Steve looked flustered, his face growing slightly red which was accented by his gray hair. "I don't know, but we should."

"For all we know," Danny said, "the police were who killed Professor Davis."

Uncle Steve started to say something, but Danny held up his hand. "We don't know, do we?"

Uncle Steve just shrugged.

"We're not in the United States, remember." Danny patted the backpack he had carried with him from the room. "And we have no idea just what's in these notebooks or how valuable they are."

"Valuable enough to kill for," Craig said, shaking his head and looking worried. "That's for sure. We need to read them, find out why."

"Agreed," Danny said. "And that's the plan for the day."

After breakfast, they went back to Uncle Steve's room.

When Danny opened the first book bound in leather and full of his father's writings, he was almost instantly disappointed. This was going to be a lot more difficult than he had thought.

The notebooks were in a combination of English, Italian, Latin, and Egyptian hieroglyphs. Danny knew his father was fluent in all four languages, plus a few others, including some Arabic, since he had worked so often in Egypt. Clearly, he had no trouble writing in all the languages as well and had done so from one paragraph to another, changing without any seeming reason.

Danny knew some Latin and some French, but that was all. Not much help.

"Who can read what language?" Danny asked, handing the notebook to Craig and picking up another to see if it was the same. It was.

"A little Spanish," Craig said, shrugging.

"Nothing," Uncle Steve said, looking apologetic. "It would figure my brother would protect his notes with something like this. He always did like to show off how smart he was."

Danny ignored the old family chant he had heard his uncle say hundreds of times. "Well, let's read what we can and figure out how to get help with what we can't read later."

Danny took back the first notebook and started into the record of the last ten years of his father's research. It felt like reading his father's private thoughts was snooping on something his father had never wanted him to see.

Three hours later, Danny put down the last notebook and sat back, trying to make sense of what he had been able to read.

It seemed that his father had been focused on finding archeological records of what he had started to call "The Fountain." That was short for the Fountain of Youth.

Danny had been around his father and his work enough

*"Valuable enough to kill for," Craig said, shaking his head and looking worried.*

to know that with any myth coming up through history, there was usually some sort of factual basis somewhere in the past. His father clearly didn't believe in any water that could keep a person youthful, so he was searching for the start of the myth.

And why the myth existed the way it did.

Somewhere, in the second year, the word Taccola had come into the notebooks. Danny knew a little about Taccola because his father had been so interested in him when Danny was ten. Taccola was an engineer in the late fourteen century in Siena, and his inventions were amazingly ahead of their time. Many of the inventions concerned moving water to the city of Siena, which was a landlocked city without a good water supply.

But later in Taccola's life, he had been interested in finding older inventions and had led expeditions into parts of

Egypt, where he vanished without a trace somewhere around 1458.

His father had underlined a phrase that bothered Danny a great deal. "Could Taccola still be alive?"

That was the last mention of Taccola in the notebooks, at least in the parts that Danny could read.

The next book dealt with Napoleon's interest in ancient culture and the archeological searches he funded and went on in Egypt and other areas around the Mediterranean. It seemed that, as with Taccola, Napoleon was focused on water in his searches, possibly even something that was rumored to give his men an invincibility.

At one point, his father had written "He was searching for the Fountain."

It was in the fourth journal that the words *Hydra Journals* were written, then underlined.

Danny couldn't tell from what he could read in English what the Hydra Journals were about, but from that point onward, they seemed to be a focus for his father. Five years of intense focus, as a matter of fact, from what Danny could tell from the dates in the notebooks.

The very last entry in the last notebook had been in English. It had basically said that Danny's father had made a breakthrough, but somehow he was going to have to keep his find from the *Hydra League*.

Then he wrote a few notes in Egyptian hieroglyph and the journal ended.

From the last date in the notebook, Danny's father had taken them to

Professor Davis for safekeeping the next day and then vanished two days later.

Danny stared at the words *Hydra League*.

Was the red-hooded man who killed Professor Davis part of that league?

Was it the league that had taken his father?

Hydra, an old Greek legend was about a snake with many women's heads.

Hydra Journals. Water. Fountain of Youth. Taccola. Napoleon. Hydra League.

Danny sighed, sat back, and closed his eyes while Craig and Uncle Steve kept reading.

At least he knew a little more of where his father's research had taken him. But now Danny was more confused and scared than he had been last night.

And he had no idea what to do next.

# CHAPTER FIVE

*August 18, 1970*
*Gizera Hotel, Cairo, Egypt.*

**THEY HAD SPENT** the entire previous day reading what they could of the notebooks a second time and talking about them and what they contained. They hadn't left the hotel and had turned in early to get rested, with the understanding that at breakfast they would decide what to do next.

Danny barely slept, even though he was exhausted. Every time he closed his eyes, a red-hooded snake with many-heads would come up out of a black pool of water and chase him.

He wasn't sure he was having a vision dream, as his grandfather would sometimes call vivid images like that, or just a nightmare. Danny had a hunch it was a little bit of both.

But he did know that he was his father's only chance of survival if he was still alive.

And Danny had to believe his mother that his father was alive. Somewhere, being held by someone.

And now, just like his father, Danny was in too deep. There was no turning back, no going home, back to the easy life of going to school.

Across the restaurant table the next morning, Danny looked at his best friend and his uncle, then laid out simply what he thought they should do next.

"Uncle Steve, Craig, I want you two to take a flight from here to London, then on home."

"What?" Craig asked.

Danny held up his hand. "Let me finish. Uncle Steve, I need you to get my mother out on your boat into the upper areas of the lake. The old cabin up on the point should be safe for a time. Lock up the house and just go, get on that boat and stay away from contact as much as possible.

Uncle Steve shook his head and Craig looked disgusted.

"We're not leaving you," Craig said. "And who do I have to go home to? My drunken father?"

Danny knew Craig was right. There was no one at home for Craig. His mother was dead and his father spent more time in bars than at home. Craig pretended to live with his father, but in reality, he spent most of his time at Danny's house. Not only were they best friends, but Craig was like the brother Danny never had. And Danny's mother considered him her second son.

"Your mother would kill me if I left

her son over here alone," Uncle Steve said. "And she'd have a right to."

"Uncle Steve," Danny said, "the men who took my father, and who killed Professor Davis, are not going to stop at the border of Egypt. They know we're here, they know we left my mother alone. Once they can't find us, where do you think they're going to go next?"

Uncle Steve's skin turned a sickly white and he instantly started sweating. He clearly hadn't thought of that.

Danny stared into the fear-filled eyes of his uncle. "Someone needs to protect my mother, and you're the best man for that. Get out on the boat on that lake and up to the cabin on the point."

"But you can't stay here alone," Uncle Steve said.

"He's not going to be alone," Craig said, his voice full of anger. "I'm staying with him and there's no argument on that point."

Danny looked at his best friend, then smiled. He had been hoping that Craig would say that. Together, they had more of a chance then Danny did alone, that was for sure.

Craig then turned to Uncle Steve. "But Danny's right, you have to go back and get his mother safe."

Uncle Steve sighed and slumped in the booth.

Danny knew that he had put his uncle in an impossible situation. He either had to leave two boys he still considered his "babies" in danger in a foreign country, or he had to live with the fact that if he didn't go back, Danny's mother more than likely would be killed.

"Remember," Danny said, "we may be young, but we are considered adults. We'll be fine."

Uncle Steve didn't even nod at that,

just stared down at his hands.

"One other thing," Danny said. "We're going to need money at times if we're going to try to find out what happened to my father and stay hidden from the men after the notebooks. Craig and I can live pretty cheap here, and stay out of sight easier if it's just the two of us than if you are with us. But even still, we're going to need someone we can contact for money."

Uncle Steve again just sighed, but this time he nodded as well.

Danny knew that his uncle had a pretty good sum of money stashed from the settlement from his wife's death.

"You're going to be our anchor," Danny said. "You and my mother have to stay safe, and yet be in contact with us. And from the looks of these notebooks, there's no telling where this is going to take us, or how long it's going to take."

Craig laughed. "I suddenly feel like I've been tossed into a quest fantasy."

"I just wish this was a fantasy," Danny said, smiling at his friend. "It's just a little too real and deadly for my tastes."

"No argument there," Craig said.

# CHAPTER SIX

*August 19, 1970*
*International Airport, Cairo, Egypt.*

**LATE THAT NIGHT,** just after midnight, the three of them went back to the international airport. Uncle Steve booked them all tickets to London, then on to Seattle. From there Uncle Steve would drive back to central Idaho. The idea was that if the men who were after the notebooks thought all three of them had left, they would follow Uncle Steve to Seattle.

"Are you sure you want them after you?" Danny had asked his uncle when he suggested the idea.

Uncle Steve nodded. "Don't worry, they'll never find your mother and me after we get on that lake. The old cabin has no entrance road and no one really remembers it's out there. Besides, looking for you in Seattle will keep them off your trail here for a while at least."

Danny didn't like it, but he had agreed to the plan.

The plane didn't leave until six in the morning, so for the rest of the night, the three of them sat in a secluded place where they could see people in the international airport coming and going. They planned as much as they could during those hours, including how and when Danny and Craig would check in with Uncle Steve and his mother.

The first thing Danny and Craig had to do was try to get new identification. Uncle Steve left them with enough money to last them for a few months in Cairo, and they set up how more money could be wired to them.

As Uncle Steve got ready to go through customs, he turned to Danny. "You're mother's going to kill me, you know."

Danny laughed. "Just make her close up the house and get away from there."

"Oh, I will," Uncle Steve said, the worry in his lined face clear. "Twelve hours after I reach home, we'll be gone."

"Good," Danny said. He gave his uncle a hug, then Craig did the same.

"Be careful," Uncle Steve said. "And find my brother, would you?"

"We will," Craig said for both of them.

Uncle Steve nodded, then with a worried smile, turned and headed into the customs area.

Danny and Craig stood off to one side, watching all the people coming and going through that area of the airport. No one seemed to be paying them any attention, so after a good half hour, they went out the door and took a cab into the old heart of Cairo, right to the Khan Al-Khalili bazaar.

Neither of them spoke on their ride into the center of the city. Danny felt completely overwhelmed by what they faced, and very much afraid. Chances were he and Craig would be killed far before they found Danny's father. But they had to try.

They had no other choice.

*Continued next month…*

*If you liked the novel* **THUNDER MOUNTAIN** *in this issue, you might also like these Jukebox stories.*

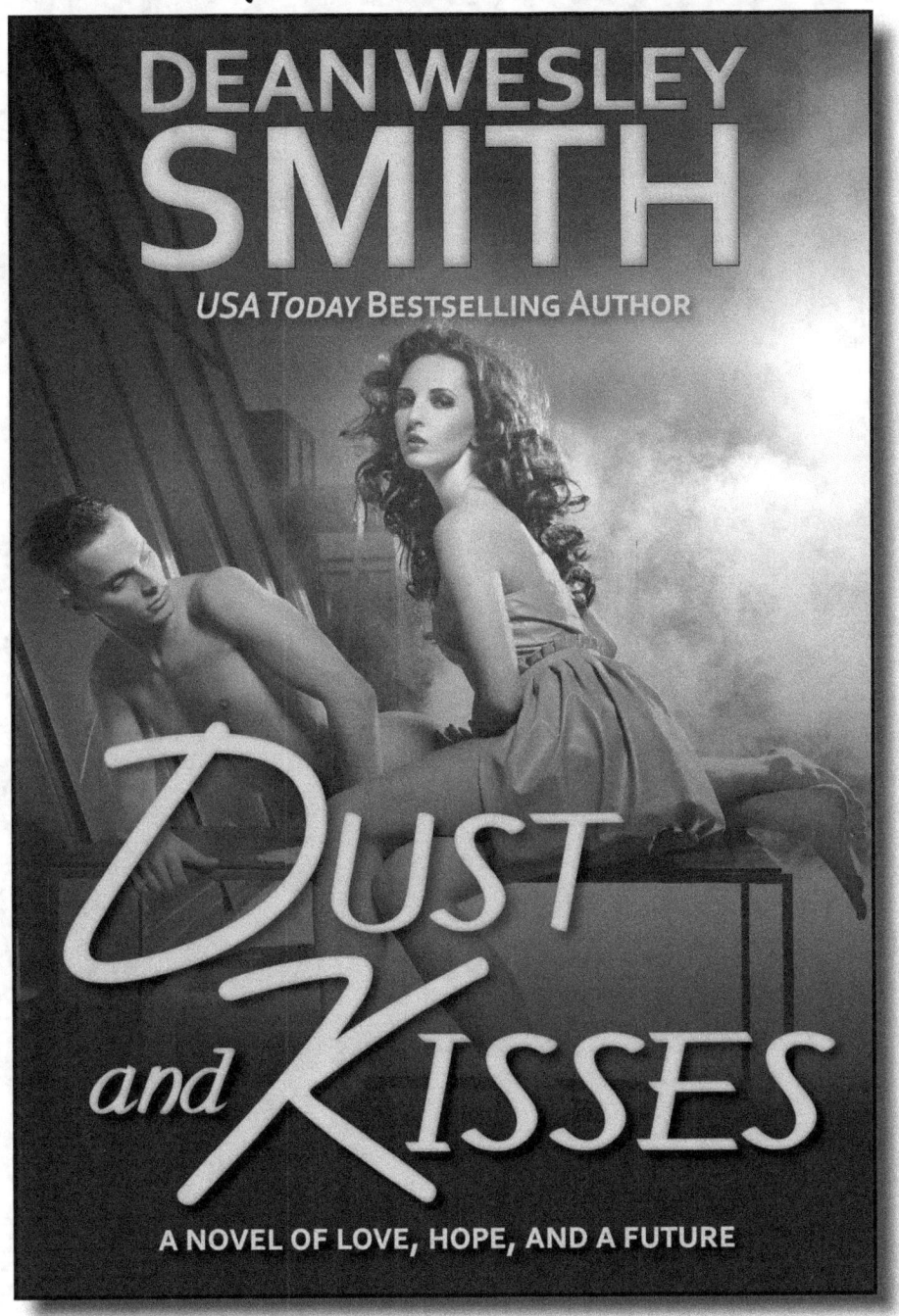

# DEAN WESLEY SMITH

A MATCHBOX AGENDA

Can a very special match,
if used correctly, save a life?

*BEN TRAGER SUCKS as a person, a father, a husband. And he knows it. Everyone around him knows it as well.*

*Lost, he stumbles into a Denny's Restaurant and gets a special box of matches. Very, very special matches.*

*Matches, that if used correctly, will save his life.*

*USA Today bestselling writer Dean Wesley Smith opens the door to a simple Denny's Restaurant and gives us all a tiny peek into Rod Serlings' Twilight Zone world just one more time.*

# MATCHBOX AGENDA

**THE SOUNDS** of the crowded Denny's Restaurant faded around him as Ben Trager stared at the little red box with the black stripes on both sides. The cardboard box held his entire life.

One match his luck, another his loves, another his actions. Everything his future held, all bundled up in the dark in nice neat rows. Each match facing the same direction, each match having the same potential, each match promising the same opportunities.

This morning he had felt like one of the matches: Wooden, explosive, and ready to burn up at any moment. But unlike his real life before now, the matchbox was full, giving his life a newness, a freshness he could have only dreamed of a few minutes before.

This morning, when leaving his four-bedroom home in Stevens Heights, his life had basically been over. His future was clouded and meaningless. He had nowhere to go, no place to be, nothing he wanted to do.

He and his wife had argued again, he had hit her again. His two teen-aged children hated him for good reason, he hated his job, and he hated himself for hitting his wife and messing up his life so completely.

He had driven around, lost, directionless, until he saw a Denny's Restaurant. He had pulled in and got out of his van, standing there staring at the newspapers in their dispensers trying to decide if he should go in and eat or not. It didn't seem to matter either way.

How could he, a man with a good college degree and wonderful potential fifteen years before, end up like this? Where had he gone wrong, what had he missed, how could he have been so stupid?

Then, as he stood there, staring at nothing but a blank future, a man coming out of the restaurant asked if Ben needed some matches.

Ben had only shrugged. He wasn't even thinking clear enough to tell the man he didn't smoke.

The guy tossed him the box of matches hitting Ben in the chest. "Decided to give up smoking while having breakfast," the guy said, shaking his head. "No smoking, no matches."

With that the man walked off leaving Ben standing there holding the box of unused matches from a man who had made a decent choice about life.

It wasn't until Ben sat down inside that he understood that his future had been given to him. He had been tossed the secret to putting his life in order.

He turned the box over and over in his hands, not even daring to set it down on the Formica-topped table. The sounds of the wooden matches inside were reminders of all the possibilities ahead. He could either start something fresh and growing, or sputter out useless and spent. It would be up to him.

The damn box held his life.

What was he going to do with it?

"You going to play with those things all mornin'?" the waitress asked, putting a large glass of water in front of him. "Or you want some breakfast?"

Ben placed the matchbox carefully down on the table and glanced up at her.

She was early forties, about his age, with a wonderful, welcoming smile. She had on a blue uniform, a blue hat that sat slightly tipped on her blonde hair, and rings on every finger but the important one. The empty skin of that finger glared at him as she held her order pad and waited for him to move.

He smiled back at her and managed to not glance down at her chest any farther than her name badge. "Jenny," he said. "Nice name."

Her smile got even larger. "Thanks."

Today, with a new life in front of him laid out in the box, he knew that everything was possible again. Even good sex.

Of course, he had his future in the box, she had her life stretched out ahead in order tickets hung on a swirling ring that took her life into the kitchen and then sent it back, burnt and overcooked.

But who knew what might happen with a carefully chosen match.

"Bacon and eggs, eggs over easy, bacon crisp, wheat toast light."

"Drink?"

"Small orange juice," he said.

She raised an eyebrow as she wrote that, then gave him a large smile and turned away.

The orange juice had been the perfect touch. Had he given her the hint that her ringless finger needed? He doubted his marriage could be saved, not with his past actions, so it sure wouldn't hurt him to start thinking of other chances.

Wow, what a difference a box of matches and a future could make, and he hadn't even used up a match yet.

He took off his overcoat and adjusted his tie. If he was going to keep his job with the county auditors much longer he was going to have to shape up there as well. No doubt that would take a match or two.

Wait. Was that worth it? Or should he use a few of the matches to find a new job, one that he would like to do. Suddenly the possibilities were endless, and he loved that feeling. It felt young, healthy, vibrant.

He picked up the box and rattled it carefully, not wanting to damage any of his future chances. The morning felt brighter, some of the weight was lifting off his shoulders.

He took a deep breath and kept staring at the matches as the waitress placed his orange juice on the table, smiled at him again, and left.

Good contact, no wasted match.

He slowly opened the box and looked at the neat row of sticks there with their bulging ends. One match seemed to stand out more than any other, and he touched it with one finger, then picked it out of the box.

He slid the box closed and put it on the table, staring at the one match. Such a simple little thing to have such possibilities.

It could light a cigarette for a man who would die of cancer.

It could start a camp fire to keep a family warm on a camping trip.

It could light a gas stove to feed hungry children.

It could start a raging forest fire.

For him it could do so much more. This box held his plans for the future.

He held the match between his thumb and index finger of his left hand. The first thing he needed to do was settle the situation left over at home.

One match in one hand.

One problem to fix.

He pulled out his cell phone with his right hand and punched in the number for home.

The phone rang until the machine picked it up. He didn't blame Gloria for not answering, if she was even still there. More than likely she had already left, going who knew where.

When the message machine came on he said calmly, "I know you understand I am sorry for what happened this morning, but sorry is no longer enough. This afternoon I will find a counselor who will take me on an emergency basis, and I will check myself into a hotel until I can be sure I will never strike another woman again. If I have to check myself into a hospital, I will solve this problem. I know this will take time. I don't expect you to forgive me or even help me. I'll call you tonight to let you know where I am."

He clicked off the cell phone, surprised at the words that had come out of his mouth. He had always been adverse to counseling.

The last flame of the match burnt his finger slightly and went out.

He stared at it the burnt remains, shocked at those as well. He didn't remember lighting that match. Yet the burnt smell of sulfur mixed with the smell of coffee and bacon as a faint wisp of smoke vanished into the air.

*Wow, what a difference a box of matches and a future could make, and he hadn't even used up a match yet.*

"Hey, no smoking in here," the waitress said, sliding his plate of food in front of him, then almost dropping the smaller plate covered in toast.

"Not smoking," he said, smiling at her. "Sorry about that. Didn't mean to light it." He pushed the last of the burnt match away.

She smiled and winked. "No more accidents, honey," she said, putting her hand on his shoulder. She turned away, letting her hand linger a fraction of a second longer than it should.

He watched her walk, her ass moving in a very fine fashion under the tight uniform. There, in that blue uniform, was a future that might be fun exploring.

He stared at the matchbox. He had used a match, a possibility in his new future, and it felt good to be on the right road. No matter what happened at home, or with this waitress, or any other woman, he would never allow his temper to run loose again. He would find a way to control it. The match had made sure of that.

He dug into the eggs, hash browns, and crisp, perfectly cooked, bacon, staring at the box of matches in front of his plate while he ate. To have a future again felt so wonderful he wanted to just shout to the world.

About halfway through the eggs he opened the box so that he could stare at the pile of matches, and all the possibilities laid out there in neat rows.

His hopes.

His dreams.

A saved marriage, a better job, a new house, more money, respect for himself. All of those things were there, one match after another.

For the first time in years he felt less angry about everything.

He finished his eggs, crunched on the wonderful taste of the last piece of bacon, then washed it all down with the orange juice. Perfect breakfast for a day of major life changes.

"Done?" the waitress asked, appearing at his shoulder and reaching for his plate.

"Just beginning," he said, smiling up her. If she could only see all his dreams and hopes and roads to travel, she would screw his eyes out tonight.

She was smiling at him, not looking at the table, when he said "Just beginning."

She stopped suddenly, the plate halfway off the table, then went to put it back down, clearly thinking he meant that he wasn't done with breakfast.

But she wasn't looking at the plate, but instead into his eyes.

The edge of the plate hit the large glass of water and tipped it over, pouring the water into the open box of matches, washing away everything in a pool of ruin.

"Shit, shit, shit!" she said, tossing a dirty towel she had with her into the puddle of water. "Sorry, I'll get some more towels."

She turned to the counter as he just sat there, the water dripping coldly onto his suit pants and down into his crotch.

He didn't even shout, he didn't cry, he didn't even move.

He just sat there starting at his water-soaked, scattered future, ruined on the table.

The room grew dark as his anger flooded back.

Clumsy bitch had ruined everything.

The waitress grabbed a few towels behind the counter and headed back his way.

He wanted to hit her, break her damn neck.

He didn't dare let his anger come out at her. Not here, not now.

He stood, took out his wallet, and put twenty bucks into the puddle. Then he turned, leaving his future on the table, and walked out the door.

By the time he reached the sidewalk outside, he could barely move his feet. He felt as if he were walking in quicksand, the anger gone as quickly as it had come.

Nothing mattered anymore.

He had hit his wife.

His children hated him.

He was about to lose his job.

He hated himself.

There had been enough matches in that box to help him, but he had let those chances be wasted as well by flirting with a woman instead of paying attention to what mattered.

His entire life was a waste.

He climbed inside his van, put the keys in the ignition, but didn't start the car.

He couldn't think of any reason to start the car. He had nowhere to go.

So instead he just sat there, staring blankly ahead, a man with no future.

No hope.

No matches.

~

# DEAN WESLEY SMITH

## USA Today Bestselling Author

## the First Tee Panic

### AND OTHER VERY REAL GOLF STORIES

*Former PGA golf professional and USA Today bestselling writer Dean Wesley Smith walks you step-by-step, club-by-club from your car to the first tee and beyond in a laugh-out-loud style that not only teaches, but entertains.*

*In the first three parts last month, we successfully got you from your car and through the pro shop.*

*Now it's time to keep moving toward the first tee, through the really scary parts of getting ready to play a round of golf.*

# THE FIRST TEE PANIC
## *And Other Very Real Golf Stories*

## PART FOUR:
## HELP! WHICH CLUB SHOULD I HIT FIRST ON THE DIVING RANGE?

**YOU'VE FOUND THE MASSIVE** open green expanse of the hitting area of the driving range, parked your cart along the edge of the concrete path, and have gone around to the back of the cart to your bag to get a club.

But which club to hit first?

You have fourteen clubs to choose from. If you have more than fourteen, maybe from your kids tossing extras in, make sure to take them out before you get to the first tee. Rule is, only fourteen clubs allowed. And actually, at the moment you only have thirteen to pick from. You're not going to be hitting any balls with your putter on the driving range. And if you even think about it, you made the wrong turn at the front driveway. You wanted the course with the castles and the big clown mouth that opens and closes.

So, thirteen clubs to pick from.

But which one first?

You glance around at the others hitting balls, sending those clean white spheres into the air with a sense of beauty and purpose you only can hope for. There doesn't seem to be any logic in what clubs they are using, since they arrived at different times before you. Some are hitting drivers, others flip wedges, others long irons.

Don't panic, there is a real reason for starting with certain clubs first in a warm-up practice session. And if you follow the basic guidelines I'm about to give you, not only will your warm-up be good for your body, but it will help you get off that dreaded first tee.

First, grab a seven iron.

Your goal with this club is to just get your body lose enough to swing a golf club. You have no intention of hitting good shots right off the bat, so don't even think about it. Just take the seven iron to the teeing area nearest your cart, do a few basic warm-up stretches to get muscles loosened, then generally hit a ball with about a half swing.

Half swing means the club doesn't go above head high on the back swing.

This going slow on the first swing is so that you don't pull tired and car-weary muscles. Last thing you need on this special day of golf is to be hauled off in an ambulance with a wrenched back. And trust me, I've seen it happen more than once from these first swings.

Let me repeat, you don't care if you hit the shot right or not. Don't even look. Just half-swing and make contact.

That's success at this time of the morning.

*Some are hitting drivers, others flip wedges, others long irons.*

Take another half swing and hit another. Then on the third take a little fuller swing. Repeat this for five to ten balls until your hands can feel the club, your grip doesn't feel like you're holding the head of an alien snake, and your back stops cracking.

If you are going to be the very first group off the tee, the grass is still damp with dew, and you have on two sweaters and a thick windbreaker, make this first part of the practice at least twenty golf balls, or until your hands stop stinging every time you hit the ball.

Now, you're a little looser and warmed up, so go back to the cart and get a nine iron.

It's time to start hitting shots directly at a target.

Golf is, after all, a game of targets.

Never hit a golf shot after the first ten or so warm-up balls without a target clearly in mind. If you can actually keep a target in mind for every shot of the round, you will cut strokes off your game. But that lesson is for another time. Right now you are practicing to get off the first tee, and picking a target is critical.

There should be signs on the driving range in front of you, or different colored flag poles stuck into pretend greens. Those are targets. Pick the one that says 100 Yards and aim at it. With about a three quarter swing with the nine iron, fire away.

Five or ten balls, you should be narrowing in or over that sign, and if you're pretty strong, maybe even bouncing the nine irons in front of the 150 yard sign.

But don't push, don't try to hit anything hard. Work on just making smooth, comfortable swings, time after time, repeating the same swing over and over and over.

After being a game of targets, golf is secondly a game of repeating an impossible movement of your body. It is a very physical game, so don't ignore that aspect. You are warming up now to have a great, injury-free day, and get that first shot off the first tee.

Go easy.

Another tip: Step away from the ball between every shot. Don't just pull another ball to you and fire away. Put another ball in place and then step back, as if this next shot is your first shot on the course. Pick a target and just repeat the word *smooth* over and over.

If you don't understand what I mean by smooth, just think about Fred Couples' golf swing. It don't get no smoother than that.

Now after ten balls or so with the nine iron, get a five iron, pick a target just beyond the 150 yard sign and do another ten balls, again working on staying smooth. Just like the nine iron, make sure you step away from the ball between each shot, line up a target, swing smooth.

If you miss a shot, forget it, laugh, and focus on target and being smooth on the next shot. This is golf, not rocket science. You are going to miss more shots than you are going to hit. Don't worry about it.

Relax, pick a target, swing smoothly.

After that, try a few fairway woods, then grab the big wood, the driver, which is more than likely made out of metal these days, but they still call it "The Big Stick."

This is, most likely, the club you will hold in your hands on the first tee.

Don't think about it.

Just pick a target and have at it. There just ain't nothing more fun than powering drivers on a driving range, swinging away at a fairway in front of you so wide they could put the entire O'Hare airport on it. And no matter how bad you hit these drivers, you don't have to chase the ball. You just tee another ball up and hit again.

Happy, happy, joy, joy.

You're warmed up, you're swinging smoothly.

Go for the fence. On the range, you have nothing to lose.

*PART FIVE:*
# HELP! WHAT CLUB SHOULD I HIT LAST ON THE DRIVING RANGE?

**OKAY, TO BE HONEST,** the jury is out on this question.

If the first club you're going to hit on the first hole is a driver, many professionals think that a driver should be your last memory on a driving range, so that when you get to the first tee, you can bring back that fresh memory and repeat.

How does this line of thinking work? Actually, fairly logically, and you're going to use this when you get to the first tee, so pay attention.

While on the range, swinging away with your driver, you are bound to hit one perfect shot, a ball that feels sharp and hard on the club face, that flies straight at your target like you've been playing the game for a hundred years. When that happens, stand there and remember, no memorize the feeling of the swing, watch the ball fly away, and then land. Hold your follow-through like you're posing for a picture done by a guy who hasn't yet figured out his new camera.

Memorize the feel of the shot.

Put the image of the shot in your mind's eye.

Then put the club away in your bag. Don't try to repeat that perfection until you get to the first tee. All you'll do is screw it up and confuse the issue.

The other side of the argument for which club to hit last votes for one of your wedges. Many professionals think a cool-down is needed in a pre-round practice session. They believe a player should work back from a driver down to a wedge, then a half wedge, then a few chip shots off the end of the driving range tee after that perfect drive.

This thinking assumes a few things. First, you are at a country club that furnishes unlimited practice balls. Or you bought a really big bucket of balls. If you bought the small bucket, make the good driver your last shot, even if that perfect last shot is three balls from your last ball. Hit the good shot, stop, and walk away.

The second thing cool-down thinking assumes is that you are there on the range far enough ahead of your tee time to take the extra time. Make sure you save some time for putting, remember.

So, let's assume you have the range balls and the time, why not work back down the clubs? It only seems like a logical way to practice. And what can hitting a few more golf balls hurt?

Again, let me repeat. While you are doing this, focus on targets and swinging smoothly.

So, to answer the question of this chapter, always end with a driver on a great shot if you bought a small bucket.

Or with a big bucket of balls, end chipping a dozen or so balls twenty yards off the end of the tee, but do that only after you have ended the practice with the driver with that perfect shot. Either choice is right, either will work, both make you look like you know what you are doing.

And more importantly, both will help you in different ways get off that first tee with success.

## *PART SIX:* HELP! HOW MANY PRACTICE PUTTS IS TOO MANY?

**THE ANSWER** to this question is very, very simple. You have hit too many practice putts when you are suddenly late for your tee time and have to rush to the first tee, thus causing you to be upset and likely miss the first shot.

Otherwise, a golfer can never practice putting enough.

Ever.

Let me add some personal comments here.

I used to be a really great putter back when I was young and had a lifetime of extra time. I wasn't that strong from tee to green, but get me on the green and I had a belief that I could make any putt from any distance.

And I often did.

How did I get like that? Simple, actually. I spent hours and hours and hours, day after day, year after year, on putting greens. I would bet my friends ten cents a hole on a putting contest around the eighteen holes on the putting green.

(Later that became a buck a hole, and more even later when I turned professional, but I won't go into that aspect of the game here.)

I even have many memories back in high school of starting my parent's car, aiming the headlights at the putting green, and practicing until after midnight. Of course, back then I needed a real life, and a few more dates, but not having a social life sure helped my putting.

The upshot was that when I got to the golf course and stood over a putt, I never thought of the mechanical movement of putting, I simply just knew the ball was going into the hole because I had made a thousand putts just like the one I had in front of me. And if the ball didn't go in, chances are I just read the break in the green wrong.

This kind of practice needs to be done long before you get to a country club for a big match like we're talking about here. The goal of practice putting when you are at a country club isn't to make your putting better, it's to get the "feel" of the greens.

How fast are they?

How slow?

Do they have grain? (Which way the grass grows because if you can see which way the grass is growing, putts break more that way and less against the grain. Bet you always wondered what those announcers were talking about when they said, "The grain got him.")

So, to be deadly honest, there is no amount of putts on a practice green right before a big match that are going to help you that day. Your putting is either going to suck or be great, depending on a few factors that have nothing to do with the amount of putts you hit before the round.

First, it depends on how much you have practiced your putting at home, on your home course, in your office, or in long hallways when staying at a hotel.

Second, how good you are feeling that day.

Third, and never forget third: Luck. Often great putting is just some luck.

So, before you start the round, just get the feel of the green, the sense of the speed, the look of the hole by hitting a few dozen putts from different distances, then give it up, head back to your cart, and go grab a snack and a bottle of water while you wait to call your group to the first tee.

But, one final tip. Always end your practice putts on a putt you made. Just like the great driver on the green, it will put a positive image of the ball going into the hole in your mind.

Everything about golf is a mind game, so don't fight it.

Just play along.

*Continued next month… We finally get to the first tee!*

# A TRUE STORY FROM THE FRONT LINES

## *MY BEST AND WORST TEE SHOT EVER WAS THE SAME SHOT*

**BACK UP IN TIME** a little to the fall of 1972. Palm Springs, California.

I was a young golf professional, just starting to be taught how to really play the game by Zell Eaton. I was also struggling to make ends meet, since I had no real money when I got the job with Zell.

My best friend, Jim Kiser, had helped me get from Idaho to Palm Springs and get set up for the job in an apartment. Jim was a college student at the time, headed to a great career in law, and he was a fine golfer. Just don't tell him I told you.

In Palm Springs during those days was a par three golf course, called an "executive course" for reasons lost in time. I have no memory of the name of the place, and I know it doesn't still exist, long ago replaced by an expansive big course and expensive homes. But in 1972, this big square piece of desert had been turned into a dry, hard golf course, fenced in from the tumbleweeds and blowing sand.

And it had one feature that got it a lot of play.

It had lights.

And it stayed open on some nights far past midnight.

For a young, avid golfer like I was at the time, this was heaven. A place to go to practice my short game until all hours of the morning. Needless to say, I spent a lot of time on those dry, dusty fairways and small, hard greens.

One night, my friend Jim, before heading back north to school, decided to go along and play a round with me. We were somewhere on the back nine, facing a hole about 120 yards long, which was fairly long for that course. It was past eleven in the evening, but we were young, strong, and had nothing better to do.

If I remember right, Jim teed off first and missed the green to the right.

I stood up there, and with the swing that Zell Eaton hoped to make worthwhile, tried to hit an easy wedge, planning to make the ball land short and bounce up onto the hard green.

To say I missed the shot would be a very large understatement.

I bladed it, which means the leading edge of the club cut into the ball like a knife.

The ball bounced once or twice just getting off the tee, hit something off to the left of the hole, while bouncing, and then just kept bouncing.

And bouncing.

And bouncing.

First right, then left, then back right toward the green.

I think there had to be a hundred gopher holes out there in that rough for the ball to do that.

It was still bouncing and moving at a pretty good speed when it reached the green, slammed into the pin, and dropped into the hole.

Hole-in-one.

The only perfect shot in golf.

I had been playing for almost twenty years at that point, and that was my first hole-in-one.

I have played for decades since, and that is still my only hole-in-one.

Witnessed by Jim.

Near midnight.

On a course that no longer exists.

I don't often talk about the shot, to be honest.

But it did teach me a lesson that I never forgot. The only thing that really matters is the score on the card.

I was watching Arnold Palmer play a few holes at Indian Wells Country Club later that winter in the Bob Hope Desert Classic. On one hole, the first hole where I joined his "Arnie's Army" gallery, he duck-hooked his drive. It would have hit a home and gone out-of-bounds if it hadn't hit a palm tree instead.

Standing under the palm tree, he rolled his next shot across the fairway. The ball bounced off the brick side of a house, and barely got back in bounds in the rough.

I had watched him for exactly two shots and all I could see was a real hack of a player. He then hit a really nasty shot that barely got off the ground and just sort of rolled up onto the front edge of the green of the short par four.

I had now watched three shots and Arnie had hacked all three of them.

Then he stood up there and made the putt and walked off with a par.

And the lesson of my hole-in-one earlier was again pounded home.

It doesn't matter how pretty, how ugly, or how just plain lucky a shot is, what counts is the final score on the card.

But, that said, I sure hope your holes-in-one are a little more attractive than mine was.

And maybe at a better time of day.

*More golf stories next month…*

# DEAN WESLEY SMITH

**USA TODAY BESTSELLING AUTHOR**

# THUNDER MOUNTAIN

A SCIENCE FICTION NOVEL OF THE OLD WEST AND TRUE LOVE

*USA Today **bestselling writer** Dean Wesley Smith weaves a science fiction tale of love and survival of two modern professors dealing with the past they both love and study.*

*Offered a free trip into a remote Idaho wilderness that she loves, Professor Dawn Edwards can't refuse. On the trip she meets Professor Madison Rogers and they fall for each other before they even reach their destination.*

*But living in the Old West proves to be a brutal task at times. Somehow, Dawn must survive to rescue herself, her friends, and the man she loves.*

*A science fiction novel of love and survival and the Old West as only Dean Wesley Smith can write.*

# THUNDER MOUNTAIN
*A Science Fiction Novel of the Old West and True Love*

## PART ONE

## CHAPTER ONE

**DAWN EDWARDS STOOD** on the edge of the narrow trail, staring at the metal plaque attached to a flat stone among the tall pines. She couldn't believe she was actually here, at the Roosevelt Cemetery, one of the most remote and difficult to find cemeteries in all of Idaho.

Maybe in all of the United States.

Around her the day was going to turn hot before it was finished, but the sun had yet to clear the tall mountains towering over her and there was still a chill to the crisp, clear air under the tall pines. Monumental Creek ran about twenty feet below her, the beautiful mountain stream filling the air with a relaxing sound of water over rocks.

This August morning couldn't get any more perfect as far as she was concerned. The smell of the dried pine needles seemed extra strong. She had managed to get into one of the most remote places in the country, a long distance inside the River of No Return Primitive Area. And she had found a tiny cemetery she knew existed, but never thought she could find.

A perfect morning.

She had on jeans and her old comfortable hiking boots. At the moment she still had on her parka, even though it was early August. But she would shortly shed that and the light sweatshirt under it as well for the white hiking shirt and sports bra under that.

She and two old friends from college were camped back up the stream above the lake about a half-mile. She had wanted to come down to the lake and cemetery on her own this morning. They hadn't cared and were both still sound asleep in their tents when she left.

She kneeled down and brushed some pine needles reverently away from the plaque.

The engraved metal plaque had been installed in 1949 by the Pioneers of the Thunder Mountain Gold Rush. That gold rush had happened from 1901 to 1909 with the peak years being 1902-1907.

Five very short years.

The small cemetery was roped off between trees framing a small square area of brush and dried pine needles not much bigger than a small front yard on a suburban street. The rope looked to be only a few years old, brown, but not frayed yet, so someone still sort of took care of the place. She wondered who that might be and if she could find that person or group.

There were still a few wooden grave marker boards, all weather-beaten and brown with names long worn away. They marked a few graves and she could see a few other unmarked graves where the

ground under the needles had settled in. One grave kept drawing her eye, the depression closest to the stone, but she didn't feel it would be right to cross inside the rope and get closer.

There would be nothing to see.

She knew so much about this area and had been studying it for two years for her new book *The Great Secrets of the West*. The remains of the Roosevelt mining town under the lake between her and her camp was one of those secrets. It would be a great chapter in her book.

The problem was there was very little to research. Very, very little, actually was known or written about this area. Even though as a college professor, she had special privileges at the Idaho Historical Society and access to the records of papers of towns that no longer existed, including the few copies of the *Roosevelt Avalanche* that managed to survive, she could find very little.

Now she was lucky enough to actually get in here and see it for herself.

For some reason, this area really had pulled her more than any other place she researched. It felt magical.

And special.

Which is why she had funded this camping trip into this wilderness and paid for two of her old college friends to come with her.

It had taken them a two-hour drive yesterday to get to the recreation town of Cascade, Idaho, from Boise where they all lived. Then it took another three hours to get to the remote old mining town of Yellow Pine on mostly dirt roads.

They had had lunch there in an old bar that looked right out of 1900. Everything in it seemed authentic right down to the two horses that were tied up outside and the dried smell of old cigars inside. There were guns and animal heads hanging on the walls along with old rusted mining equipment and a large wagon wheel.

She found it wonderful and familiar. Her friends found it "quaint" but they loved the fantastic cheeseburgers made on an old grill. Dawn had to admit, her cheeseburger was one of the best she could remember. And the fries were greasy and covered in salt, just as she liked them.

From Yellow Pine, it took three more hours of horrid driving on a one-lane winding dirt road to get through another ghost town named Stibnite and up to the Monumental Valley Summit.

The road had switchbacks so tight, she had to back the van up to get around them. The road scared the hell out of her two friends and if she hadn't been driving, it would have scared her as well.

Her research made vague references to a grand hotel that stood on that summit at one point, but there was no sign of the ruins now, and no record was really sure where it had been.

Or even if it had existed at all.

Sometimes history could be so elusive. Especially history of the Old West.

She had walked among the trees on the flat top of the ridge, getting the strangest feeling that she really knew the place. Yet she had never been here before.

Weird. Not creepy.

More like she had come home. It was so beautiful. You could see seemingly forever in all directions. And the views of the mountain ranges going on and on just took her breath away.

That ridge summit marked the edge of the River of No Return Primitive Area, but a mining claim inside the primitive area had managed to keep a road open, so she could drive down the two thousand foot drop on a frighteningly steep road into the Monumental Creek drainage.

Once in the bottom of the valley, the road wound leisurely along the stream among the tall pine trees. They passed a lot of ruins once they got to the valley floor.

They camped about a mile above the lake that marked the death of Roosevelt, Idaho in 1909.

Now, this morning she had seen the lake and taken pictures of the remains of the old ghost town under the water.

And now she had been fantastically lucky and found the cemetery below the lake on a small hillside.

The plaque attached to the rock on the edge of the cemetery read:

**Roosevelt Cemetery**
**In Memory of**
**The Thunder Mountain Dead**
**Of Whom Thirteen Are Known**
**To Rest In This Cemetery.**

There were ten names on it with an inscription about three unknowns that were also buried here.

Two of the names were only last names.

She had a picture of this plaque blown up and framed on her office wall at Boise State University and she knew those names by heart.

She had managed to find family history on eight of the names, but the two without first names remained elusive as well as the three unknowns.

Again, she reverently brushed away more pine needles, then she took a few pictures of her own of the plaque.

And a few pictures of the sunken grave closest to the rock.

Then she stood and looked around, taking long deep breaths of the clear air, enjoying the smell of pine and forest.

What was it about this place that had her so fascinated?

What kind of connection? It had been with her since the first moment she heard of this valley and the lost town.

She sat again next to the plaque on the dirt beside the trail, her back against the base of a large tree and pulled out a bottle of water.

The peacefulness of the forest and the tall mountains around here just seemed to relax her, like she belonged here in these high mountains. She took a drink, savoring how the water took the dust out of her mouth.

Then slowly and carefully, she looked around, studying the trees, the hillsides, and the stream below her, trying to memorize every detail of this perfect morning.

She could almost imagine this valley alive with people instead of forgotten by all but a few.

She wished she could see this valley when it had seven thousand people in it, when the town of Roosevelt was a booming mining town, when the sounds of the pianos playing in the dozen saloons and two dance halls along Main Street echoed through the trees and the high peaks at all hours of the day and night.

For over six years, until a mudslide blocked Monumental Creek and backed water up over Roosevelt, this valley had been alive and booming, one of the great secrets of western lore.

And then it had died.

Quickly and without anyone really remembering it.

Or writing about it.

Now, legend had it that on a calm night sitting beside Roosevelt Lake with the remains of the town visible through the clear water, you could still hear the pianos from the saloons.

Tonight, as the sun dropped behind Thunder Mountain, she planned on sitting beside that lake and listening.

And maybe, just maybe, if she listened hard enough, she would hear the music.

At least she hoped she would.

# CHAPTER TWO

**DAWN EDWARDS SAT** in her office on the Boise State University campus working on the lesson plan for an honors program on western history she started teaching in September. She had on a t-shirt with the logo "Read a Book, Save a Mind" and jeans. She had kicked off her tennis shoes when she came in. Today, since she had walked down to her office from her apartment, she had her long brown hair pulled back off her head.

On her desk she had a large glass of iced tea with too much sugar as far as her friends were concerned. But she exercised enough to keep her weight level, even at thirty-two. No kids, no marriage, no relationship. She figured she could do what she darned well pleased.

She loved her office, tucked in a corner on the third floor of one of the older buildings in this sprawling campus. She was closer to Capitol Boulevard than the wild football-stadium-side of campus. The building used to be an old administration office and they had converted a break room on the third floor to her office.

Two large windows looked out over a wide stretch of lawn that ran to the edge of the Boise River. Beyond the trees that framed the river and filled the park beyond, she could see the Capitol Building and the tops of a few of the taller downtown buildings.

She had installed dark wooden bookcases on three walls and had her grandfather's old wooden desk brought in to command an area of the room.

She had found some used couches and a couple of chairs to form a sort of sitting area with a scarred-up wooden coffee table that was now normally covered with books.

In one corner sat a small fridge and microwave and a shelf of various teas.

The place always smelled like a library and her tea, even after she had been gone for a time.

She had spent many a late night up here reading. She tended to like her office more than she did her small apartment up the hill just off Vista Avenue. Her apartment seemed lonely and sterile, mostly because she had never bothered to fix it up. Her office, on the other hand, was warm in the winter and comfortable in the summer. And close to a couple of her favorite restaurants as well.

She had more than enough family money to buy herself a nice house somewhere. Three or four houses, actually, but so far the desire just hadn't struck her. Her office was enough of a home for now.

A knock at her open door startled her.

In early August there just weren't that many people on campus beside football players practicing and she hadn't heard any steps coming down the hall outside.

She looked up into the smiling face of Bonnie Kendal.

Bonnie and her fantastic husband, Duster, had been friends for two years, since they discovered at a lecture how much Dawn loved the Old West and the history of the people of the west.

It seemed that both of the Kendals were experts on western history and lore and often gave her directions to explore with her research that she would have never found without their advice. In fact, she was thinking of adding them to the acknowledgements of her next book.

Bonnie was a striking woman, with deep brown eyes and long brown hair, almost as long as Dawn's. Bonnie stood a good three inches taller than Dawn's five-eight. And Dawn loved how Bonnie carried herself, as if she were in charge of everything and everyone around her, even though she was the nicest and most unassuming woman Dawn had ever met.

Bonnie just had a confidence about her that seemed to go far beyond her 35 years. Dawn admired that and hoped that some day she could command that same feeling in people around her. But most of the time she just felt insecure.

"How was the trip into Roosevelt?" Bonnie asked as Dawn motioned for her to come in.

"Grueling, long, and just flat-out wonderful," Dawn said, smiling as she stood and came around the desk to hug Bonnie. She indicated Bonnie should take a seat on the couch. "Water? Diet Coke?"

"Water," Bonnie said, smiling as she sat down. "It's getting warm out there."

"Who would have thought?" Dawn asked. "August in Boise."

Bonnie laughed. "So tell me about it. Not many people have ever seen that valley you were in."

"There's something magical in that valley," Dawn said, getting a cold bottle of water from the fridge, then grabbing her own ice tea from her desk, and joining Bonnie in the seating area surrounded by high shelves of books.

"Magical?" Bonnie asked, smiling and looking intently at her. "Never heard it described like that before."

"Magical." Dawn could feel herself being pulled back into the sensations, the smells, the visions of that area as she talked. "Monumental Summit felt like the top of the world and the entire valley felt like it could come alive for me at any moment. My two friends who went with me thought it creepy, but I loved it."

She then continued on for the next five minutes, lost in the wonderful memories of being in that valley, describing everything she had seen, and what she wanted to have the time to see on future trips. For example, she hadn't made it down the valley the extra couple of miles to the site of the old Thunder Mountain City mining town. There seemed to be more information surviving on Thunder Mountain City than its much larger neighbor Roosevelt.

Bonnie smiled all the way through and nodded until Dawn finally came back to the world of her office and realized she had been talking for a while.

"Sorry," she said, feeling embarrassed as she took a sip of her tea and didn't look Bonnie in the eyes. "Just not many people I can talk to about that kind of history and actually getting to see it."

Bonnie laughed, the sound filling the office and making Dawn smile and feel less embarrassed. "Oh wow, do I know that feeling. Duster and I hoped you might feel that way."

Dawn took a drink of her very sweet tea. "I'm so in love with that area and the history around it, I've decided that only one chapter in my book isn't enough. I'm thinking of doing an entire book on the area."

"Wonderful," Bonnie said. "There really isn't one."

"I know," Dawn said. "How well I know."

Bonnie suddenly looked more serious. "So you going back in there again this summer?"

Dawn shook her head, feeling sad. That was the one major disappointment she was going through. She had over a month before classes started. She had the time and the money and the desire. "Can't find anyone to go with me."

Then she looked at Bonnie's now smiling face. Something was going on. She knew Bonnie well enough to read that much.

"So what do you and that gorgeous hunk of a husband of yours have dreamed up?"

"Just a little trip," Bonnie said. "Back to Roosevelt. But you are going to have to keep something about the trip very, very secret. Is that possible?"

Dawn damn near came off the couch and floated in the air in her excitement. Her mouth went instantly dry and her mind just wouldn't let the idea in much. She had resigned herself to not being able to get back into Roosevelt for another year. No one she knew even slightly would go with her, and she wasn't going into that wilderness by herself.

"I can keep a secret," Dawn said, smiling. "With the best of them. So you and Duster thinking of taking a trip in there?"

"We are," Bonnie said.

"Oh, my, oh, my," Dawn said, trying to catch her breath.

Bonnie just kept smiling and talking, thankfully ignoring how Dawn was suddenly acting like a kid promised a new toy.

"And we're going to pay all expenses. We hope to bring along one other friend. Have you ever met Professor Madison Rogers from the University of Idaho?"

Now Dawn's heart leaped even more and her mouth got even drier if that were possible.

She took a quick drink to clear some of the dryness.

"I heard he is working on a book on the mining wars of Montana and Northern Idaho," Dawn said. "And I've read two of his books on Utah history. He's a good researcher. I'd love to meet him."

Dawn was sure she would feel intimidated by him, but she could get past that. He only had one more book than she did. And they both had their areas of expertise. More than likely he would be focused on the mining in the Thunder Mountain area while her interest lay in the people who lived in that remote valley.

And the ones who died there.

"Fantastic," Bonnie said, standing. "Can you leave tomorrow? We'll only be gone a few days."

"Of course I can," Dawn said. "I can't begin to thank you. This is so exciting."

"We'll pick you up in the parking lot here tomorrow morning at 5 a.m. That work?"

"Perfectly," Dawn said, even though she hated the idea of getting up that early.

She hugged Bonnie.

"Thank you," Dawn said. "I so wanted to see Roosevelt one more time this summer."

"Oh, you can see it more than that if you want," Bonnie said, laughing.

With that she turned and left, leaving Dawn bouncing with excitement.

She quickly shut down her office and locked it. The lesson plan could wait until she got back. Tonight, she had packing to do.

She felt like a little girl at Christmas as she half-walked, half-skipped down the hallway toward the stairs.

# CHAPTER THREE

**MADISON ROGERS** dozed slightly in the front seat of Duster Kendal's big Cadillac Escalade. Groggy didn't begin to describe how he felt. Barely awake was an understatement.

Behind him, Duster's wife, Bonnie sat also in silence. Too damn early for any of them to talk much.

The big car rode smooth as glass as Duster wound it through the empty, early-morning streets of Boise from Madison's home down toward the campus of Boise State University. It seemed that Professor Dawn Edwards was joining them on their adventure into the mining areas of central Idaho.

Madison had always wanted to see the Yellow Pine, Stibnite, Edwardsburg, and Roosevelt areas. It was the last big mining run in the lower 48 states and it actually didn't end until around 1910. It seemed that Professor Edwards was an expert on the area, not the mining, but the people and history. He couldn't imagine how the mining and the history could be pulled apart much.

Bonnie and Duster had agreed to take him and Professor Edwards into the area, and since he had time before his classes started in September, he couldn't say no to Duster.

Bonnie and Duster had been friends for two years now, and one of the major supporters in his work. They seemed to know an uncanny amount about things in the Old West, and they had funded two of his trips so far. And they were completely funding this one. And they asked for nothing in return for their help.

Duster was a tall man, more than six feet. He tended to always wear cowboy boots, a cowboy hat, and a long duster-like brown coat, even in the summer. More than likely that was where he got his name.

Bonnie was a tall woman with long brown hair and a smile that seemed to light up rooms. Together, the two of them just sort of controlled a power and confidence that Madison had never experienced before. And he was very glad they were his friends.

He would do anything for them. But he had to admit, this getting up at 4 a.m. was not his thing. He rarely, even with classes, crawled out any earlier than ten or eleven in the morning. And only taught afternoon and evening classes.

Even though he taught up at the University of Idaho in Moscow all winter, Madison still had a home here in Boise where he spent the summers. It had been his parents' home and they had just given it to him when they retired to Arizona. They seldom came back. In fact, they hadn't been back to Boise now in three years.

He liked the place and had remodeled it for his own, with huge rooms full of research books and desks covered with paper. His parents kept asking him if he was ever going to have a woman join him in the house, but he was in his early thirties now and pretty set in his ways. He'd had relationships in the past, none now.

He was a night person. It was silent at night. People left him alone to research and write and he liked that.

He hated getting up this morning, which was the middle of his night. And perky morning people drove him crazy. In fact, he often wore a t-shirt that said, "If you laugh before noon, I'll have to kill you."

Bonnie was in the back seat and thankfully not talking much. Duster just drove and smiled, as if he were enjoying every minute of this early hour and how he was torturing Madison.

The Cadillac bumped into the parking lot, forcing Madison to open his eyes. He must have dozed for a few blocks because he didn't remember turning off of Capitol Boulevard into the University area.

The sun was barely lighting the sky and it was still just slightly before five in the morning. The last time Madison saw this hour of the day, it was from the night side.

Duster swung through the empty faculty parking lot and pulled up beside a woman standing in a dark jacket next to a dark minivan of some sort. There was a backpack at her feet.

She looked like she was fairly experienced in backwoods just at a glance at how she was dressed. She was about his height and clearly in shape. She bent down and swung the pack up onto her shoulder as Duster got out to help her load the pack into the back.

And as she swung the pack up, Madison caught a look at her face and his heart leaped and he was instantly awake.

Instantly.

Better than ten cups of coffee awake.

She was about his age and maybe the most attractive woman he had seen in a long, long time. She had brown eyes that seemed to stare at him in surprise for a moment, then look away. Her hair was long and brown and pulled back off her face.

72

Holy crap, Professor Edwards was a stunner.

The breakfast bar he had managed to choke down before Duster and Bonnie picked him up felt like lead in his stomach. Never in all his life had he had a reaction to a woman like this. He prided himself on being alone most of the time because a social life got in the way of his passion, which was his work.

He had had a few longer relationships through college, but they had all left telling him he was basically married to his work and history.

He hadn't argued with any of them, and honestly didn't miss them. They had been right.

He sat up straight and took a couple deep breaths. He was going to need to get a grip on himself quickly, or this was going to be a very long few days.

Duster shut the back hatch and Professor Edwards got into the back seat beside Bonnie and behind Duster. He watched.

How was it possible? He must be having a nightmare or a hallucination because of getting up so damned early. She just couldn't be even more stunning in the light of the car. Her face was slightly tanned and her nose small and perfect.

She laughed at something Bonnie said about morning.

Then she said in this perfect voice, "Anyone who likes to get up at this hour should just be shot."

Madison managed to get himself in control and shifting around slightly against his seat belt, he extended his hand. "I agree completely, Professor Edwards."

She took his hand and he felt like a jolt of electricity had run through him as she looked into his eyes with those wonderful brown eyes of hers.

"Dawn," she said. "Call me Dawn, Professor Rogers, and no jokes about the time of day."

He actually laughed and it only sounded slightly forced to his ears. He loved her voice, her eyes, and the feel of her hand.

What was wrong with him?

"Call me Madison."

And with that he had to let go of her hand, even though he would have rather just held it.

The light in the car dimmed as Duster started out of the parking lot and Madison forced himself to turn back around from staring into her eyes and face forward.

He just hoped she hadn't noticed he was sweating at five in the morning. The car just hadn't been that warm a minute ago.

Duster was still just smiling about some unknown joke as behind him the most beautiful woman on the planet sat.

And she hated mornings as well.

And she loved history, was an expert in it, wrote books on the topic.

Was a woman like her even possible?

This was most certainly going to be an interesting few days. Far, far more than he had expected.

Now, if he could just quit sweating and calm down.

# CHAPTER FOUR

**DAWN SOMEHOW,** after only getting a few hours sleep, had managed to make it down to the parking lot at the University ten minutes ahead of time. She hated mornings and being as excited about this trip as she was, she hadn't slept more than a few hours last night.

The crisp morning air smelled like wet grass from the sprinklers going on the wide lawn between the office building and the river. Nearby Capitol Boulevard, normally one of the busiest streets in the city, had no traffic on it. The streetlights just lit up the pavement in an odd orange glow.

She was a little worried about meeting Professor Rogers. She had no idea what he looked like, but had heard through friends that he was a great teacher and very focused on his work. But honestly she was more worried at the moment about falling asleep and snoring and drooling all the way to Cascade.

She had tried a cup of coffee and a doughnut on the way from the apartment, but neither had helped much at all. Sandpaper was grating at her eyes. She was going to have to doze a little, of that she had no doubt. She just hoped Bonnie and Duster didn't mind.

Thank heavens this time she wasn't driving as she had done on the trip into Roosevelt last week.

Duster and Bonnie drove into the parking lot just a few moments after she had got out her pack and locked up her van. They were driving a big Cadillac SUV and she had no doubt it would have the power to handle the roads into Yellow Pine and over Monumental Summit. That was good.

Their car was huge, far big enough for the four of them to have enough room with all their supplies and gear.

As Duster stopped the car and opened the door to come out and help her, she remembered how handsome and powerful Bonnie's husband was. He seemed to dominate anyone around him and his smile and confident manner was fantastically attractive, even at this ugly time of the morning.

If she could find a man like Duster, who could put up with her and her research, she would be in heaven. Bonnie didn't know how really lucky she was.

As Dawn swung the pack up onto her shoulder, she caught a look at Professor Rogers in the front seat, turning to look at her.

It was like she had been shot.

She froze, staring into his eyes.

He was the best-looking man she had ever seen.

Period.

No exceptions.

Better than even Duster, if that were possible.

How was that possible?

Why hadn't Professor Rogers put his picture on his books? At least she would have been warned about how good-looking he was. Of course, she didn't put her picture on her books either.

He looked just as shocked to see her as she felt to see him.

She suddenly felt a lot less tired.

A lot less.

The pack swung up on her back, and somehow she managed to turn to move to the rear of the SUV to toss the pack in without falling down or doing anything really, really morning stupid.

Duster helped her and then she moved around on the driver's side to get into the back seat behind Duster.

Bonnie was in the other back seat, behind Professor Rogers, and Dawn managed to not look at Professor Rogers for a moment as she worked with her seat belt, a task almost impossible at this hour of the day.

Bonnie laughed and asked her if she was awake yet.

"Anyone who likes to get up at this hour should just be shot," Dawn said, then suddenly got worried that Professor Rogers was a morning person. Oh, God, had her very first sentence insulted the man?

Professor Rogers laughed and turned to her, extending his hand. "I agree completely, Professor Edwards."

She touched his hand and somehow managed to just not sigh and melt into the car seat. He had dark brown eyes, longish brown hair, and chiseled features, including a perfect dimple on his right cheek when he smiled.

Holy crap, she was shaking hands and staring into the wonderful eyes of a flipping Greek God. He even smelled fantastic, like faint orange peels and rich chocolate.

How was that even possible at five in the morning?

"Call me Dawn," she managed to choke out, hoping that her voice didn't sound too stupid. Control at this time of the morning was not one of her strong suits. Combine that with facing a man so handsome, she wanted to melt, and control wasn't a word she would use.

"Call me Madison," he said.

And as Duster started the car forward, she sadly had to let go of Madison's firm hand as he turned to face forward and the interior car light went dim.

She stared at his profile for a moment in the dim morning light, then turned to look at Bonnie.

Bonnie was smiling, the smile reaching her eyes and every inch of her face. Then Bonnie pretended to fan herself, indicating that she thought Professor Rogers was hot as well.

Dawn nodded and tried not to laugh. She leaned over and whispered to Bonnie. "You could have warned me."

Bonnie laughed softly and then said, "What would have been the fun with that? I didn't want to miss your reaction."

All Dawn could do was shake her head and laugh softly.

And then she sat back and stared at the profile of the man of her dreams in the front passenger seat.

Holy smokes was this going to be a long drive and a very strange trip. Not at all what she had expected.

# CHAPTER FIVE

**MADISON COULD FEEL** Dawn's eyes looking at him from behind, but damned if he could think of any small talk to give him an excuse to turn around and look at her. It was far, far, too early in the morning and he felt like he was back in middle school and just meeting a girl for the first time.

Stupid, just flat stupid. He was too old for this, yet he couldn't seem to shake it.

She was amazing and he didn't even know her.

And she smelled wonderful as well. Like a fresh bakery and a rich cup of coffee. Perfect smells for this time of day.

So without one stupid thing to say, all he could do was sit and stare out the front window as Duster headed through the mostly empty city streets toward the freeway.

Duster finally took him off the hook when he said, "Okay, folks, we have a little side trip to make on the way to the Thunder Mountain region."

"Side trip?" Madison asked, turning slightly to face Duster. Madison couldn't figure out why Duster was smiling. It was like he and Bonnie had some fantastic joke they were pulling or something.

Beyond the joke of asking the most beautiful woman in the world, who was also smart and loved history, to come along.

"We want you both to see a place very special to us," Bonnie said from the back seat and Duster nodded.

"It's in Silver City," Duster said.

"Silver City?" Dawn asked from the back seat.

Madison glanced back and could see that she was as surprised as he was.

Silver City was an old ghost town that sort of now functioned as a tourist stop in the summer months. It had been one of the major mining towns in the late 1800s. There were still a few mines active in the area, but the town was mostly gone except for a few buildings that had made it through the one hundred and fifty years of weather. The town was in the Owyhee Mountains on the Oregon border. About an hour of fairly rough road off any major highway if Madison remembered right.

"It's the secret we asked if you could keep," Duster said, smiling as he headed the big SUV west on the freeway.

"Can you tell us about it now?" Madison asked, not really sure if he were happy with the idea of such a long side trip. It would take them almost four hours to get up to Silver City, and a good three of those hours would be out of the way, so this would be a six-hour side trip at least.

He had no doubt they were going to have to stay in McCall tonight if they got that far, even though they had started early. Duster had told him this trip was going to only take a few days, but now he wondered.

Of course, with Professor Edwards along, a longer trip seemed like it might be better. Duster and Bonnie were paying all the costs. So why not? He had the extra time.

He forced himself to take a deep breath and relax into the idea of spending more time with two friends and a beautiful woman he wanted to get to know.

"You wouldn't believe us on the secret if we told you," Duster said.

"I'll second that," Bonnie said. "You two are going to be the first two people we show this to."

"Besides my family," Duster said.

"So we are trusting you both a great deal with this secret," Bonnie said.

Duster nodded. "We feel that the work both of you do could really, really be helped by what we are going to show you. But you have to trust us for a few hours first."

"Our research?" Madison asked.

He glanced back at Dawn who looked just as confused as he felt. She was fantastic-looking even frowning.

Duster nodded. "More than you can imagine, actually."

"Are we still going into the Thunder Mountain region?" Dawn asked.

Madison could hear it in her voice that she was worried. Clearly her passion was that area.

"We are," Bonnie said, then laughed. "More so than you can even dream of right now."

"Wow, that sounds very secret-agent-like," Madison said, staring at his friend Duster.

"Much, much more important than any secret agent stuff," Duster said. "Much more."

Madison glanced back at Dawn again. In the dim light he could tell she was worried. As much as he was.

He shrugged at her and she smiled at him and said, "Why not?"

He laughed and turned to face the front again, watching the empty freeway in the early morning light flash past. "Looks like you have two adventure-lovers with you on this."

"We hoped you would both say that," Duster said.

"We were pretty sure you both would," Bonnie said, laughing.

"So is this secret actually in Silver City?" Madison asked. He had been up to the old ghost town a number of times and had studied it a lot. He liked focusing his work on lesser-known areas of the history of the Pacific Northwest region. Now the people who owned the buildings in the actual remains of Silver City were very, very protective of the property and the history of the city was clearly documented.

"Nope," Duster said. "It's in a mine on Florida Mountain above Silver City. Now, no more on that until we get there because we honestly can't explain it until you see it, and even then it's almost impossible to believe."

"Breakfast at that fantastic little café in Murphy?" Bonnie asked.

"Please," Dawn said in that wonderful voice of hers. "I don't care where."

"Never been there," Madison said, "but breakfast in an hour does sound perfect."

"Mind if I doze off until then?" Dawn asked.

Madison was very glad she asked that, because the shock of meeting her was starting to wear off and he didn't want to be rude by just dozing on his own.

"No problem at all," Duster said, his voice happy and filled with far, far too much energy for this time of the day. "I'll get us there, but if you are all snoring, I might turn up the music."

"Deal," Madison said, leaning back and closing his eyes.

With the most beautiful woman he had ever seen on this crazy trip, he was going to need to be as rested as he could be. Not counting whatever crazy secret Bonnie and Duster had in store for them on the mountain above Silver City.

Behind him he heard Dawn say softly, "I hate early mornings."

All he could do was smile.

She was more perfect than he had even imagined a woman could be.

And he didn't even know her yet.

# CHAPTER SIX

**THE DRIVE** into Murphy, Idaho, seemed to be instantaneous.

Dawn had dozed off right after the announcement they were going to Silver City first. She'd never been up there, so the idea kind of excited her, as long as they were actually headed to the Thunder Mountain area and Roosevelt after that.

Duster pulled into the café parking lot and shut off the car, then said, "We're here."

She managed to sit up and wipe the sleep from her eyes a little and run her fingers through her hair. Then she quickly checked to make sure she hadn't been drooling.

Bonnie was doing the same thing as she climbed out the other side.

The sun was up and was promising a hot August day as Dawn stepped onto the concrete and stretched. There were in front of a one-story old building with a faded sign on it and dust-covered windows. The sign said, "Highway Café" which was about as original as it came in these parts.

She had pulled off her coat and had been using it as a pillow. Now she was only dressed in a white cotton blouse tucked into her jeans with a sports bra under that.

The air wasn't cool, even though it was just barely after six in the morning. The day was going to be hot. Very hot.

The air around the small town of Murphy smelled like sagebrush and the wind was barely rustling the tops of the nearby cottonwoods.

On the other side of the car Madison seemed to almost be staggering as well and his hair was mussed up. She smiled, liking the fact that he was as much a night person as she was.

"No talking about the secret at all," Duster said to her and Madison as they headed for the front door of the old Highway Café. "Or any mine. Or Silver City for that matter. The people here think we have a ranch up in the hills."

"We actually own one," Bonnie said, laughing as she stretched. "Cattle and all."

Dawn nodded, actually surprised that Bonnie and Duster would own something like that. It showed how much she didn't know about them. They had offered to fund some of her research once, so she knew they had money. She did as well, actually. So much that she didn't really have to teach if she didn't want to. She actually had a vast amount, in the millions, which had been left to her from her grandmother. When they had offered the funding, she had thanked Bonnie and Duster, but said no.

But they had insisted on paying all the expenses on this trip and she didn't feel like arguing. She really never let anyone know just how rich she really was. It always caused more problems than it was worth.

Dawn stretched and ran her hands through her hair, working to shake the sleep from her mind.

Madison was doing the same thing.

God, even half asleep, the man was fantastic. She couldn't remember when she had been this attracted to a man in just a physical way.

And he seemed attracted to her as well, which meant they were both going to have to be careful on this trip if they didn't want to spoil the few days for Bonnie and Duster with wild and noisy sex.

She honestly wouldn't mind the thought of that, but she really liked Bonnie and Duster and wanted to keep them as friends.

Inside, Duster got them a scarred-top booth looking out the dusty front window while she and Bonnie and Madison all headed down the narrow hallway toward the restrooms. Pictures of the area in cheap frames covered the hallway walls, but Dawn was far too tired to stop and look at them.

Bonnie made it to the sink first and splashed water on her face, pulling out a comb and working on her hair while Dawn used the toilet.

Then they switched positions.

Dawn let the water in the sink run cold for a minute, then splashed water on her face. The ice-cold water felt perfect, knocking back the sleep some, enough to get her through the rest of the day and more than likely into a hotel room in McCall later this evening.

"You know how hard it is to not ask about this secret thing?" Dawn said softly to Bonnie as they headed down the narrow hallway back into the restaurant.

"I got a hunch," Bonnie said, laughing. "But trust me, it will be worth it."

"I am trusting you," Dawn said to Bonnie as she sat down in the booth next to Madison.

At a glance he looked like he had splashed water on his face as well.

She suddenly felt like a first date back in high school, all afraid to talk or get too close to her date for fear of even brushing an elbow.

So instead she glanced around at the café.

It was one that looked like it had been here and functioning since the 1950s. It had a few stuffed animal heads on the walls, two deer and a large elk, and lots of pictures of various things along the Snake River that ran nearby.

Murphy was founded out here in the middle of the desert, away from the river in 1890-something when a rail line came in. Now it wasn't more than a stop on the two-lane highway.

The menu for the place was covered in plastic and tattered from use.

There were only two other customers in the place sitting with their backs to them at the counter. She could see a cook behind an open counter and a waitress in a blue apron over jeans and a blue blouse. The waitress looked like she had had a tough life with far too much time in the sun for her skin.

Looking at the menu and smelling the wonderful breakfast smells of bacon and coffee, Dawn suddenly realized she was very hungry. More so than she expected to be at this time of day.

All four of them ordered basically the same thing. Eggs, bacon, toast, hash browns, and a small stack of pancakes. It was called "The Basic" on the menu and Dawn had no doubt there would be far, far too much food to finish. But it all sounded so good.

"So," Madison said to Duster, "exactly where is this ranch of yours and how big is it?"

Duster and Bonnie talked about their ranch, the house on it, and everything, like proud parents for most of the time it took for the food to start arriving, which thankfully wasn't that long. Dawn was afraid to even sip on the coffee in front of her until she had some food in her stomach.

*God, even half asleep, the man was fantastic. She couldn't remember when she had been this attracted to a man in just a physical way.*

Beside her, Madison didn't touch his coffee either. And even after sleeping like that in the car, he smelled wonderful. She wanted to just lean over and put her head on his shoulder and let his soft smell fill her nose, but she had no doubt that would just freak him out.

It turned out that Bonnie and Duster's ranch was a historical ranch and she recognized a few of the names that Duster and Madison were mentioning. The history of this area just hadn't been her focus, but it was still history of the Old West and she loved anything to do with that.

Then as they started eating, Duster asked Madison how his research on the mining wars of Northern Idaho was going. Madison talked about that for a short time with both Duster and Bonnie asking very pointed questions at times that surprised Dawn. Those two really, really did know their western history.

They had done the same with her a few times.

Dawn mostly sat and listened and ate and was happy for that.

She was mostly lost in Madison's clear and wonderful voice and a couple times found herself just staring at him beside her as he talked.

She flat-out loved that dimple on his right cheek when he smiled.

And just as two kids on a date, they both avoided any physical contact in the small booth. She wasn't sure what she was so afraid of with touching him. Maybe just bursting into flames.

It had been a while since she had spent any physical time with a man. Too long, in fact. More than a year if her memory served, and even that hadn't been any good.

So maybe she should be afraid of bursting into flames with a man as hot and good-looking as Madison.

It would be kind of embarrassing if he touched her arm and she just had an orgasm right there in the booth.

Bonnie and Duster would never let her forget it.

# CHAPTER SEVEN

**THEY ONLY MADE SMALL TALK** after they left the café and Murphy and headed east along the river. Madison had managed to get through breakfast sitting next to Dawn without doing anything really stupid, or even touching her in anyway.

He was afraid to, honestly. Even though all the way through breakfast it felt like it would be natural to reach down and just touch her leg or her hand on the table.

But he hadn't.

Amazing self-restraint on his part, not because he wanted anything from her, although he did, but because it would have felt so natural to touch her. Part of him just felt at home with her, at ease with her.

His feeling for her scared him more than he wanted to admit. It had been a long time since his work had allowed him to even meet a woman he was interested in.

Dawn hadn't said much through breakfast, and now he was afraid to ask her about her work, even though Duster and Bonnie had talked with him about his work. And as most discussions with them, he had been stunned at how sharp their knowledge about western history was.

They had surprised him a couple of times with questions just over breakfast. They seemed to do that a great deal with him.

Duster slowed and turned the Cadillac SUV off the highway and onto a dirt road that led up and over War Eagle Mountain and then down into Silver City.

The road was gravel, but wide, clearly two-lane, smooth, and well kept. Madison was surprised.

"Wow, they really improved this road."

Duster nodded. "A couple years back they started working some of the old mines up on War Eagle. They were sifting the tailings, actually, and finding enough to make it worthwhile. They needed to have a good road to get the big trucks up and down, since they were doing the sifting at a plant down on the river. The road up is two lane and pretty smooth gravel all the way up to the top of the mountain now."

"Thankfully," Bonnie said. "This used to be a terror ride."

"That's my memory of it," Madison said.

Duster then went on to tell him the history of the mines that had opened back up and now were mostly closed again, and why they had closed, and the politics of the entire thing.

It wasn't until they left the improved road and started down the narrow, winding old wagon road into Silver City that Duster turned to talking about their destination. Madison was glad he was, because the road from the top down was the terror that Bonnie described and what he remembered as well. Basically not much more than a trail working along a cliff face.

"We're not actually going into Silver City," Duster said. "We're going to take another road from Jordan Creek a mile south of Silver City and go up on Florida Mountain."

"How far up?" Madison asked, looking down at the drop beside his passenger window as Duster expertly took the big SUV around some corners. He clearly knew this road.

"About eight hundred feet up to an old mine my family has owned for a long time."

"It's called The Trade Dollar Mine," Bonnie said from behind him. "It officially played out around 1871, one of the first to have the gold vein pinch off, as they used to say."

Madison nodded. He had heard that term a lot. Gold veins often just went down to slivers and then stopped. The mine owners usually dug a little farther hoping the vein would start back up, but it seldom did.

Duster got the SUV to the bottom of the twisting road and then he slowed to a stop just short of a wide wooden bridge, letting the dust around them die off slowly. Ahead of them on the other side of the bridge the road went in three directions.

To Madison it looked really warm outside the window and it was still three hours before noon. It was going to be one really hot day.

"You ever been up here before?" Bonnie asked Dawn."

"Never," Dawn said. "A lot drier than I imagined. I like the central Idaho area better for that alone."

"Yeah, this is dry," Bonnie said. "But not as high. "This is just over six thousand feet here. Monumental Summit is around eight thousand."

"Higher," Dawn said.

Madison twisted around in his seat a little so he could see Dawn. Again she just shocked him with her looks and his attraction to her.

"This is Jordan Creek," Bonnie said. "And down the valley a few miles are the ghost towns of Delemar and Dewey. Up the creek about a mile is Silver City."

"You can get out of here by going down the stream and through those two towns," Duster said, "but the road out to Jordan Valley on the Oregon side is so rough, I wouldn't want to try it."

"I agree with that," Bonnie said. "Scared me something awful the one time we did try it."

"We're headed straight," Duster said as he started the SUV up and bounced them across the rough wooden bridge with a loud clatter and up the road. "We'll be there shortly now."

"And then we can see this secret?" Madison asked, smiling at Dawn who smiled back before he turned to face forward.

"I can promise you that you won't believe it, even when you see it," Duster said, laughing. "I sure didn't."

"You should write mystery novels," Dawn said.

Beside her Bonnie said softly. "Nope, this would be science fiction."

Madison wanted to turn around and look at Bonnie and ask her just what she meant by that, but didn't dare considering the road Duster was powering them up. It had more washouts and ruts than it had smooth spots.

Even the huge Cadillac was bouncing like a wild bull.

And the term road was not really accurate. Trail would be a generous description, actually.

And holding on for dear life was Madison's plan at the moment.

# CHAPTER EIGHT

**DAWN DID** everything she could to hold on as Duster bounced them up the roughest road she could ever remember. The Cadillac had great suspension and was normally a smooth ride. Even with that, she felt like she was inside a dryer set to tumble dry. If it hadn't been for the handle over the door and the seat and shoulder belts, there would have been no telling where she would have ended up. More than likely she and Bonnie both would have ended up in a broken pile on the floor.

Thankfully the rough part didn't last very long, even though it seemed like it did.

Duster finally turned the car onto what looked like nothing more than an old wagon trail that wound through a stand of scrub pine going across the mountain and slightly up along the top of a ridge.

It was smoother, but on this trail it felt like the car was going to roll over and not stop until it reached the valley below. She wanted to hold onto Bonnie who seemed to be above her at the moment.

She could tell that Madison wasn't riding this out any better than she was.

Bonnie seemed indifferent to it, like it was just something to get through and not worry about.

Finally Duster turned the car into an opening in some brush under some thin pine trees and stopped.

"We're here," he said, shutting off the car and letting the silence of the mountain crash in on them. "This is as close as I can get with the car."

"You get the plate on that truck that hit me?" Madison asked, slowly easing his grip from the handhold above the door.

"Yeah," Dawn said. "I'd like that as well."

Duster laughed. "No worry, it's easier going back down."

"Oh, great," Madison said.

Dawn laughed.

She loved the fact that on the surface the two of them had a lot in common. They both hated mornings and rough car rides and they both loved studying history. Might not be enough for a relationship, but she figured it was more than enough for some great sex.

She shook her head of that thought and opened the door into the hot, dry, and very thin mountain air.

Everything around her had the wonderful smell of sage and warm pine needles. It reminded her of so many great memories of being in the mountains as a kid. Her parents used to take her up outside of McCall in central Idaho and on hot summer days near the lake, this is what it smelled like.

She loved it and those wonderful memories. More than likely all those childhood trips were why she loved being in the mountains so much.

Right now the air around her felt hot, and she had no doubt it would get much, much warmer before the day was done.

"Wow, this is wonderful," Madison said from the other side of the car, also breathing deep. "That's almost worth the ride up here."

"Wait until you see the mine," Duster said, going around back and opening the rear of the SUV. He took out Dawn's pack, then Madison's, and then started unloading some supplies.

"Can we get it all in one trip?" Bonnie asked.

"I think so," Duster asked. "Grab your packs, guys, and then some food or a case of water."

Dawn looked at Bonnie who nodded. "Trust us, we're going to Central Idaho and Roosevelt. You'll see."

Madison glanced at Dawn, shrugged and picked up his pack and slung it over his shoulder. Then he took a case of bottled water.

Dawn swung her pack up on her back, and grabbed two sacks of what looked like groceries.

Bonnie picked up a large pack and swung it to her shoulder, then tucked under her arms two huge bags of smoked jerky and turkey from Smokey Davis Meats.

Dawn had no doubt there was enough jerky in those two bags to sustain a couple of people for a month or more with enough water.

What in the world was going on?

Duster took a large pack as well and the remaining supplies, locked up the car, and then said, "Follow me."

"I have to tell you that you two are worrying me a little right about now," Madison said.

"Same here," Dawn said, trying to force the butterflies down in her stomach.

"You'll see shortly," Bonnie said.

"In about a hundred yards, actually," Duster said.

He led them through the trees and out onto a trail cutting across an open and fairly steep hillside.

Dawn almost froze. She wasn't afraid of heights by any sense, but that trail across that hillside looked darned thin. And way down the slope was the ghost town of Silver City.

She could see beyond the ruins of the town the large War Eagle Mountain and the Treasure Valley in the distance. On a really clear day she had no doubt she could see parts of Boise from here.

"Now that's a view," Madison said.

"It gets better," Duster said as he led them to what looked like the top of an old mine tailing. An old cabin with no windows or doors sat on top of the tailings, clearly long abandoned and leaning slightly into the hill. Its wood stained by weather into a light tan with dark streaks.

Dawn had seen her share of old mining shacks and this one was authentic and more than likely over a hundred years old. A good snowstorm with a little wind one winter would turn it into a pile of wood in the next decade or so.

Dawn could see an old small-gauge mining car track coming from the side of the hill and through the old shack and toward the edge of the tailings. That clearly had been used to bring ore and rock from the mine.

The mine itself had been boarded up and looked like the mouth of it had collapsed in on itself just beyond the boards a long, long time ago.

There was nothing more to see. She had walked on dozens of old mine tailings that looked just like this one.

"Okay, here's where the secret part comes in," Duster said, putting down his pack and turning to them. "You can never tell anyone about what you are about to see."

"Way up here I find it hard anyone would care," Madison said.

Duster laughed. "Oh, they would care, trust me."

"Not a word," Dawn said, getting annoyed at all the secrecy from her friends.

"Not a word," Madison repeated.

Duster nodded and looked at Bonnie, who also nodded.

Dawn could tell that this was clearly something the two of them had thought through a great deal and was important to them.

Very, very important.

Dawn just wished like hell they'd hurry up and get on with it, whatever it was.

## CHAPTER NINE

**DAWN WATCHED** as Duster pulled what looked to be an old skeleton key from his pocket. He did something to it

and a rock just to the left of the old mine entrance slid to one side revealing a very large steel door.

"That's nifty," Madison said.

Dawn had to agree with that.

A moment later, with a thump the huge metal door slid inward and to one side.

Duster looked around, scanning the hillside.

Dawn could tell that where the door was in the hillside, no one from below could see it, but if someone was up on the hillside above the old mine, they might.

"Follow me," Duster said, grabbing his stuff and ducking inside.

Dawn followed him, then Madison, then Bonnie bringing up the rear.

Behind them the huge and very heavy metal door slid closed, plunging them into darkness for a moment before the lights came up.

"Smart," Madison said. "At night no one would see the lights."

"Exactly," Duster said.

Dawn was stunned at what she saw ahead of her. They were clearly in the old gold mine, with what looked like old wooden timbers. It stretched into the hill with a string of electric lights showing the way.

The lights and the soil and the old wood gave everything a faint gold tint that seemed appropriate for an old gold mine.

Down the middle of the tunnel was the rail for the old ore cars.

"Is this safe in here?" she asked as Madison stared at the timbers above them.

Madison nodded. "Perfectly."

Duster nodded at the same time. "All of these have been reinforced."

"And the work well-hidden," Madison

said, staring up between two timbers. "This looks very old and dangerous at first glance, but it's not."

"Thanks," Duster said, starting down the track deeper into the mine. "I did the work."

Dawn wasn't afraid of caves and mines, either. But this just felt creepy. And honestly, she was getting more and more worried by the second. She thought she knew Bonnie and Duster well, but now she wasn't so sure. There was no telling what she and Madison were walking into.

And with that huge metal door, there was clearly no way out at the moment.

One thing for certain, without Madison here, she never would be doing this. But that put a lot of trust in a guy she had never met.

"Can you open that big door from the inside?" Madison asked.

"Button right beside it," Bonnie said, pointing to a wall and a red button there. "It's only locked from the outside. Not the inside."

"That's good," Madison said.

Dawn nodded her thanks to Madison for asking that question.

They started off deep into the hillside, following the rail tracks on the floor.

Dawn was happy that Madison was thinking along the same lines she was. And the deeper into the mountain they went, the more worried she got. She was about to say something, her stomach twisting into a tiny knot, when ahead of her the tunnel turned to the right, but Duster didn't.

He just kept walking straight and went right through the wall without a word of warning back to them.

Dawn damn near choked and just froze, staring at the wall where Duster had gone.

"Hologram," Bonnie said from behind her. "Pretty nifty security trick, huh?"

Dawn eased forward like she was sneaking up on the edge of a cliff and put her hand out where Duster had vanished.

She felt nothing but air where her eyes told her the damp rock wall should be.

"Close your eyes and step forward," Bonnie said, "and you'll be all right."

Dawn took a deep breath and did as she was told and found herself in more of the mine tunnel on the other side.

Duster was a few steps away, smiling.

She looked back and could see Madison and Bonnie. Clearly Madison was having as much trouble with it as she did, easing up and feeling the air and looking worried.

That made Dawn feel only slightly better.

"Still gets me at times and I'm the one that put it there," Duster said.

She stepped forward as behind her Madison stepped through, his eyes also closed.

"I've seen a lot of illusions," he said, looking back at Bonnie, "but that's one of the best."

"Just more levels of protection in case anyone got in here," Duster said.

He pointed to a hidden panel on the wall beside him. "If either of you are in here for any reason alone, flip this switch. It shuts off the hidden alarm that is sent to our homes and to our car."

Duster flipped it off, then turned and headed deeper into the mine.

"Wow, really protected," Madison said, glancing at her.

All Dawn could do was nod.

Not a damn bit of this was making any sense to her yet. She felt like she was still dreaming or had stumbled into a strange *Twilight Zone* episode or something.

Bonnie followed as they went forward to where it looked like the mine had just flat dead-ended. Duster didn't even hesitate and stepped through the wall.

Another hologram.

"Amazing," Madison said from behind Dawn.

This time Dawn was a little quicker, but still stepped forward into what looked like a solid rock wall with her eyes closed. He stomach was twisting so hard, she felt like she might be sick at any moment.

Something about all this felt very wrong. She wanted to turn and run, but where could she go?

On the other side of the second hologram was a large cavern full of all sorts of supplies and such scattered around the walls on tables and shelves. The cavern itself looked natural and from what she could tell, the mine had broken into it.

It echoed slightly, had a flat dirt floor, and smelled of dry dirt. Lights had been strung in set places around the big cavern with low wattage bulbs making it feel comfortable. They must have turned on when someone came in.

There were period dresses and all sorts of men's period clothing and hats on hangers and a ton of supplies, mostly dried, stacked on shelves.

For the life of her, Dawn couldn't think of a reason for such a cavern to exist and be stocked like this.

Duster dropped the supplies and bags he had been carrying on a long table and indicated that Dawn and Madison should do the same thing with their things.

Dawn did, staring around at the clearly natural cavern. There were enough supplies in here to last for a very long time. That bothered her more than she wanted to admit. She wouldn't let herself

think that maybe Bonnie and Duster were going to keep them prisoner here.

"This is really something," Madison said, echoing part of what Dawn was thinking. "But why?"

"You ain't seen nothing yet," Duster said, his broad grin seeming to want to burst off his face.

"From this point forward your life will never be the same," Bonnie said.

"Now that's scary," Dawn whispered to Madison as Bonnie and Duster turned toward what looked like another mine tunnel.

"Yeah," Madison said softly.

Dawn glanced at Madison and he again shrugged. "We've come this far. Might as well see what all this craziness is about."

"Famous last words," she said.

He smiled, but the smile didn't reach his eyes. "I sure hope not."

"Me too," she said.

She and Madison followed Duster and Bonnie into a mineshaft that left the cavern on the far side. Duster was working to open a huge metal door at the end of the tunnel. He pulled it back showing only a solid rock wall about ten feet beyond the door. He walked forward and then stepped through yet another hologram.

Bonnie followed him, leaving her with Madison.

She glanced back. They could cut and run now. Whatever was beyond that third hologram was very, very protected in some very creative and effective ways.

What could be so important?

So she stepped through just ahead of Madison and into a sight she could never have imagined in all her life.

Ever.

It was a huge cavern that seemed to tower over her and stretch off into the distance toward the center of the mountain. She could see no end to the cavern.

Almost every inch of the walls and ceiling was covered in rose crystals of various sizes and shapes. Some were huge, upwards of four or five feet long, others tiny, almost too small to see. Most were growing in clusters and some clusters seemed to grow on each other, easing out into the room a little.

The floor was flat dirt and twenty steps inside the door there was an old wooden table with a device in the middle of the table with wires running from it along the floor toward one wall.

Dawn blinked, trying to clear her mind, but the cavern around her and the fantastic beauty of all the crystals didn't go away.

They seemed to be lit with their own power and the entire place sort of sparkled. She could see no lights or source of energy. The crystals themselves were glowing.

The crystals were the energy.

Bonnie and Duster stood to one side of the table, smiling like proud parents showing off their new child in a hospital.

Madison was clearly as stunned as she felt.

He stood beside her gazing around, his mouth open.

She walked about thirty steps farther into the cavern, right down the center, past the long wooden table. There was no end in sight. The cavern just went on and on, slanting slightly downward.

She forced herself to take a deep breath to calm her nerves.

She then turned back to Bonnie and Duster.

"What is this place?"

"It's all of history," Duster said.

"And all of time," Bonnie added.

Dawn had no idea what they had just said.

And honestly she was scared to death to ask.

But the fact that this place was very, very special was clear.

And it was fantastically beautiful.

Madison hadn't said a word.

She just went back to staring and attempting to grasp just a tiny bit of what she was seeing.

And after a moment she decided that was impossible. No one could grasp this place.

# CHAPTER TEN

**MADISON JUST COULDN'T** seem to wrap his mind around the crystal room.

The crystals covering the walls seemed to glow with a life of their own, giving off a faint, soft light. Every inch of walls was covered and the cavern was huge. It stretched downward into the distance as far as he could see.

He started to move toward one of the walls and Duster said, "Don't touch any of the crystals."

"Why," Madison asked, glancing first at the shocked look on Dawn's face, then back at Duster and Bonnie.

"Each crystal represents a timeline," Duster said.

"A what?" Dawn asked.

"A timeline," Duster said, but Bonnie put a hand on Duster's arm. "We have to show them before they will really understand what this room actually is."

Duster nodded. He moved over the table and indicated that Madison and Dawn should join him.

Madison stumbled in the direction of the table, not really looking away from the fantastic beauty of the cavern of rose-colored crystals.

On the table was a metal box that looked like it was more of a kid's idea of a control panel. It had two terminals on one side with nothing hooked to it and a face with a number of dials and read-outs that made no sense on first glance.

The entire thing was about the size of an old-fashioned large computer tower without any monitor or keyboard.

Duster took off an expensive Rolex watch and sat it on the wooden table beside the box. He put on thick leather gloves, then strung the two cords over to a smaller crystal on a nearby wall and carefully attached the ends to the crystal with small soft clamps that looked like they could expand and not fall off.

"Okay," he said, pointing to the front of the big box. "See the date?"

Madison glanced at the date May 1st, 1878 that was on the side of the machine.

"Why that date?" Dawn asked.

"That's a date just about one year after we built all this protection for this place and put in this machine," Duster said.

"And started stocking that other cavern with supplies," Bonnie added.

Madison was about to ask the first in about a billion questions, but Duster stopped him and smiled. "You'll understand more after this quick little trip."

Madison glanced at Dawn. Her beautiful eyes looked as puzzled as he felt, and worried as well. He wished he could just reach over and hold her hand, but again, he didn't. He was in the strangest place he could remember being in and still focused on her.

Duster picked up the two wires that were attached to the crystal. "Everyone touch the box, please."

Madison wasn't certain, but he leaned in beside Dawn, who sort of leaned against him slightly. That felt great. Having her experiencing this at the same time gave him more strength.

Bonnie leaned in as well.

Duster attached one wire to one terminal.

"Black to black," he said to them, pointing to the black wire and the black terminal as if expecting they would be doing this at some point in the future.

Then with one hand on the box beside Bonnie's, he attached the red wire to the red terminal.

Nothing seemed to happen. Maybe a slight shimmer, but that was it.

Duster and Bonnie stepped back, smiling.

Madison and Dawn both took their hands off the box and looked around. As far as Madison was concerned, nothing in the big crystal room had changed in the slightest.

The two wires were still attached to the box.

"Welcome to 1878," Bonnie said, smiling.

"Yeah, right," Dawn said, shaking her head.

Madison looked back at the box and then noticed that the Rolex was gone.

"Where's your watch?"

Duster smiled. "In the summer of 2014, where I left it, of course."

Madison again couldn't grasp what Duster was talking about, but that watch had vanished and Duster had been nowhere near it.

"Come on, we'll show you," Bonnie said.

She turned and headed back for the outer cavern followed by her husband.

Dawn looked at Madison. "Is this weird or am I just dreaming."

"If you're dreaming," he said, "I wish you'd come up with better things for us to do. I could think of a few thousand right off the top of my head."

"Yeah, me too," she said, laughing slightly as they turned to follow Bonnie and Duster out of the fantastic cave of crystals.

Madison noticed that even though they had left the door open to the outer chamber, Duster had to open it again. Then he went toward a rack of men's clothes while Bonnie went toward some women's clothes.

Duster handed Madison a men's jacket clearly from the mid-1870s.

Bonnie handed Dawn a woman's dress from the same period. "Just slip this over your clothes."

"We're only going as far as the cabin in front of the mine," Duster said. "but in case someone sees us from a distance, we want to generally look like we are just two couples out for a stroll."

Madison looked at Duster. "Are you seriously trying to tell us we really are in 1878?"

He really liked Bonnie and Duster as friends, and he loved that amazing cavern full of crystals, but traveling in time wasn't possible and the fact that Duster and Bonnie both thought it was worried him a great deal.

"Just slip this on," Duster said, "and we'll show you. I won't need to tell you."

*"If you're dreaming," he said, "I wish you'd come up with better things for us to do..."*

He slipped on the jacket as Duster put on a long oil-cloth duster and a cowboy hat. He gave Madison a cowboy hat as well.

Bonnie and Dawn took a moment longer, slipping on the dresses over their clothing, but not bothering to even buttoned them up in the back.

They all then headed down the mine tunnel toward the surface.

At the big iron door, Duster looked through a type of scope, then showed both Dawn and Madison how to do it as well.

Through the scope Madison could see that there was no one outside the mine on the tailings or anywhere near the old cabin. Strangely, that old cabin now didn't look so old and still had doors and windows.

Duster showed them both the button that would open the door and then he pushed it.

The big metal door slid inward and out of the way and they stepped outside.

The air was biting cold and the sky overcast. The mountain was no longer covered in trees and near one edge of the mine tailing there was a small drift of snow that hadn't melted yet.

The air smelled of rain and wood smoke.

Madison could not let himself believe any of that, but yet his eyes told him it was right in front of him.

He had gone into that mine on a hot, summer morning. Now it was cold out here, the cabin looked far newer, and there was still snow on the ground. They had not been inside long enough for someone to do that much work out here as a practical joke.

Madison took a dozen steps out onto the flat top of the mine tailings to a spot near the edge and just stopped.

He could not believe what he was seeing. And his legs would not allow him to move another foot.

Finally he just sat down on the dirt and rocks, staring at the most impossible site he could ever imagine.

Behind him Dawn just gasped and said softly, "Not possible."

Across the slope where they had parked the Cadillac in a stand of pine trees, there was nothing but open hillside. The car, the trees, everything was gone.

All over the hills were new mine tailings, clearly freshly dug. But what was spread out below Madison was what he couldn't believe.

His mind would not accept what his eyes were seeing.

"Silver City just after its prime," Duster said. "May 1st, 1878."

"How?" Dawn asked softly from beside Madison as she too sat down on the dirt mine tailings, staring at the valley below.

Spread out below Madison was a bustling city with hundreds of buildings and smoke curling up from many chimneys. The sounds of people working and horses and activity echoed through the valley.

Somehow, below him, Madison had no doubt he was looking at Silver City, Idaho, in its prime. Not a ghost town as it had been when they arrived.

Bonnie laughed as she moved over beside Dawn and sat down on the dirt as well. "As I said, welcome to 1878."

# CHAPTER ELEVEN

DAWN WALKED in what felt like a stunned stagger back into the mine and then through the holograms and back to the big room. Her mind would not let her grasp what she had just seen.

None of it was possible. It had to be some sort of major illusion or some drug that Bonnie and Duster had given them.

Madison looked as stunned as she felt. She caught a glimpse of his eyes and they looked almost haunted. She had no doubt her eyes looked the same way.

She really just wanted to go over to Madison and lean into him for comfort.

Bonnie helped her slip out of the dress she had put over her clothes, then she followed Duster and Bonnie back into the crystal room.

"We're still in 1878," Duster said.

Dawn would not have believed it before, and she wasn't sure if she did yet, even after seeing what had been outside the mine.

The endless crystal cavern was as stunning as the first time, maybe more so on this second time into the room. The scale and the beauty of it just took her breath away.

What she saw outside wasn't possible, but neither were this fantastic cavern and all the beauty of the crystals.

On the wooden table in the middle of the room the machine still sat, wires running over to a wall and attaching to a small crystal there. She had to admit, the table looked slightly newer, but nothing else was different.

"Everyone ready to go back to 2014?" Bonnie asked.

"Might as well," Duster said, smiling. "Now focus on where I put my watch on the table in 2014."

He then took off one connection.

There was a slight shimmering and the big watch appeared on the table again.

The moment before he did that, Dawn had been standing next to Madison just inside the room. Suddenly she found herself leaning against the machine next to Madison without any sense of being moved.

Duster, Bonnie, Madison were also touching the machine in the same way they had been when Duster plugged in the machine.

How did she get those ten feet across the room?

Madison coughed.

"We're back in 2014," Duster said.

Dawn didn't know what to think. She just stepped back trying to make herself take long, slow breaths.

Duster carefully removed the other cable, then with gloves on, he moved over and took the ends of the wires off the crystal on the wall.

"We were gone for exactly two minutes and fifteen seconds," Bonnie said.

"We have no idea why it is always one-hundred-and-thirty-five seconds," Duster said, picking up his watch and slipping it back on. "It doesn't matter how long we are in the past, we only age two minutes and twelve seconds in our regular timeline."

"It took us about thirty minutes to get out there, look at everything, and get back," Madison said. "But we only aged two minutes and fifteen seconds?"

"Actually, in that timeline," Duster said, pointing to the crystal on the wall where he had attached the crystal, "we all aged about thirty minutes. We just reset when we came back here, to this timeline. But we remember that timeline because we were touching the machine when we started."

"You built that?" Madison asked, pointing at the machine.

"We did," Duster said, nodding and indicating Bonnie as well. "We both have degrees in physics, math, and theoretical physics."

"We both have a number of doctorates in physics and math, actually," Bonnie said, smiling at her husband. "That's how we met, down at Stanford."

"Is there some place we can sit down and talk about this?" Dawn asked. Her knees were feeling weak and her mind was reeling just trying to get some sort of hold on what she thought she had seen. And what they were claiming had happened.

And the massive beauty of the crystals around her wasn't helping. She just kept wanting to stare at them.

Bonnie said, "Sure, this way."

Thankfully, Bonnie took Dawn's arm and together they left the crystal room, moving back into the large storage cavern. All Dawn focused on was putting one foot in front of the other.

That seemed like a massive task at the moment.

"Stunning, isn't it?" Bonnie asked. "We worked our way into understanding it slowly, over a few years. We were worried that it would be too much for anyone to grasp at once."

"It might be," Dawn said, her voice soft as she worked to keep herself moving forward. She normally prided herself on being firm and solid in reality, even though her friends and parents and few former boyfriends accused her of living far too much in the past.

Now she had actually seen the past, or that's what Bonnie was trying to get her to believe. And by actually seeing the past, Dawn had lost all footing and belief in the here and now.

There were sounds of a couple switches flipping and an area off to the back of the big supply cavern lit up that she hadn't noticed before. There was a seating area with three couches, a coffee table, and a large reading chair and lamp. Slightly closer to the cavern was a large dining table with six chairs around it and a stove and fridge in a kitchen area. It was all tucked into a side nook in the cavern.

Bonnie moved her over to the table and Dawn sat with a sigh of relief. At least now she wouldn't have to worry about her legs giving out under her.

Madison dropped into a chair across from her.

He looked as stunned and shaken as she felt. His handsome chiseled face not hiding any of the emotions he was feeling. He just stared at the table in front of him.

They were both in a form of shock. Dawn had no doubt about that.

Bonnie got them both a cold bottle of water, then asked if they would like some lunch. "I know it's just a little after ten in the morning, but we ate breakfast early. I have cold meat sandwiches and chicken soup."

Dawn asked for both. Madison only wanted a sandwich. Duster opted for both.

"So," Duster said after taking a long drink from a bottle of cold water. "That's our little secret. See why we couldn't tell you ahead of time. You wouldn't believe it."

"I honestly don't believe it now," Madison said.

Dawn nodded. "I'm afraid I don't either. Or another way of putting it, I don't know what I believe at the moment."

"Figured that would be the case," Bonnie said, laughing. She looked at Duster. "I know it's been a long time, but remember how we felt when we discovered what those crystals could do and then took the first trip in time?"

"I do," Duster said, nodding. "Scared me to death."

"Me too," Bonnie said, laughing.

"So how about starting from the beginning?" Madison asked, shaking his head slowly from side-to-side.

Dawn glanced up at the man she so wanted to spend time with. She just hadn't expected this kind of adventure.

"It's time travel," Duster said, smiling, a twinkle in his eye. "There is no beginning."

Madison actually smiled weakly at that, but Dawn wasn't sure if she liked the sound of that concept at all. But she was going to let Madison lead this questioning. He seemed like he was slightly ahead of her in grasping what had just happened. She was just trying to not drop to the floor and curl into a ball.

"So you own this mine? Right?" Madison asked.

"In this timeline, my great-great-grandfather bought it in 1877," Duster said. "He actually planned on opening it

> *"It's time travel," Duster said, smiling, a twinkle in his eye. "There is no beginning."*

back up, but never got around to it. My great-grandfather took a hand at it in 1902, and found this cave. His son, my grandfather, during the Depression, took another shot at finding gold and opened up the crystal part of the cave."

"Luckily he was wearing gloves when he touched those crystals," Bonnie said. "Otherwise you wouldn't have been born."

"What happens when you touch the crystals with your bare hands?" Dawn asked before Madison could, trying to clear her mind and find some answers, no matter what those answers might be.

"We're not sure," Bonnie said. "We think it might vaporize a person from all the power. We've never tested it."

Duster nodded and went on. "My father showed me this place the year after Bonnie and I met and because of our background in physics and theoretical math, we started to realize what it might be. So together we spent the next two years working on that machine and testing it."

"What exactly is that machine?" Dawn asked, almost afraid of the answer.

"Well, there's no easy answer for that," Bonnie said, sliding a sandwich in front of her and Madison. Dawn glanced at it, but honestly didn't feel much like eating.

Duster leaned forward looking at both of them with those intense dark eyes of his. "You understand the principle of the conservation of matter and energy? Right?"

Dawn nodded. Basic high school stuff.

Madison also nodded.

"There are theories that time is connected to that rule as well," Duster said. "Matter, time, and energy are all linked and must be conserved when moving from one state to another."

"So every crystal in that crystal cave is the physical representation of another timeline," Bonnie said. "When you decided to come up here, an alternate timeline started where you decided to not come with us."

"And because of all the small and larger decisions made by others ahead of us," Madison said, "in billions of timelines we decided to come here and in billions we didn't."

"Exactly," Duster said, smiling. "We believe those caverns in there go off into other dimensions, extend basically forever. This cavern, under this mountain is just a physical location of the crystals in this tiny area of this universe."

"Oh, God, my head hurts," Dawn said.

She was actually understanding most of what they were saying and that bothered her. She didn't want any of this to be real. She wanted to wake up in her bed and shake her head and wonder where this dream came from.

She forced herself to take a bite of the ham sandwich to try to ground her body and mind in the moment. She had done all right in physics, but hadn't really needed to go that far since her love was history. Timelines and alternate history had never been her interest. She had a hunch that after today she was going to be studying up on it some.

"So," Madison said, shaking his head to clearly try to manage a thought," you figured out a way to travel back in time by touching that machine, inside one of the varied timelines already existing on the wall?"

"We did," Duster said, nodding. "Exactly right. We have even gotten it close enough to set dates of arrival within a week or so."

"So how does the machine exist back in 1878?" Madison asked.

Dawn was impressed. Madison was asking questions she never would have thought about. Ever.

"My grandfather, my great-grandfather, my dad, and the two of us built all of the precautions you see to protect this mine back in 1877. We set the table up and locked it into position. The machine is our connection and travels with us in some fashion or another. We are not sure how, exactly."

"So you could visit millions of timelines that look exactly like this?" Dawn asked. "Actually, there are millions of timelines where we are sitting here talking?"

"There must be billions," Madison said, nodding.

"Exactly," Duster said. "Actually, unlimited amounts. Every small decision every person makes creates an alternate timeline. The crystals in the area around the table are just all close to these events. If you went deeper and deeper into the cavern, the events and alternate histories might move slightly away from this one."

"Have you tried that?" Madison asked.

"Nope, no real interest yet," Duster said. "Exploring our own history is just too much fun."

Dawn just couldn't grasp numbers like that, so she changed the focus. She had a couple of human questions she needed answers to.

"How many times have you gone back to the past?" Dawn asked as Bonnie put the chicken soup in front of her.

The soup smelled wonderful and even though she had choked down one bit of the sandwich, now she felt hungry.

"I looked it up because I figured you would ask that," Bonnie said. "We've made four hundred and nine trips into the past, four hundred and ten if you count the one a few minutes ago."

"A number of the trips were building this place and protecting it all," Duster said. Then he looked up at his wife. "You figure out how old we really are? Wait, I'm not sure I want to know."

Bonnie smiled at her husband. "Will you still love me if I tell you?"

"Forever," he said, laughing.

Dawn really liked their relationship. She just hoped she could find one like it. She glanced at Madison and he had been looking at her. He smiled and that wonderful dimple of his appeared, then he turned back to face Bonnie.

Bonnie sat down at the table, a sandwich and bowl of soup in front of her. "We are both 35 in this world, just a couple years older than both of you. In thirty-to-fifty-year increments in the past, we have lived just under two thousand years as best as I can figure. We've done that in the last two years real time."

"Great years, I might add," Duster said, smiling at his wife.

"For the most part," Bonnie said, smiling back at her husband and winking.

"Two thousand years?" Madison asked, his voice soft.

Dawn could see that if he wasn't in shock before, now he really was. She was feeling the same way.

How could she actually be sitting here with two people who had lived for two thousand years?

How was that possible?

Then it finally sunk in.

She put down her spoon and just sat there staring into her soup, letting the reality of it all wash over her.

There was living history right outside that mine opening. Not just book history, but the actual thing.

And the door to that history, to living in that history, was that machine in the crystal cavern.

When Bonnie and Duster had promised her a trip into the Thunder Mountain region, they hadn't meant going in 2014. They meant she could do it in 1902, when the mining town of Roosevelt was first in its prime.

She could be there when the valley was alive and booming and history was being made.

And when there were no bodies in that cemetery yet.

# CHAPTER TWELVE

**MADISON SAT AT THE TABLE** in the big cavern trying to eat some lunch and let his mind just grasp a tiny part of what Duster and Bonnie had said. If they had actually lived that long in the past, it was no wonder they knew so much about western history.

They had lived it.

They were basically immortals.

But in all his research, he had never run across anyone like them living anywhere in the west.

He had to ask. "Okay, a little help to get me to understand what you are saying,"

Duster and Bonnie both nodded as they ate.

Across the table from him, Dawn seemed in as much shock as he felt. She had asked a few questions, then just suddenly stopped and gone to staring at her food, clearly lost in deep thought.

He turned to Duster and focused on asking his questions instead of just staring at Dawn.

"So you go back in time," Madison said. "How come in all my research, I've never seen references to either of you?"

"Because in this timeline we never did go back," Duster said. "When we go back, we start a new timeline with us in it."

"And a new crystal forms on the wall," Bonnie said. "And the crystal we are hooked to sometimes will grow when we are gone."

"So you never run into yourself because every trip back you are always in new timelines?" Madison asked, slowly starting to understand.

"That's correct," Duster said. "But there do seem to be what we call 'echoes' from one timeline to the next, things we do that sometimes show slight hints in this timeline later. We have no idea what causes those echoes, but it's one of the reasons we got interested in your research."

"So you change history?" Madison asked.

"Oh, sure," Duster said. "Can't help it. But that just creates new timelines."

"We will attach the wires to a small crystal," Bonnie said, "and by the time we return, just over two minutes later in this time, there may be thousands of crystals in and around that one we started with."

Madison nodded. He understood that the theory of timelines completely solved all time paradoxes. The fact that Bonnie and Duster could always return to their original timeline was amazing.

"What happens if you get killed back there?" Dawn asked, suddenly looking up.

The question sent shivers down Madison's spine. Dawn had a distant look in her eyes and a very worried expression on her face.

"You find yourself standing, touching the machine back in the crystal cavern," Bonnie said, staring at her sandwich. "Just over two minutes after you left."

"So you can't be killed?" Dawn asked.

"Oh, you can be killed in a different timeline," Duster said, also not happy with the subject. "But it doesn't kill you in this timeline, your main timeline."

"Oh," Dawn said and went back to staring at her food again, picking at her sandwich.

"How many times have you both died in the past?" Madison asked.

"Too many," Duster said, also not meeting Madison's gaze. "Dying in the Old West is never fun, so try to avoid it, even though you end up here just fine."

"Never a fun memory," Bonnie said, shivering slightly while she worked at her soup.

"So what happens," Dawn said, asking a second very pointed question, "if say all four of us went back and someone came in here and unplugged the machine from the crystal?"

"We would all appear right back here, just over two minutes after we left," Duster said. "Never an exception to that rule it seems. On some things time and physics are very firm."

Dawn nodded and kept eating.

Madison was impressed. Her questions were spot on the money and focused on the people aspects of all this, not the actual physics of it all.

"So you're thinking we should all go into the Roosevelt area together, in 1902?" Dawn asked, looking first at Duster, then at Bonnie.

Both Duster and Bonnie nodded.

"That was the idea," Bonnie said, looking worriedly at Dawn.

Madison sat back. Wow, that was something he had not thought of. There was no doubt that was what this had all been about. With two of them introduced to the entire thing, and a set goal like that, it would allow both of them to get used to this crazy idea.

"I'll go back about five years ahead of that," Duster said. "Get set up, get what we need for the trip, then the three of you come through in early May of 1902. I'll meet you here."

"We should be able to make it into Roosevelt in about a week," Bonnie said. "We can take our time, spend most of the summer, and get back here before the snow flies. Neither Duster or I have ever been there, so we're kind of excited to see it as well."

"And we'll only be gone from her just over two minutes?" Dawn asked.

Duster nodded, smiling. "Kind of fun, isn't it?"

"And we'll hit the same timeline as you are in ahead of us?" Madison asked.

"Yes," Duster said, nodding. "We have a way of doing that and we have tried it a number of times and it works fine."

Bonnie pushed her half-finished bowl of soup away and looked first at Madison, then at Dawn.

"We've never told anyone about this because we didn't think anyone would believe us. And we are telling you now because we feel that having access to history like this will help the richness of both of your works."

"I would think so," Madison said, his stomach twisting at the idea of actually going back into history itself.

"But we will completely understand if you decide not to use this," Duster said.

"Now that you know about it, Bonnie and I will be glad to make research trips for either or both of you to help in your work."

He smiled at them both. "Remember, we can spend years living there and only be gone two minutes from here. So the resource would be pretty amazing and very quick research for you."

"Life in the Old West is not an easy life," Bonnie said. "Especially for women."

She looked at Dawn, who was nodding.

"And you have to be careful on what you reveal about the future," Duster said. "It can quickly warp a timeline."

Madison could completely understand that as well.

They all sat there in silence for a moment around the dining table. The cavern around them felt comfortable to Madison. If this were all real, if he really could travel in time and see the history he loved to study so much, the possibilities were endless.

He looked across at Dawn, the most beautiful woman he had seen in memory. And a woman he wanted to spend a lot more time with. No matter what the year was.

She glanced up at him.

"You want to go spend a summer in 1902 in Roosevelt, Idaho, Professor Edwards?" he asked.

Her eyes lit up a little, and she smiled for the first time since they got back from their first little jaunt into the past. "Are you asking me on a date, Professor Rogers?"

He laughed and a ton of the tension he had been feeling sort of just drained away in the face of the fantastic smile across the table from him.

"Couples in the Old West tended to do better as teams," he said.

"That they did," she said, still smiling.

"So why not a date?" he asked. "Might be the strangest date in recorded history in this or any time line, but sure, a date."

"It will most certainly be different," she said, smiling at him.

"So when do we leave?" Madison turned to Duster and Bonnie, who were both smiling.

"As soon as we're ready to go," Duster said. "We should be ready by about noon in this time, but it's time travel, remember? We're only going to be gone just over two minutes."

"And a lifetime in a summer," Dawn said, clearly suddenly excited about the coming adventure.

"That too," Bonnie said. "That too."

# CHAPTER THIRTEEN

**MADISON STILL** partially felt like he was walking in a dream as they prepared for a summer living in the past.

Duster basically had saddlebags, a change of clothes, and a bunch of gold pieces from the time period in different parts of his clothing. He had an oilcloth dark duster and a brown cowboy hat. In that outfit he looked striking and someone to not mess with in any time period.

He wore jeans from the time and flannel shirts. He packed two extra pair of jeans and four extra shirts, a lot of extra underwear and socks, plus a bedding role.

"One of my cheats from this time period," he said, showing Bonnie and Madison his bedroll. "If no one is around, I tap this button and the thing blows up to a nice cushion so I don't have to sleep on the rough ground all the time. It's in your bedrolls as well."

He then showed them what looked like a simple toothpick. But when he struck it against the rock wall it flamed.

"Nifty," Madison said.

"We both try to use what we can from the time we are in, but these things come in handy. And they are light to carry. You both will be carrying them as well."

Then Duster showed them his Colts as he strapped them on his hip.

"How good a shot are you?" Madison asked.

"Scary good, aren't you, Marshal?" Bonnie said, smiling.

"A lot of years of practice," Duster said.

"Marshal?" Dawn asked.

"He likes to become a marshal," Bonnie said.

Duster shrugged. "Keeps me busy."

"You ought to see his collection of tin stars back home," Bonnie said, kissing her husband on the cheek.

"Can you fire a revolver?" Duster asked Madison.

"I know how to fire one, but hitting something besides my own foot would be another matter," Madison said. He had fired pistols on a range for a time, but he hadn't been that good at it.

"Good enough," Duster said, giving him a wide belt with a revolver in a holster on it.

Madison looked at it, but didn't touch it. He wasn't sure if he wanted to wear it, to be honest. "I'd rather not unless that's a problem?"

"Not a problem," Duster said, smiling and putting the guns away on a shelf. "I'll have saddle rifles for all of us on each horse when you come through."

Madison felt better about that.

Dawn and Bonnie spent a lot of time on Dawn's wardrobe off on one side of the cave. It seemed that Duster and Bonnie had been planning for this for some time and had brought back with them on a number of trips clothes and undergarments and everything that Madison and Dawn would need to get started. The rest they could buy along the way.

Then Duster took them back out of the mine and into the heat of the summer day.

Madison could see the Cadillac in the trees on the ridge and below Silver City was only a ghost town.

"This is so strange," he said, remembering how the last time he had stepped out of the mine it was cold and that town below had been alive.

Dawn could only nod standing beside him as she too stared down at the ghost town.

Duster closed up the mine, then showed them how to unlock the mine if they got separated and had to get back here.

"You will always end up back in the cavern in this time eventually, no matter what," Duster said. "But better to do it on your own terms if you need to. Worse-comes-to-worst, you just grow old and die and then end up back here."

"Only two minutes older," Madison said, shaking his head trying to imagine that.

"Only two minutes and some seconds older," Duster said.

He handed each of them two of the special skeleton keys. One to keep on them, one to hide in a special pocket of the leather saddlebag they would be taking.

Bonnie and Dawn would also be taking traveling cases, as was the custom of the time for women to carry when traveling.

Duster then showed them were he had hidden a key up the hill.

"Make sure no one follows you up the hill when you come up here," Duster said.

Then they went back inside to finish packing.

All four of them had modern medicine tucked into secret pockets of their saddlebags. And stomach drugs for the adjustment period between modern food and the food of 1902. For the most part, they packed a lot of what they would need to start off with.

And pills to clean water. It seemed humans from 2014 were a lot more delicate than those from 1902.

"Don't worry," Duster said. "You get used to the food and water with time."

"The process just isn't pleasant," Bonnie said. "With luck, we won't be gone long enough for any of that to matter."

"Speak for yourself," Duster said, smiling. "I'll have been back there for five years before you three arrive."

"Oh, yeah," Bonnie said, smiling at her husband. "Are you going to miss me?"

"Every day," he said.

Bonnie laughed. "Great husband answer."

Madison glanced over at Dawn who was looking sort of shocked at the idea that Bonnie and Duster could be apart that long and be fine with it.

To be honest, Madison had to admit he was having a little trouble with that idea as well.

But considering that they had lived for a couple thousand years back in the past, what was five years here and there?

That thought just made him shake his head.

From the time they had decided to make the trip, it took just over two hours real time to get ready.

It was still just around noon on the first day of their trip.

"Anyone hungry?" Bonnie asked as she and Duster headed for the kitchen area, hand-in-hand.

Madison glanced at Dawn and she shrugged. "One last supper."

Then she laughed.

"This is going to be fun," he said, smiling at her as they turned and headed across the cave behind Duster and Bonnie, walking side-by-side. He just wished they were holding hands as well.

And for some reason, he was now excited about going into the past.

Scared to death, but excited at the same time.

And a lot of that excitement came because he was going with Dawn.

## CHAPTER FOURTEEN

**DAWN FOUND** herself standing in the crystal room, next to the machine on the table, dressed as a lady of 1902 who would be riding horses. The undergarments felt strange when she tried them on and she had decided instead to just go with her normal underwear and work later to get used to the standard for the era.

No point in being chapped in places she didn't want to be chapped in.

Bonnie had agreed that would be a good idea.

The blouse and riding pants felt soft, but the boots were slightly uncomfortable, even though they were brand new boots manufactured here to look like they were from 1902. They were completely waterproof and very light. She was supposed to tell anyone who asked about them that they were deer hide and made specially for her in Denver.

She was glad that Duster and Bonnie had put so much thought into their wardrobe.

Dawn also had a hat and a long black coat that she would put on against the weather, both of which were also made modern to look period and both were completely waterproof as well.

And she had gloves. Thin, lady gloves, but gloves. She also had a pair of modern thick gloves in her saddlebag and dresses and changes of clothes, as well as enough supplies to make it through three periods without resorting to 1902 methods of dealing with that problem.

Madison had complimented her on how good she looked as they headed for the crystal room and Duster had seconded that opinion.

Duster looked striking in his oilcloth duster and cowboy hat. He wore cowboy boots like he belonged in them and she could see him being a marshal.

But what had surprised her was Madison. He also had on a long duster-like jacket over his suit coat, and when he put a cowboy hat on, she thought she might have trouble breathing. He was almost as tall as Duster, but not as rugged-looking. But damned if he wasn't handsome. More like a gentleman you would find in a top hotel than a marshal of an old west town.

"Wow," Bonnie said as Madison walked up to them, dressed and ready to go.

"I'll second that," Dawn said, smiling at him.

For a second she thought Madison had blushed.

"Ready?" Duster asked, looking at all of them.

"This just can't be real," Madison said. "But I'm as ready as I'll ever be with that belief."

Dawn laughed because that was exactly how she was feeling.

And she was flat scared to death.

She just kept repeating over and over that no matter what happened, they would all end up back here two minutes and some seconds after they left.

No matter what.

Damn that was hard to believe.

Duster kissed his wife long and hard, then told them he'd see them soon.

He connected the cables to a crystal on the wall, then picked up everything he wanted to take with him and with one hand on the box, he connected the other wire.

And vanished.

"Shit!" Madison said, "This is real."

In all her life Dawn had never been so scared.

She couldn't breathe, she couldn't swallow, and more than anything else she just wanted to turn and run.

She almost dropped half the supplies she had on her back and in her left hand.

Bonnie, with gloves on, quickly moved to the box and changed the date to May 1st, 1902, leaving the wires completely connected.

Then she pulled her glove off and told them to make sure they were holding everything they wanted to take, then touch the box on the count of three.

"One. Two. Three."

Dawn put her hand down on the box at the same time as the other two.

The room shimmered and Bonnie stepped back.

"Let's see if we made it or not," she said, smiling at them.

She turned and headed for the door to the supply cavern, carrying her supplies. The door was closed and she opened it, going into the cavern ahead of Dawn and Madison.

"I was wondering when you three would show up," Duster's voice came from the living area of the cave.

He stood from where he had been napping on the couch and limped toward them, smiling.

Dawn was shocked that he looked older and frailer. Not the Duster that had left the cavern a moment before.

Bonnie rushed toward him and they kissed. Then she pushed him back.

"What happened to you?"

"Horse got spooked by a rattler and tumbled on me three years ago outside of Boise. Broke my foot. I've been laid up in the Boise Hotel for most of the last three years."

"Getting waited on hand and foot, I suppose," Bonnie said, smiling but clearly worried.

"Great food, good poker games, not much more a man could ask for except the company of his beautiful wife."

Then he kissed her again and turned to Madison and Dawn. "Welcome to May 1902."

"How far did we miss," Bonnie asked.

"It's May 12th," Duster said.

"Are you sure you are going to want to do this, Duster?" Madison asked a moment before Dawn could.

He laughed as Bonnie looked at him with a very serious expression. "Of course. I plan on being on horseback most of the time and if I do have an issue, I'll just work my way back up here and wait for you three to get back."

Bonnie looked Duster in the eyes.

He smiled at her. "Honest. I can make a summer."

Dawn didn't like the sound of that at all. He didn't look good.

"No," Bonnie said, shaking her head. "We reset and all come into this year at the same time."

Duster started to object, but Bonnie would have nothing to do with it.

Dawn suddenly saw the very powerful woman that she was.

"Make sure you got all your supplies in your hands," Bonnie said as she turned for the crystal cavern.

"Sorry, guys," he said. "It would have been easier with me going in earlier if this hadn't happened."

A moment later the room shimmered and Dawn found herself touching the machine back in the crystal cavern.

Man, that was strange, being in one place and suddenly being in another.

Duster was back to his old self, looking fit and as handsome as ever.

"Thanks," he said to Bonnie, moving over and kissing her after she finished unhooking the cables from the crystal. "That feels a lot better."

"After two thousand years, Marshal Kendal," she said, "I know you. And know when you are just putting on a good face."

Dawn glanced at Madison, who was just standing there in his long coat and cowboy hat, saddlebag draped over his shoulder, looking handsome.

"So give me some time to pack again," Duster said, smiling at them as he and Bonnie headed for the supply cave. You can leave your stuff in here if you want."

"Now that was amazing," Madison said. "We were in there, then in here. He was healthy, then injured, then healthy, all in the space of a minute."

"I think flat weird describes it better," Dawn said as the two of them dropped their supplies and turned to follow the most amazing couple in all of time.

She only wished that some day she would have a relationship half as good as the one she had just watched in action.

She looked over at the handsome man beside her and he smiled at her.

She so wanted to kiss him, but somehow managed to not do that. But instead she said, "I'm so looking forward to spending time with you, getting to know you."

"I feel the same about you," he said, still smiling. "And I have a hunch that a summer in the Idaho wilderness in 1902 is going to give us that chance."

"And the time," she said laughing. "If we can ever get out of this cave."

He laughed, his dimple showing clearly, and together they went to see what they could do to help Duster pack for the second attempt at 1902.

# CHAPTER FIFTEEN

**DAWN FELT** almost as scared on the second attempt to go back to 1902 as she had the first time, even though she got to watch the return happen firsthand and how she and everyone ended up right back in the cave just a few minutes after they left.

But having Duster get seriously injured reminded her of just how serious this trip was. Of course, any of them could have gotten hurt going into Roosevelt in the Cadillac. And that would have been a forever injury.

On this trip, they got to reset if something happened.

She liked that idea, but it didn't ease the fear at all because honestly she just flat didn't believe it.

"Ready?" Duster asked as he checked to make sure all of them were holding their supplies.

Dawn glanced around.

They were a strange sight, that was for sure. All dressed in period clothing, standing in a fantastically beautiful crystal-covered cavern. There would be more supplies waiting for them in the supply cavern, but all that was basic stuff that Duster and Bonnie went back periodically and replenished from the future.

And there were no clothes there that would fit either Madison or Dawn. They all were going to have to buy more on the trip to Roosevelt.

When Duster connected the last wire to the machine, there was a shimmering, but nothing seemed to change.

"Here we go," Madison said, smiling at her.

Dawn could see the smile didn't reach the worry in his eyes.

They all moved out into the supply cavern and dumped the stuff they were carrying on the big sorting table. Then Duster headed for the front of the mine to check on the weather and if anyone was out front while the rest of them dug into the stored supplies for more to take with them on the coming ride.

"Looks like we are close to May 1902 again," Duster said as he came back in. "I'll go down and into Silver City, see if I can round up some horses to buy. I'll be back in five or six hours, so you all get some rest."

With that he turned and headed out, his duster swirling around his legs, his hat pulled low on his head.

"He really loves it back here, doesn't he?" Dawn asked Bonnie.

Bonnie laughed. "We both do, actually. We tend to start in 1878 and stay as long as health lets us."

"Do you always stay together?" Madison asked.

Again Bonnie laughed. "Oh, heavens, no. For the first few hundred years we did, exploring the country and different parts of the world, then we started going our own ways. He likes to stay up here in the Pacific Northwest, being a marshal and playing cards and living in plush hotel rooms. I tend to like nice apartments in San Francisco or New York and the life there."

"Wow, that's a lot of trust," Dawn said.

Bonnie sort of smiled at her and then got a faraway look. "What happens in the past, stays in the past. We agreed to that a long time ago if you count that in lifetimes lived."

Dawn felt shocked, so all she could do was say, "Oh."

"Makes sense if you look at it," Bonnie said, smiling at what must have been her shocked look at learning about Duster and Bonnie's open relationship. "In the present, it's only the two of us. And no matter what happens in the past, we must return to the present where it is only the two of us."

There was silence in the cavern as they finished digging out some supplies they could pack on horses, including a number of solid tents that Dawn wasn't sure she could set up correctly, but she had no doubt she was going to learn how to do it before the summer was over.

Dawn did not want to look at Madison, but from the corner of her eye she could tell he was as surprised and shocked as she felt at Bonnie's revelation. And she liked that he was shocked.

But who was she to judge two people who had lived for two thousand years?

"What was your longest time in the past?" Madison asked.

Bonnie smiled and glanced around to make sure Duster wasn't close by. "I went back in 1878, then headed for San Francisco. I met this wonderful man named David Carr, a banker. I died of old age and consumption in his arms in 1926."

"And you never told Duster?" Dawn asked, shocked again to her core. She had no idea where she got some of the beliefs she held, but wow was Bonnie challenging them.

"We came back that time, didn't say a word to each other. We just hooked up a new crystal and went back. After a few more lives like that, there didn't seem to be much point in telling him."

"And you don't ask about his relationships either?" Madison asked.

Bonnie glanced at him and smiled. "What happens in the past stays in the past. We have that luxury since none of it matters in this timeline. We just come back here as we were two minutes earlier."

"But with another lifetime of memories," Dawn said. "Seems like that matters a great deal."

"It does," Bonnie said, nodding. "But what matters more to both of us is the time to keep learning and studying as well. Duster and I value learning more than anything it seems, which is the main reason why we're trying to help you two."

Dawn nodded.

"And for that we thank you," Madison said.

"Especially for trusting us with this secret," Dawn said.

The more she started to believe that all this was real, the more amazing the trust that Duster and Bonnie showed in them was.

When they finished the packing, all three of them headed for the sitting area tucked back in the corner. There were three couches there. Bonnie gave each of them a blanket, then curled up on one couch.

"Try to get some sleep," she said. "The first couple days on horseback is always tough."

Dawn stretched out on the couch and looked over at Madison.

"We agreed we wanted an adventure," she said, smiling at him and wishing she was curled up on that couch with him instead of alone.

"That we did," he said, smiling back.

Damn she wished she had the courage to just get up and go cuddle with him. But she knew, without a doubt that if she did that, neither of them would get any rest at all.

And she needed the rest. Even though it was only about one in the afternoon

their real time, four in the morning in Boise, Idaho, seemed like a decade ago.

Actually, it was about a hundred and twelve years in the future.

She pushed that thought away and with one last look at Madison, she turned over and curled up and went to sleep for the first time in 1902.

# CHAPTER SIXTEEN

**MADISON HEARD** Duster come in and softly moved over to wake up Bonnie. She stirred, reached up and kissed him, and then whispered "Get horses all right?"

"I managed to buy just one," he said.

She stood and moved over with him so that they wouldn't wake up Madison and Dawn, but he was already awake.

He swung off the couch and gently touched Dawn's shoulders. She was facing away from him and rolled over slowly, yawning. Then she looked up at him and smiled. "I was having a great dream about you," she said, then yawned.

He couldn't believe how beautiful she was as she woke up. He hoped to see that a lot in the future.

"You're going to have to tell me about that later," he said, smiling back at her. "Duster's back."

She nodded and sat up.

He offered her a hand getting off the couch and again just touching her sent an electric shock through his system.

He could tell she felt something too, but instead of just holding her hand there as he wanted to, he let go and they turned to join Bonnie and Duster.

"In 1902 there isn't much left down in Silver City," Duster said to them as they approached. "I managed to buy one horse from the owner of the hotel that a guest a few months back had traded for a room for a month."

"Not much of a horse, huh?" Madison asked.

"Not much," Duster said, nodding. "I'm going to need to go down to Murphy and a horse ranch there to get us what we need. That's going to take a couple of days."

"We'll be fine right here," Bonnie said, kissing her husband. "How much more daylight out there is there?"

"Only a couple of hours and it's damned cold," he said.

She nodded. "Bed the horse down in the side tunnel and you can get an early start."

He shook his head. "No point in that. Let's just give this one more try, and I'll go back only a year ahead and be here waiting and healthy with everything we're going to need when you come back through. That will only take a few minutes for all of you."

She looked at him, then smiled. "If you don't mind the year."

"You know how much I hate it back in the Old West," he said, laughing.

Madison was just stunned. These two really knew how to deal with all the aspects of time travel.

Dawn was just shaking her head, looking puzzled, clearly not wrapping her mind around what Duster had just suggested.

Bonnie kissed him long and hard, then turned to Madison and Dawn. "Grab your stuff. Make sure you are holding it all. Third time's the charm."

They all headed back into the crystal room carrying their saddlebags and supplies.

Duster pulled a wire.

The room shimmered. Madison had been about ten feet away watching. Suddenly, all four of them were touching the machine. Madison had a hunch they were once again back in 2014.

But there wasn't a darned thing in the crystal cavern that allowed him to easily tell when they traveled over a hundred years.

Then with gloves on, Duster went over to the wall and put the connections on a brand new crystal.

Bonnie motioned for them to all step back. "Be ready to go quickly again," she said. "Just as we did the first time."

Madison nodded, as did Dawn beside him. He still had all his supplies on his shoulder and in his left hand. She was carrying all of hers as well.

Duster reset the time on the machine for May 1901 and kissed Bonnie. "See you in a year."

Madison just couldn't completely wrap his mind around the fact that Duster would live a year in the next few seconds.

"Try not to break anything this time," she said.

"I'll try," Duster said, smiling.

Then, with one hand on the machine, he connected the wire and vanished.

"Wow! That is just amazing," Madison said.

"Creepy," Dawn said, shaking her head.

With gloves on, Bonnie quickly changed the date to May 1902. Then she took off the glove.

"On the count of three again," she said. "One. Two. Three."

Around Madison the room shimmered again as he touched the machine.

All three of them stepped away from the machine at the same time and headed back toward the supply room. The door between the crystal room and the supply room was open, so someone was there.

As they walked in, Duster again sat up from the couch and came forward, giving Bonnie a huge kiss. This time he didn't look any the worse for wear, but he was wearing different clothes than a few moments, and a hundred years, before.

"Any problems?" Bonnie asked as all three of them moved over to the packing table.

"Not a one. I have four great horses and two extra packhorses. And I have a bunch of supplies already, so we don't need much but the personal stuff you brought through. I got everything out there and ready to be tied to the horses."

"Perfect," Bonnie said. "How long have you been waiting?"

"I got back up here on a clear day about the 20th of April. I set up a camp outside like I was just using the old cabin and have the horses there. It's the first of May now."

"Perfect," Bonnie said. "What time of the day is it?"

"My guess, about sunrise," he said. He smiled at Madison and Dawn. "You two ready to see Roosevelt and other parts of the Old West?"

"You mean there's more to it than the inside of this cave?" Madison asked, winking at Dawn.

"I guess that means they're ready," Bonnie said, laughing.

"I guess we are," Dawn said.

Then she reached over and squeezed Madison's hand.

It surprised him and felt wonderful.

"An adventure?" she asked, smiling at him.

"An adventure," he said, smiling and looking deeply into those wonderful eyes of hers.

She let go of his hand and ten minutes later they were out into the biting cold of the May 1st 1902 morning.

# CHAPTER SEVENTEEN

**BY THE TIME THE SUN** was nearing the horizon in the west, getting ready to set, they were out of the Owyhee Mountains and down on the edge of the Snake River.

Dawn felt like she might never walk again.

Ever.

So far it had been most of seven hours on a horse, plus a few more hours leading a horse, or sitting on logs wishing someone would just come and shoot her.

Duster had picked out a campsite for them near the Snake River and figured they could make it out to it fairly easily on the first day.

Well, it had been easy for him, Dawn could see that.

But for her and Madison and Bonnie, the day turned into a very long journey. She had just kept thinking over the last three hours that at any moment she would just lose all feeling in her legs and fall off the horse.

They had rested every hour. After the first couple of hours, that hadn't helped much.

The worst part of the trip was coming down off of Florida Mountain right at first. They had actually walked the horses down a scary trail, and Dawn had quickly learned how much the footwear of a "lady" in 1902 was not suited for hiking, even though her boots were modern made.

And the riding outfit she had on wasn't suited for pee breaks either. The first stop had flat been embarrassing, since Bonnie had had to help her get out of the pants and then also help her button them back up again to make sure she knew how to do it.

As Bonnie said on one stop, they were a long ways and a lot of years away from a public restroom beside a road.

At the campsite, Duster mostly set up camp, showing Madison and Dawn how to set their tents. Dawn doubted she was going to remember much of it.

"Now that we're down on the valley floor," Duster had said, "We can take our time."

Both she and Madison and Bonnie all agreed that would be a very good idea.

Even though Duster had a fire going, Dawn splashed some water on her face and arms, ate a cold dinner of jerky and a sandwich, went into her tent, took out an extra blanket, and pumped up her air mattress. Then she took all her clothes off and crawled into her cloth bag. She didn't care that it wasn't appropriate for a lady to sleep in the nude in 1902. She had to be out of those clothes for just a little while.

She lay down, pulled the extra blanket up around her chin, and the next thing she remembered, there was light outside the tent and Madison was asking from outside if she was all right?

"Breakfast is on," he said.

"It will take a few minutes," she said, her voice sounding hoarse and her throat dry.

She rolled over and took a drink from her canteen. She could feel the bite to the early-morning air on her exposed shoulder.

She managed to find a clean pair of underwear in her saddlebag near her head and then she slipped into her pants.

She had brought a number of sports bras because, as Bonnie had said, "Who was going to know." Dawn slipped one of those on, then a white blouse over the top of that and then a suit coat and then a jacket.

Then she carefully took her feet, washed them off with a little water from her canteen, applied some antiseptic to most of the bottoms and a few red spots on the sides, and put on a pair of her favorite socks, then pulled socks more suited for the period over them, and finally her riding boots.

As she stood, every muscle in her body complained and she damned near ended up sitting down again.

She carefully limped out into bright sunlight, feeling like her legs would never be the same and she would walk funny the rest of her life.

Duster and Bonnie were sitting beside the campfire while Madison worked at something in a pan. Wow, not only was he the most attractive man she had ever seen, he could cook over a fire. More than likely just one of the many secrets she was going to find out about him on this trip.

"Women's restroom?" she asked, her voice still rough and dry.

Bonnie pointed to a grove of trees about fifty feet away and along the side of the hill.

"You need help getting there?" Bonnie asked.

"I think I'll make it, but if you don't see me in a couple hours, send help," Dawn said. "Riding a horse is something that should be done in small doses at first."

"I'll second that," Madison said, smiling at her.

She limped back ten minutes later to the heavenly smell of whatever Madison was cooking. Some sort of bacon, but she didn't remember them bringing any bacon along. More than likely it was from the supplies that Duster had ready for them.

Not only did her joints ache, but she felt like she was covered in two layers of dirt and grime. And this was only after one day. It was a long way from Murphy, Idaho, to Roosevelt, Idaho.

A very, very long way.

And she was starting to wonder if she was up for this kind of journey.

She must have moaned slightly as she sat down on a log beside Bonnie.

Bonnie patted her knee. "We are still a ways up river from the ferry. There's a hot spring about five miles from here. We'll camp there for the second night and give us all a rest."

She couldn't believe Bonnie said hot springs. "Oh, thank you," Dawn said. "That sounds heavenly."

"Wait until you see it," Bonnie said, smiling. "One of my favorite places. Very few people in this time period know about it, and it's a perfect temperature."

Madison turned over something in the pan, then said, "If I would have known I was going to be riding horses this summer, I'd have practiced."

"You get used to it in a few days," Duster said. "Sorry about that long first day, but we needed to get off that mountain in case a storm came in. It's been known to snow up there in early May."

Dawn looked at Bonnie, then simply asked once again to make sure she had heard correctly, "Hot springs?"

All she could think about was soaking in hot water, washing off the grime, and somehow getting closer to feeling human again.

Bonnie and Duster both laughed.

"Hot springs," Bonnie said. "There are a bunch of them along the way to Roosevelt, but this first one is the best."

"Heaven," Dawn said.

And again Bonnie laughed and agreed.

# CHAPTER EIGHTEEN

**MADISON HAD BEEN GLAD** to see Dawn was as sore as he was when she came out of her tent. Riding that much on a horse without being in shape was just flat brutal. He felt like he could barely move or walk, for that matter.

But even limping and clearly not awake, Dawn still looked fantastic. Stunning actually.

There was no doubt that he was completely taken with her.

He had offered to cook breakfast and moving around for a few minutes and getting loose was helping. Bonnie and Duster had let him, giving him a few tips as he got started. He managed to impress Dawn, and that made him happy, more than he wanted to admit.

They all took their time, the feeling of rushing to get out of the mountains completely gone now that they were down on the Snake River.

He was still having a hard time believing it was 1902. That would take more than a few days and a ton more evidence to sink in.

The air was cold and the sky gray and overcast, but it didn't feel to Madison that a storm was coming.

They packed up camp with Duster and Bonnie adding in all sorts of tips to make the process shorter. Then when they were about to start off, Dawn looked at

Duster and said, "Is it going to be possible to walk most of the way today?"

"Planning on it," Bonnie said.

"Oh, thank you," Madison said, completely relieved and Dawn laughed. He had not been looking forward to climbing back on that horse anytime soon. In fact, he wasn't certain he could even do it, he was so sore.

Duster had spared no expense both on horses and saddles, getting them the best that Madison knew existed in this time. But even the best saddles were tough at first.

Duster took the two packhorses and started off riding ahead of them down the wagon trail they would be following, promising that he would have camp set up by the time they reached the hot springs.

It was a very well-traveled wagon road and was full of deep ruts, clearly well-used. But so far they hadn't run across anyone else. For the moment Madison was happy about that. He wanted to get his wits settled a little before having to deal with someone from 1902 directly.

As they walked slowly, all three of them leading their horses, the morning slowly turned warmer.

After about a mile Dawn took off her heavy coat and Bonnie did the same. Madison hadn't started out with much of a coat on beside the light duster, so he left it on. He liked the feel of it, actually.

Bonnie and Dawn walked ahead, side-by-side, talking and laughing at times. He walked behind them, catching glimpses of Dawn past the two horses. She seemed to be relaxing into the adventure. He hoped he would as well fairly soon.

At about the two-mile point, as far as he could tell, a man and family in a wagon passed them. The man had on a work shirt, suspenders holding up jeans, and a cowboy hat. His wife wore a faded blue cotton dress and protective sun hat. The two kids sitting on the supplies looked to be in the four- to six-year-old range.

Both Bonnie and Dawn nodded to the family as they passed and Madison tipped his hat to the man, not looking at the woman or children at all.

The man nodded at them and the woman smiled while the kids waved.

Madison wondered who they were going to grow up to be.

Dawn looked back at him after the wagon was a distance past and said, "Think we might know any of those kids' great-great-grandkids?"

Then she laughed and turned back to face forward and say something to Bonnie he couldn't hear.

It took him a moment, but he realized that she might be right. If those young kids had kids of their own in 1920, and those kids had kids in 1940, and those kids had kids in 1960, the great-great-great-grandkids would be about his age or a little older in 2014.

Wow, that was a sobering thought.

He did his best over the next mile to try to even grasp that thought.

After about three hours he was starting to get hungry and thinking of digging into the jerky in his saddlebag when Bonnie pointed off the road and led them down through some cottonwood trees toward the edge of the river.

From what Madison could tell, it looked like they were about a hundred feet above the river at this point on a bluff overlooking the fast-moving Snake River below them.

Bonnie led them down a trail that was barely visible and clearly seldom used to a small meadow that looked out over the river. The meadow was covered only with dried scrub weeds and nothing else.

Duster had all three of the tents set up and a fire going in a pile of stones to one side of the camp. He was happily working on some lunch. He had taken off his hat and duster and hung them on his tent. He looked completely at home and in his element.

"Horses over there," he said, pointing to where he had his horse and the packhorses tied up in a grove of trees about fifty paces from the camp. "Brush them down and settle them in. We're here for the night."

Then he pointed in the other direction. "Shallow latrine dug over there about sixty paces. Paper and shovel next to it."

"Wow," Bonnie said, smiling at her husband. "All the comforts of home."

By the time Madison got his horse settled and helped Dawn with her saddle, he also was starting to feel more at ease. He had spent his share of time camping. In fact, on a number of his research trips, he had spent almost a month camping near an old ghost town up in western Montana. He had actually enjoyed the trip and the camping.

Now, on this trip, he was with a woman he wanted to get to know more than he would admit and with experienced guides. He really needed to relax and just enjoy the adventure.

Thirty minutes later, they were all sitting around the small campfire on the cool afternoon in May 1902, talking about who that family might be that had passed them and eating a wonderful hot sandwich of fried beef with tomatoes that Bonnie had packed.

Duster said he figured the older man was the son of a guy he had met in a few

timelines who homesteaded up the river beyond the turn-off to Silver City.

"So, with modern locators, where exactly are we?" Madison asked.

"Well," Duster said, "We're on the Snake River about three miles north and a little east of the brand new town of Murphy. At this point, Murphy is only a few years old, founded around a rail head."

"We ate in Murphy, right?" Dawn asked and Duster nodded.

"But we're not going to see Murphy this trip," Duster said. "It's a ways from the river and we have to keep going downriver to a place called Warren's Ferry to cross. That's where the bridge will be built, but it's not there yet."

"And that wagon trail out there?" Madison asked. "Will that turn into any part of Highway 78 that we came in on?"

"Not this area of it, nope," Duster said. "The highway will be built farther inland now that Murphy is there. This wagon trail will just vanish into history in a few years."

"You really must have to know your places and times in history," Dawn said.

"Actually," Bonnie said, "when we go back, we just live in the moment and let the history develop around us instead of thinking about what will be in the future."

Duster nodded. "Makes it a lot easier and keeps you from making mistakes. But remember, it took us a number of trips to get to that way of thinking."

Bonnie nodded. "That it did."

To Madison, that made sense.

Then Bonnie pointed at a path that led toward the river. "That leads over to a trail down about fifty feet to some hot springs on the bluff face."

She stood and held out her hand to her husband, who took it and smiled at her.

"You guys get to do dishes," Bonnie said, flipping a couple towels over her shoulder and picking up a change of clothes she had gotten from her bag earlier. "Then when we get back you two can have the springs. It's only big enough for two at a time."

"Water, soap and dish towels there," Duster said as Bonnie pulled her husband along the trail.

Madison felt his stomach twisting as he thought about being in a hot springs with Dawn.

He turned back and glanced at Dawn, who just smiled that wonderful smile of hers that melted him and made him want her more than he could think about.

"An adventure, remember?" she asked.

He laughed, his worry broken. "An adventure," he said, nodding, "but the real question is who is washing and who is drying?"

"Depends on what you are talking about washing," she said, smiling at him, a twinkle in her eyes.

He was fairly certain he turned bright red before he stuttered out, "Let's start with the dishes."

She laughed and that wonderful sound carried through the trees as she turned to get the pot of water and soap.

All he could do was stare at her.

# CHAPTER NINETEEN

**DAWN WASHED THE DISHES** and Madison dried, their hands touching at times as they passed the cookware between them. And each time that happened she got more and more excited about sitting in that hot springs with Madison.

She wanted to just jump him right now, kiss him, drag him into a tent and make love to him now. And from his reaction, he wanted the exact same thing.

If Bonnie and Duster didn't get back pretty soon, neither she nor Madison would make it to the water. But Dawn really wanted to wash a layer of the last two days on the trail off her before Madison touched her for the first time.

Somehow, they managed to keep talking, learning a little about each other with each question. With the dishes done, they both dug out clean clothes and towels.

Finally, after what seemed an eternity, Duster and Bonnie came back up the trail, looking pleased and flushed.

"Water's pretty warm," Duster said.

Bonnie shook her head and laughed. "It's perfect, trust me. Time for a nap, now."

With that they ducked into their tent and closed the flap.

"Clean?" Dawn asked, smiling at Madison.

"That sounds heavenly," he said, smiling back at her and letting that wonderful dimple of his come into full force.

"I got the towels, you got the soap?" she asked.

"Got it," he said.

Then he led the way down the trail.

The day had warmed up to almost comfortable. It was still mostly overcast, but no threat of rain and the winds were light from the east. Perfect as far as she was concerned.

She followed Madison, staring at his wonderful butt in those 1902 jeans. And the loosely tucked-in dress-shirt just made him look sexy. His brown hair was ruffled and he clearly hadn't shaved. She had a hunch that if he grew a beard and moustache, she was going to like it on him.

A couple places along the trail he paused and then helped her down a step or two on the rocks, his hand touching hers. But thankfully, the hot springs wasn't far below the edge of the canyon and had a fantastic view out over the river that was running pretty high and fast from spring run-off.

The hot springs itself was nothing more than a small pool formed among some rocks. About twenty feet up the hill, steam rose from where the water bubbled out of the ground and ran down over mossy rocks and into the pool. Then it went over the edge of rocks that framed the pool and on down toward the river.

It smelled like moss and wet dirt.

There was a sort of flat area to the right of the pool with a couple of stones that looked like they could be used as seats. The ground in the flat area was still wet from Bonnie and Duster.

"I wonder if this is still here in 2014," Madison asked, looking around and out over the river. "It's really amazing."

"More than likely it is," Dawn said, "but I'd wager it's on private property."

"Yeah, good point," Madison said.

She put the towels over a branch and then let her hair loose.

Madison had stopped, turned back, and was staring at her. She smiled at him as she started to unbutton her blouse.

"Anyone ever tell you how fantastically beautiful you are?" he asked.

She actually could feel herself blush and she wasn't sure what to say to that.

Then Madison closed the two steps between them and kissed her.

And kissed her like she had never been kissed before.

They seemed to just fit together and she pushed back into his kiss and into his body.

He felt wonderful.

Oh, god, did he feel wonderful.

Never, in all her life, did she remember a kiss like that one.

After what seemed far too short a time and an eternity at the same moment, he broke the kiss.

He smiled, letting the dimple come back strong as he said, "I've been wanting to do that since the first moment I saw you outside the car."

She kissed him again, this time slower.

It was as wonderful, maybe better than the first time.

Then breathless, she stopped and said, "Trust me, the feeling was mutual."

He kissed her again until finally she pushed him back about a foot. "Get undressed and get in the water. I need someone to scrub my back."

He laughed and said, "I thought you would never ask."

She watched him and he watched her as they undressed. Her hands were shaking and the unfamiliar buttons on the blouse slowed her down.

He had his shirt off first.

She wondered for a minute if she could breathe. He was in amazing shape, only a very slight sign of any love handles above his belt. Just stunning for a man in his early thirties.

She pulled off her blouse and put it on the rock as he worked on stripping off his pants. Under them he had on boxers that looked more modern than this time period.

Then he pulled off his underwear and she just stared at him.

He was clearly aroused and looked perfect in all ways.

She managed to strip off her riding pants and then her sports bra as he eased into the water and settled in to look back at her.

A smile was plastered on his face as he watched her take off her underwear and then step down into the hot water.

Bonnie was right, the temperature of the water was perfect. But the naked man sitting across from her had her so hot, she wasn't sure if she was going to be able to stand the water for long.

"Anyone ever tell you how fantastically beautiful you are?" he said, looking across the water into her eyes.

"This guy just recently back in 1902," she said, smiling.

Then they were together again in the middle of the small pool of hot water, kissing.

For a moment, she just kissed him, holding his head in her hands. Then she let her hands roam over his smooth skin and hard muscles of his back and he did the same for her.

Finally he pushed her away, clearly breathless and said, "Turn around. You wanted your back washed and you're going to get it."

She did as she was told, pushing back against him in the water and feeling his hardness against her back as he used the soap and rubbed it all over her back.

She ducked her head under the water and washed her face as he kept working on her back and shoulders and sides, his hands sometimes going to breasts and washing them as well.

She was so hot she was about ready to explode, and it wasn't from the water.

Finally, she raised up a little and pushed back and sat down on his hardness.

He slipped inside her.

His hands stopped moving and he pushed his face into her back just below her neck.

She couldn't believe how wonderful, how completely natural that felt. She wanted to keep this moment with her forever.

"Don't move," she managed to choke out.

"You're kidding, right?" he asked, his voice hoarse.

His hands moved around to her breasts and cupped them, but he did as she asked and didn't move.

Slowly, the feeling of him against her and holding her and inside of her built up in this wonderful wave of sensations.

And built.

And built.

And then there was no longer any ability for either of them to hold still.

# PART TWO

# CHAPTER TWENTY

**DAWN HAD FOUND** the week after they made love in the hot springs fantastic and difficult at the same time. With Bonnie and Duster with them at all times, she and Madison found it completely impossible to have any intimate private times except late in the evening. And even then that had become a challenge as they stayed in hotels along the route.

She was traveling as a single lady and he a single man, so they had to be very careful as to how they acted around others. She didn't much like that. She would rather walk along with his hand in hers, or reach over and just kiss him at times.

That day in the hot springs had been fantastic. Never had she imagined making love could be anything like that. He was perfect in all ways, even though he warned her a couple times that he was not a perfect person by any means. She was in lust with him and she knew it and as far as she was concerned, at the moment he was perfect.

And their lovemaking hadn't seemed to dim his interest in her as she worried it might. It had actually increased it, and she found herself liking that extra attention from him.

Also, getting used to the various aspects of living in 1902 was difficult. The clothing seemed to just perplex her at times. For a historian who focused on the human side of history, she was amazed that she had never really thought much about clothing before this trip. It clearly influenced a great deal. She had so much to learn and clearly Bonnie and Duster were right about how much a trip into the past would impact and influence her writing and teaching.

Thankfully, for the trip she had decided to just stay with her modern underwear. The boots, the socks, the riding pants, the blouses and coats and hats all seemed like far too much. But at the same time, she was loving all the learning about how women of this time period just dealt with this as normal.

On the fourth day out of Silver City, they reached a railhead near a farming town of Caldwell, Idaho. Duster had booked them on a train getting them up beyond a place called Emmett, where a wagon road was being built north up to the mining camps in the central region of Idaho.

The train ride had been rough, but interesting. She had sat facing Madison and the two of them compared notes on the time in soft conversations.

And they talked a little about the people around them in the passenger car.

Dawn knew that Colonel Dewey in 1902 was in the final stages of building most of a wagon road from the Emmett railhead clear into the Monumental Valley. He never made it all the way with the full wagon road because the state had backed out of their promised share of the costs.

But by the middle of the summer, not only would Dewey have heavy stamping equipment hauled into the valley by mule to process ore from the mines, but also the saloons would be filled with pianos hauled in over those same trails.

Roosevelt, Idaho, would be a booming town when they arrived and the closer they got, the more excited she got.

They had followed the wagon trail up out of Emmett and crossed the Payette River at a place called "Smith's Ferry." Then they had worked their way up the wagon trail and into a huge mountain valley. It was the south end of the same valley where McCall, Idaho, existed, the town where she had spent all her summers as a child.

The weather, even though it was still early in May, was being nice to them. It had only rained one morning and they had just stayed in a hotel near Caldwell for the time, not leaving until after the rain stopped.

The huge mountain valley smelled of marshlands and pine trees and she couldn't get enough of it as they rode along.

She was now much more used to riding and her aching muscles had eased. She was very glad she was back riding, actually, since they seemed to be crossing small streams every hundred steps.

It had taken them most of another day in that high mountain valley before they started back into the mountains just east of the future site of the town of Cascade.

From there they went back to alternating between walking and riding over the ups and downs of the wagon trail, since they were in no hurry in the slightest.

And along the way they took breaks often.

Both Bonnie and Duster said it was the way they liked to travel and Dawn didn't seem to mind at all. When you have all of time at the tips of your fingers, there really didn't seem to be much point in hurrying.

As the week went on and they spent more and more time around other people, it started to finally completely sink in that she really was in 1902. Madison mentioned that a great deal as well, that he believed this finally.

They were often passed on breaks by wagons and other groups, mostly men headed into the last great gold rush of the lower forty-eight states, hoping to strike it rich.

Dawn found it fascinating to sit and watch the men and a few families go by. Everything about her work and research was about the people of this time period and now she found herself actually getting to see them.

*And their lovemaking hadn't seemed to dim his interest in her as she worried it might.*

And she hoped in Roosevelt to get a chance to talk with them as well.

On the other hand, Madison was fascinated by some of the equipment they were carrying and was looking forward to seeing Dewey's stamping mill in action.

It took them almost two days after leaving the large valley near Cascade before they made it to the small mining town of Yellow Pine.

She was stunned beyond words. The exact same saloon she had ate lunch at in 2014 earlier in the summer was there, newer, less smoke-smelling, but exactly the same.

She just sort of walked around staring until Madison asked her what was wrong and she told him in whispers so that the owner of the place wouldn't hear her.

From Yellow Pine they started the long two-day climb the next morning toward the Monumental Summit. They all rode for most of that, resting the horses often, with a stop for a time in the new mining camp of Stibnite, which forty years later would be a major producer of different minerals for the Second World War before finally falling into ruin.

Dawn had made it from Yellow Pine to the top of that summit in a van in 2014 in just under four hours.

Now it was going to take them two days on horseback.

The night air going up that mountain was always cold, and twice it snowed lightly on them as they got closer and closer to the top.

Snow still blanketed almost everything and was piled in drifts under the trees. In a number of places the streams they had to cross were rushing torrents over rocks. That bothered Dawn a great deal, but her horse managed them just fine.

"We wouldn't make it in here much earlier," Duster said at one point, pointing at a snowdrift to one side of the wagon trail.

"Usually didn't open until real early May at the earliest," Dawn said. "And everyone who stayed in the valley was snowed in from the middle of September onward."

"Wow, that's a long winter," Madison said.

"And a brutal one," Dawn said. "Which was why after the first major year, this year, actually, not many people spent winters in here. The snow and the cold pretty much stopped the mining except in the big mines like the Dewey."

It was in the middle of the eighth day after leaving Silver City that they finally reached the Monumental Summit. Nine miles ahead of them and down one thousand feet was Roosevelt.

They decided to camp for the night on the summit on the flat area about a hundred paces to the north of the trail. The wind had kept the snow from building up in the area and the spring sun had melted what had been there, leaving a wonderful open meadow.

After they had camp set up and Duster was cooking, she stood on the edge looking down into Monumental Valley a thousand feet below them.

Madison stood beside her, holding her hand.

She could see the smoke from a few campfires in the valley winding up into the crystal clear air. On one side, Thunder Mountain loomed over the valley, its steep, rocky slopes still mostly covered in snow.

On the other side, a tall ridgeline seemed to drop over loose shale and rock straight to the floor. They could faintly hear the sound of Monumental Creek below them flowing down through the trees along with faint sounds of axes and shovels from minors working along the stream.

The newly completed wagon road ended near the other end of this ridge and from there a trail cut down the side of the valley on the left. Somehow Dewey and his men had gotten mining equipment down that trail to the valley floor.

Or up and over a worse trail to the north called the Elk Creek Summit trail.

Looking at the trail in front of her slashing through the snow across the hill, she had no idea how that was possible. About halfway down a group of men with two horses and a dozen donkeys seemed to be clinging to the cliff face as they worked their way down slowly.

The sun was still barely lighting the valley floor and the air was so clear and crisp she could see almost to the end of the Monumental drainage to the Middle Fork of the Salmon River twenty miles away. To her right, she could see to the sharp ridges and snowcapped mountains that towered over the River of No Return.

She had loved this summit when she had gone over it in 2014. She loved it even more now.

"This is magical," she said, softly.

He squeezed her hand gently. "Yes, it is. More than I had ever imagined. And I'm glad I'm standing here with you. That makes it even more magical."

She smiled at him, then glanced around to make sure no other travelers were close by. Then she kissed him, long and hard.

And he kissed her back with the same amount of passion.

She belonged in his arms.

She knew it.

And she belonged on this summit, and in the valley below.

She knew that as well.

# CHAPTER TWENTY-ONE

**MADISON COULDN'T BELIEVE** how comfortable he felt standing there with Dawn on the top of Monumental Summit. In all his life he couldn't have imagined this.

He had grown more and more comfortable as each day went on being in the past, the same past, the same time in history that had been his life's work to study. He kept waking up in the morning, looking at the tent above him, and thinking he was in a dream. But when he left the tent, he found himself actually in the past with a woman of his dreams.

Since he was a kid he had been fixated on the west, on the mining in the west, on every detail of the real Old West, not the west told in old westerns. That fixation had all started with a history lesson in the sixth grade in Washington Grade School in Boise.

His teacher gave a presentation about how a former governor of Idaho, Frank Steunenberg, had been assassinated in 1905 because of his stance against a mining union. Then the teacher had taken them to the Boise Capitol Building on a field trip to see the dome and the statue of Governor Steunenberg standing in a small park right in front of the capital.

That had gotten young Madison's interest focused on history, and he never let it go.

Now he stood here, in that history.

In May 1902, Idaho had only been a state for twelve years. Stuenenberg had just finished his term as governor a year ago, but would not be killed for his stance against the mining unions for another three years.

Below him in a valley was one of the great hidden secrets of the West, the town of Roosevelt that Zane Grey had found so fascinating he had written a novel about it.

Dawn had said that this was magical.

Madison completely agreed.

She was magical, the valley, the history, and the fact that they were together in this past moment.

They stood on that summit overlooking Monumental Valley kissing and just holding each other until Duster called out that dinner was ready.

Over a dinner of fresh grouse that Duster had shot, combined with a wonderful potato dish that Bonnie had made from dried potatoes and chopped, dried vegetables, they talked about the area.

Dawn told them a lot about the people, about what the town was generally going to look like when they went down the hill tomorrow. Madison was impressed with her knowledge of the little stuff, even though she didn't feel confident about much of it.

And Madison was really, really excited to see what Colonel Dewey was building for a stamp mill. Dewey was one of the great figures of the Old West mining, and a town below Silver City had actually been named after him.

At one point, Duster said that he knew Dewey pretty well in a few other timelines. "I know what the man likes," Duster said, smiling. "I might be able to figure out a way to get us inside the entire works."

That got Madison really excited and they agreed to come up with a backstory to tell Dewey later.

Both Bonnie and Duster were surprised that in all their trips, they had never been into this area before.

"I'm betting it's because the area just didn't last long enough," Dawn said. "The mining season is very short and in just six years the mines will be played out and that town we're going to see down there will be mostly abandoned. Then in the spring of 1909 it will be covered with water and lost to history and this entire area will be mostly forgotten."

Both Bonnie and Duster nodded at that.

"So many towns came and went that fast in the west," Duster said. "Glad we're finally given an excuse to see this one in its prime."

After that, the conversation turned to how Bonnie and Duster survived in the past, how they got money, that sort of thing. Madison actually turned the conversation in that direction because he had been wondering since Duster bought them first-class passage on that rail car over to Emmitt.

Duster laughed at the question. "We have been back here so often, we know when stocks are going to go up and when they are going to go down. When banks are going to boom and when they will go bust. We know which businesses to invest in and which to avoid."

"And which real estate to buy and when to sell it?" Madison asked, nodding. "It's because you have made so many trips, you know all of this?"

"Exactly," Duster said. "We bring a lot of gold with us to start each trip, of course. Usually more than enough to be comfortable, but even when we go different directions, we tend to do small investments to make more."

Bonnie nodded. "Since I have spent so much time in San Francisco, I know all the history there and the land and I tend to become one of the rich women of the town very quickly."

"When you are there, do you leave before the big quake?" Dawn asked.

Bonnie looked haunted again, as if the memories had overtaken her.

"I've rode it out a few times," she said.

Bonnie clearly didn't want to say more about that at all.

The fire crackled and they sat there in silence.

The night was slowly falling on the mountains and the air was chilling down. So far no other travelers had decided to stay on the summit for the night, which pleased Madison. He and Dawn could enjoy an evening completely together.

And he was looking forward to that a lot.

After a moment, Dawn sort of glanced around at the flat area of the summit through the pine. "I'm sort of surprised there is no sign of anyone building the rumored hotel up here yet."

"Rumored?" Duster asked.

Dawn nodded. "No one has ever been able to find evidence of the site of the hotel, or even pictures of it."

"Maybe it was only talk and no one actually did it," Madison said, looking at Dawn who seemed disappointed. "After all, if I understand right, this is only one of three ways into this valley."

"Yeah, they called this the Boise route," Dawn said, "and you are right, many came in from the other side through the Middle Fork of the Salmon River and still others came around over Elk Summit from Warren and up Monumental Creek. What made this trail even used was the connection between Stibnite mining areas and Yellow Pine and the Dewey road to the summit here."

"Maybe what you found was an echo?" Duster asked.

"Are you saying in our timeline no one built the hotel," Madison asked, but in others it was built?"

"Exactly," Bonnie said. "We're still trying to figure out how echoes of events in one timeline can be rumors in others, but this wouldn't be the first time we've noticed that. We just don't understand completely how it works mathematically."

"That sort of fits," Dawn said. "Back in 1998 a group came up here with sounding equipment figuring the old hotel might be a cache of old bottles and buttons and treasures. They couldn't find any evidence of the site at all, or that the ground had even been disturbed in a thousand years."

"Echo," Duster said, nodding. "Someone built a hotel here in some timeline. Just not ours."

"It would be a beautiful place for a hotel," Madison said, looking around through the trees and the piled up snow. "No customers in the winter, though."

"I can think that might be a good thing at times," Dawn said, smiling at him with that wonderful smile that promised a night of fun ahead.

"I'll agree with that," Madison said.

All Bonnie and Duster could do was shake their heads and laugh.

# CHAPTER TWENTY-TWO

**THE NEXT MORNING** they headed slowly down the long, dangerous trail into the Monumental Valley. The narrow trail that cut across rockslides scared her to death. They all walked slowly on the sometimes loose shale, leading their horses.

One slip and she would tumble a thousand feet to the valley floor.

If her horse slipped, she had exact instructions from Duster to let it go, not try to save it, and not go over the edge with it. She hadn't liked those instructions, but now that she was on the trail working her way to the valley floor, she certainly understood them.

No wonder anyone still left in this valley when the snow started to fall was stuck for the winter. This trail was scary enough fairly dry. No way would she even try it in the rain, let alone snow.

The morning had dawned very, very cold and breath from the horses and everyone seemed to just hold in the air. Even though Madison had put up his tent, he had brought his bag over after they had dinner and they had shared her tent, sleeping curled up together after making slow and quiet love.

Knowing that noise carried long distances in the cold mountain air had kept them both very silent, which had the added benefit of ramping up the intensity of the lovemaking.

Just before the sun colored the distant horizon, Madison left her, dressed quickly and went back to his tent. She hated that he had to do that, and hated when he left her.

She was falling completely for him.

So far, in a week of traveling together, she hadn't seen one thing she didn't like or that worried her about him even slightly. He was smart, gentle, and had a sense of humor that had her laughing more times than not.

And he was as passionate about history as she was and learning as much as he could about it.

They left early with only a light breakfast and while the air was bitterly cold. Even with her heavy gloves over her more fashionable ones, she couldn't get her fingers or her toes warm.

Duster wanted to leave that early to get ahead of any of the packtrains that might be headed in to Roosevelt. And he also wanted to get ahead of anyone coming up out of the valley. As he said, there just weren't going to be many places to turn around or move out of the way on that trail.

And now that she was on it, she understood that.

Completely.

She wanted to stop, stare at the fantastic view below them, but mostly the only thing she saw was the trail in front of her.

From the time they broke camp until they finally reached the valley floor and Dawn thought she could breathe again, it had taken just under an hour.

An hour full of sheer terror and fear combined with the excitement she felt about where they were.

"That was fun," Duster said, smiling at them as they moved out off the now wide wagon road that had been built up the valley to the bottom of the trail. He led them to what looked like a well-used camp in the trees and they tied up the horses to let them rest and feed.

There was snow still under the trees, but a lot of it was melting fast. Dawn could still see her breath, but the fear on the trail had stopped her from thinking about being cold at all.

"You have a very strange sense of fun," Bonnie said to her husband, smiling and clearly looking relieved. "That has to be one of the scariest trails I've ever been over."

"Worse than that one in the goldfields of Alaska?" Duster asked.

"That only had a raging river below it, not a thousand foot drop over rocks and snow."

Dawn just shook her head as she sat down on a log and took deep breaths of the crisp morning air to settle her nerves. In two thousand years, Bonnie and Duster had seen a lot of the west. Amazing they could remember half of it.

"Actually," Dawn said, "in history very few died on that trail. Not compared to the poor souls coming in over the trail from Warren and up the Salmon to Monumental Creek and then up."

"Seriously, one of the other trails in here is worse?" Madison asked.

"Much," Dawn said, nodding.

"Let's not go out that way when we leave," Madison said.

"Deal," Dawn said.

She sat and looked around as Duster and Bonnie and Madison walked down toward Monumental Creek to wash their faces. The stream was running strong from all the snow melt, yet just above where they were, on a bend in the rushing stream, she could see a man with his hands in the water, panning.

She had tried to pan for gold just once, and gave up after about three minutes because she could no longer feel her hands. Working all day in that ice water had to almost be impossible. Yet the miners did it.

She looked around. She just couldn't believe she had made it back to this valley again. She loved it here, far more than she wanted to admit to anyone, including Madison.

She looked up at the towering mountains above her. Right in front of her was Thunder Mountain, the peak that gave the entire region its name. At one point Monumental Creek had dug into the side of the mountain and actually gone underground for a distance, making the narrow valley sound like the mountain was rumbling from the water cascading down over the rocks in the cave.

The first Native Americans in the area had called the mountain Thunder because of that rumbling and the name had stuck to the entire area. The water during the middle eighteen hundreds had been diverted out of the cave by a landslide and the mountain stopped rumbling, but kept its name.

She shivered and stood, stomping her feet to get some feeling back into them.

The sun had yet to come close to the valley floor, but she could tell it was going to be a nice day. They still had a good seven miles down the valley before they reached Roosevelt.

She was so excited, she almost couldn't contain herself.

Just a short week ago she had driven into this valley, taken pictures of the ruins of Roosevelt down through the water, and sat beside the old cemetery.

Now she actually got to see the place in its prime.

She had to be dreaming.

She glanced over as Madison walked back toward her, smiling, his face red from the extremely cold water.

He was the most handsome man she had ever seen.

She was in love. Plain and simple.
In love with this valley.
In love with that man.
She was right. She had to be dreaming.

# CHAPTER TWENTY-THREE

**THEY RODE** from the bottom of the trail down the valley, walking the horses slowly, not in any hurry to really get anywhere. The morning remained bitterly cold, but the sun slowly working its way down the high mountains around them promised it would warm up some.

They just seemed like four people out for a leisurely morning ride.

The valley was surprisingly full of noise. Dawn had expected that, but not as much as was actually going on. They passed men chopping trees to build log cabins, and in one long area a crew of men were cutting down trees and stacking the lumber.

In places there was nothing but stumps for hundreds of yards up the sides of the hills.

The sounds echoed off the tall slopes that climbed sometimes straight up from the valley floor at times. In places, the valley seemed so narrow, she wondered how even a wagon road could get past the creek between the rock slopes, slopes far, far too steep to climb for anyone but a trained climber.

The air was full of the smell of freshly-cut wood and spring grass. Along this area there was very little snow left on the valley floor, but it was still clear just a few hundred yards up the hills.

In a few places, the valley floor widened out to a football-field wide, which seemed almost spacious.

Around the very next bend in the valley, they came across a large three-story building being built to the left of the road up against a rock slope.

"Stamp mill," Madison said the moment he saw it. "Where's the mine? And who does it belong to?"

"This isn't Dewey's," Dawn said as they stopped and watched five or six men work on the large wooden structure. "I can't remember the name of it right off. The mine is back across the valley and a hundred yards up the hill."

She pointed to the hill across the field of tree stumps where a road had been cut into the side of the hill and there were signs of tailings.

She felt shocked because two weeks before she had passed this site on this very road in her van. The old mill they were watching being built right now only had one wall left standing in 2014, towering into the air like a monument to a forgotten age. Everything else in and around the building was a pile of rotting lumber and rusted metal.

She moved her horse up beside Madison while Duster and Bonnie brought their horses around so they could hear her as well.

Making sure her voice didn't carry, she said, "All this wood along here is being cut for the boilers for this mill, but they never bring the boilers in and get the mill started because the mine plays out before they can. When I was in here last week, I mean back in our time, all this lumber they are cutting is still stacked along here and all the trees have grown back up around the piles. It was creepy."

"That would be," Bonnie said, nodding and looking around at all the lumber being stacked in perfect piles about shoulder high. Some of the piles ran for fifty or more paces.

"So this place never even gets used?" Madison asked, staring at the big building.

"Nope, never does," Dawn said. "They got the stamp mill in here but not the boilers."

"Then where's Dewey's mine and mill?" Duster asked.

"About two miles up Mule Creek above Roosevelt. It's where the landslide started that buried the town, actually."

"Wow, this is really something," Madison said, smiling at her with that wonderful dimple showing.

For some reason she was really glad he thought so. She had been faintly worried he would find this time in history boring, since his main focus was the mining wars in Northern Idaho and Western Montana.

Duster turned and headed down the road leading the two packhorses.

"It really is amazing, isn't it?" Dawn said, staring at the men working and then down the narrow valley framed in with high mountains on both sides.

"That it is," Bonnie said. "Can't believe I have never been in here before."

From the big mill onward they started passing more and more people. Many of them were working on log cabins, some planting small gardens, others just on their way somewhere.

Dawn had gotten her wish. She had wanted to see this valley alive and it clearly was on this beautiful spring day.

They finally stopped for lunch in a wide area that Bonnie was pretty sure she and her friends had camped in the week before, but a hundred and some years in the future.

A wide trail left the road and headed up a side creek at that point, while in 2014, that trail was a road leading up to a mine.

Within a half mile, in 2014, was marshland where a hundred years of spring run-off had filled in the upper end of Roosevelt Lake for about a mile. It was going to be very interesting to see what the valley looked like now, before the lake.

She had seen old pictures of it, but they were so few, and only focused on a small part of the town, she was convinced the pictures would not do the town justice.

She was so excited, she could hardly eat. But she forced herself to drink water and choke down a sandwich while they sat and talked under two large trees tucked against the north side of the valley.

Finally, about halfway through lunch, the sun hit the valley floor and suddenly the air got a lot warmer.

'Wow, that's amazing," Bonnie said as she stood and pulled off her heavy coat and tucked it under a strap on her saddlebag.

Dawn did the same thing, leaving on a dress jacket that matched her riding pants. She was still deathly afraid of any kind of contact with anyone from this time, but Bonnie said she perfectly looked the part of a lady.

She might look the part, but could she act and speak the part, that was the key.

"So," Dawn said, glancing at Duster, "we might want to think about where to camp tonight. Not sure how much of this from here on is owned land."

"We have a place to stay," Duster said, smiling.

"We do?" Dawn said, very surprised.

She glanced at Bonnie and Madison who both looked surprised, then back at Duster. "I don't think there were any hotels that would be suited for us at this point in Roosevelt."

Duster laughed. "Just wait. You'll see."

Bonnie frowned at her husband. "What did you do, dear?"

Again he laughed. "Just wait. We're almost to Roosevelt, aren't we?"

"We are," Dawn said, feeling very puzzled. One of her worries for the last few days had been where they were going to set up camp while in the valley this summer. At this point in time, this valley was mostly owned either because Roosevelt had been divided into lots and sold or the land fell under placer claims along the creek.

"Then let's go take a look at this mythical mining town," Duster said, taking a last drink from his canteen and putting it back on his horse.

Dawn climbed on her horse and forced herself to take a deep breath. Her hands on the reins were shaking slightly and she wanted to turn and ride away, let the dream remain a dream.

"It's going to be amazing," Madison said, smiling at her.

She hoped so. Sometimes the story of a place was far more than the actual place, she knew that.

But in the future, she had stood beside the lake, stared down into the crystal clear water of the lake at the foundations and

*Dawn had gotten her wish. She had wanted to see this valley alive and it clearly was on this beautiful spring day.*

remains of the buildings and wondered what the people who lived and worked in them were like.

Now she would ride between those same buildings on a beautiful spring day.

How fantastically strange was that?

# CHAPTER TWENTY-FOUR

**THE VALLEY** got slightly wider as they approached Roosevelt. The road was wider allowing wagons and other rides to pass them. Dawn smiled at the women, but kept her eyes forward for the men passing. If they tipped their hats to her, she nodded slightly. Bonnie had helped her with that ritual.

Monumental Creek was running down the left side against a steep slope of loose rock, barely heard in the noise of the construction and the music from the saloons and dance halls ahead.

There were more and more buildings scattered among the tall scrub and no signs of trees at all. Even the stumps were chopped down to almost ground level, more than likely for firewood during the last winter. However, the trees still covered the steep slopes about a hundred yards up the hills on both sides.

She could smell ham and eggs cooking and the smell of campfire smoke seemed to fill the air.

The sound was what stunned Dawn more than anything. She actually could hear the pianos over the noise of hammering and sawing and some shouting. The music wasn't distinct, and she couldn't pick out a song because there were numbers of pianos fighting each other to fill the air between the steep rock slopes.

What little that had been written about Roosevelt always talked about the music and how it filled the air in the valley all the time.

"Pianos?" Duster asked, turning in his saddle to look at Dawn. He had a puzzled look on his face. "How did they get pianos in here?"

"Mostly over that trail we came down," Dawn said, smiling.

Duster just shook his head.

Behind her she heard Madison say, "Amazing."

That made her smile.

Then suddenly, they came around a slight bend in the valley floor and there, ahead of them and slightly down a hill, spread out from side-to-side in the valley, was the mining town of Roosevelt.

One main road ran right down the middle of it, now filled with wagons, horses, and people.

Dawn was speechless, her heart racing. It was so much better than the old black and white images of the place. Those old pictures had been taken from up on the rocks. Where they were, they could see right down the main street of town.

The buildings were mostly only a single story tall, with steeply slanted roofs. Wooden planks ran along both sides of the street for people to walk on over the mud, and the main street itself was so choked with horses and wagons, it was amazing anything moved. Many of the horses were tied up outside of saloons with open doors.

Behind the buildings were more buildings filling the area up to the rock walls of the valley on both sides. A few of the buildings on the left side of the valley actually straddled Monumental Creek.

Right below the town the valley choked down tight. To the right side was a second wide valley where the wagon road turned and went up. That was Mule Creek. It was from that valley that the avalanche of mud and trees would come down and block both Mule Creek and Monumental and cover this town in a hundred feet of clear, cold water.

They all four moved off to one side of the road to let a wagon full of supplies go past. They stopped, staring at the bustling town ahead of them. The music was even louder here, even though they were still a ways above the main part of the town.

Dawn sat on her horse between Bonnie and Madison, just staring and smiling.

Finally she glanced over at Madison, who was also smiling.

"I really love old mining towns," Duster said. "They had so much life and energy and promise."

"And dreams," Bonnie said, staring at the town spread out ahead and slightly below them. "I love them because everyone here has a dream of one sort or another."

"I think this is a dream," Dawn said. "I can't begin to thank you enough for bringing me here."

"I second that completely," Madison said.

"You are more than welcome," Bonnie said, smiling. "I imagine both your books will be richer for the adventure."

Dawn just stared at the buildings and all the motion in front of her. She'd think about her book later.

"So we have a whole summer to explore this town and everything around it and meet some of these people," Duster said. "What do you say we get settled in first?"

"And where exactly might that be, dear?" Bonnie asked, shaking her head at her husband.

Duster turned in his saddle and pointed back up the road along the creek. Built on a slight ridgeline coming off the hill was a log cabin that looked bigger and more expensive than the standard log cabins going up along the valley floor.

Many of the small cabins they had passed from the outside looked like they were built too low for anyone to actually walk upright in them. Actually, Dawn knew that the ground inside had been dug out because it was easier to dig down than build up. And the buildings lasted longer in the heavy snow loads of the winter.

Dawn could see that the cabin that Duster had pointed to was built almost to modern standards. And it had a front porch that would look out over the valley and the town below. It also had a place along one side for the horses. It even had curtains in the windows and a large stone fireplace chimney in the center of the steep roof.

"You're kidding me?" Bonnie asked, looking at the big home and then back at her husband. "How did you manage that in one year?"

Dawn was so stunned, she didn't know what to say.

"Last summer I bought the land while in Boise."

Dawn suddenly remembered that even though it seemed like only a second, Duster had come back a year earlier than they had. She had forgotten that.

"I figured that if we were coming in here as rich landowners, we might as well act the part," Duster said. "So I hired three men that I knew were trustworthy in other timelines, assuming they would be in this one, to spend the winter in here building the cabin and then furnishing it and stocking it. I still owe them a little money for the work and supplies, but I promised to give them each a placer claim along the creek if they got it done. Looks like they did."

"How big is that?" Madison asked, clearly as stunned as Bonnie was feeling.

"Three bedrooms," Duster said, "an outhouse just outside the back door a few steps up the hill, plus a living and cooking and dining area. I figured if we were going to spend a summer here, we might as well all be comfortable. Especially on your first trip back."

Bonnie looked at her husband, then reached over and pulled him toward her in his saddle and kissed him.

"Thank you."

He smiled at her. "You are more than welcome."

# CHAPTER TWENTY-FIVE

**MADISON COULD NOT BELIEVE** he was seeing an actual mining town spread out down the valley in front of him. In all his years of research, it was this time in each town that fascinated him the most. And now he was going to get a chance, an entire summer, to talk with miners, understand them better, figure out what really drove them through the hardships, besides the promise of riches.

And now Duster was leading them back up to this huge log cabin built on the edge of the valley above Monumental Creek that he said he had built.

Or actually had built.

The idea that Duster had been back here in the past for a year ahead of them had just never really sunk in. Sure, he had the horses bought and supplies in place, but Madison was having a hard time grasping the idea of spending an entire

year back here just to get ready for the three of them to come through.

Yet Duster had thought nothing of it.

No doubt it was going to take some time for Madison to get used to this time travel stuff.

And it was really going to be difficult to grasp that no matter how long they were here in this valley, only two minutes and twelve seconds will have passed back at the crystal cavern in 2014.

In reality, it was still the same day that he met Dawn, not much after two in the afternoon on that first day, actually.

He pushed that thought away as he dismounted and tied up his horse in front of the big, new cabin and followed Duster and Bonnie up the three stairs to the wide front porch.

"This is wonderful," Dawn said, getting to the porch and looking down the valley at the main part of Roosevelt, the smoking fireplaces and the fighting music from pianos making it an amazing sight to behold and listen to.

Duster pushed open the door and Madison turned to follow him and Bonnie into the cabin.

Which actually wasn't a cabin by any means.

The insides felt more like a mansion.

A large wooden dining table filled one area of the main room with a cloth tablecloth and a candlestick centerpiece. Huge overstuffed couches and chairs filled a living room area formed by two large windows that looked out over the valley. A giant stone fireplace dominated one wall of the living room with chairs and couches facing it as well.

A kitchen with sink, large wood stove, large counters and an icebox occupied yet another side of the large front area of the home.

Cut wood for both the stove and the fireplace were stacked perfectly beside both. Unlit lanterns were everywhere and there were pegs to hang coats and hats near the front door.

The entire place had a wonderful smell of freshly cut pine and wood smoke.

The ceilings were high and the logs of the walls and rafters were stained golden. The chinking between the logs seemed to be a light brown as well, matching the logs. There were area carpets over the smooth wood-planked floors under the living area and the dining area.

A hallway with a carpet runner down the center went straight through the center of the back half of the building. Madison could see three doors leading off the hallway, two on one side, one on the other.

This wasn't a log cabin, this was a home that just shouted rich. More than likely it was the largest home in the entire valley.

"Wow," Bonnie said, laughing. "This is what I call roughing it."

She then turned and gave Duster the longest and most passionate thank-you kiss Madison had seen in a long time.

For a couple that had lived thousands of years, they sure hadn't let the passion die off. That was wonderful to see.

He smiled at Dawn who was watching as well and also smiling.

Madison took Dawn's hand and the two of them went down the hallway, checking out the bedrooms. In the large one there were two dressers and hanging rods for clothes built across corners. The featherbed was huge and had a carved wooden headboard. The two smaller bedrooms had large featherbeds in both of them as well, plus a dresser and hanging rods in each, along with the standard washbasins and pitchers.

"Front or back?" Madison asked Dawn.

She smiled. "Front." Then she reached up and kissed him and whispered. "But we'll spend the nights in yours if you don't mind the company."

"Never will I mind," he whispered back.

And he meant that.

She kissed him again and they headed back out to help bring in their clothes and supplies from the saddlebags and the packhorses.

As they got back to the living room they could hear Duster talking with some men outside.

Bonnie was on the porch, standing near the door.

Madison went past her and down the steps. As he neared the conversation, Duster turned and smiled. "Ah, this is Madison Rogers," Duster said. "He's an expert in certain types of mining and will be studying miners in this area for a book he will be writing back east."

Duster then introduced the three men who had built the home over the winter and early spring and Duster shook each man's hand.

Then Duster turned to Bonnie and Dawn standing on the porch.

"This is my wife, Bonnie, and Miss Dawn Edwards."

Madison watched as both of them bowed slightly as they should for this time period and all three men took off their hats and nodded their hellos. None of them spoke.

"So, gentlemen," Duster said, "shall we go into town and get accounts settled?"

All three of the men nodded their goodbyes to Bonnie and Dawn, then said they were glad to meet Madison, and turned and walked off toward the downtown area of Roosevelt, the closest a half-step behind Duster.

Madison watched them go, amazed at how Duster just commanded them without even trying. He was in charge and all three of them knew it and didn't question it. It might have something to do with the Colt revolvers on his hips, but more than likely it was just how he carried himself.

It was going to take Madison some time to even get close to that, if he ever did.

Now he understood why Duster liked it so much back here in the west.

Everywhere he went, he was in charge.

Even when not a person knew who he was.

# CHAPTER TWENTY-SIX

**DAWN SAT** in a large overstuffed chair in the living room of the fantastic cabin just above Roosevelt, Idaho. Madison had built a crackling fire and she and Bonnie had cooked a combination of fresh trout caught a few miles down Monumental Creek by a local merchant and potato salad spiced by dried onions and carrots.

The place smelled of newly-cut logs, a campfire, and the sweet smell of dinner.

Now, sitting around the fire, the drapes drawn, they were sipping small glasses of a sweet sherry.

"I've died and gone to heaven," Dawn said, smiling at Madison, who tipped his glass at her in agreement. She had not felt this relaxed in a very, very long time.

And excited.

Outside the windows the sounds of the pianos from seven saloons and two dancehalls filled the valley. No tune came through clear, just a distant wave of music that promised a new world to explore tomorrow.

"I am so glad you thought of building this," Bonnie said, smiling at her husband. "It had been a while since I had spent an entire summer in a tent, sleeping on the ground."

"How long ago?" Duster asked, smiling fondly at his wife.

"I could figure it out if you really want to know," she said, a twinkle in her eye.

"Will it make me feel old?" Duster asked.

"Very," Bonnie said.

"Then please don't," Duster said, laughing. "I wasn't relishing the idea of spending the summer on the ground either. So I figured this place would be the best solution and give us good cover among the people here."

"Cover?" Madison asked a moment before Dawn could. That use of the word bothered her as well. Why in the world would they need cover in Roosevelt?

"All winter the people of this valley knew that four rich people were coming into the valley. Not even Colonel Dewey has a place this nice in here. And he owns the biggest mining claim."

"And we needed it known that we were coming why?" Dawn asked, still very puzzled.

"By building here, especially so close to town and this early in the boom time," Duster said, "we become one of them. They may not know us, but we won't be treated as outsiders either. And considering some of the questions we might ask, better to be known as a valley insider than an outsider."

"Is that the way it worked in a lot of mining towns?" Madison asked.

"It is," Duster said. "If you were in first and built early, it was considered that you belonged."

"And thus protected," Bonnie said, nodding. "I've seen that a lot as well. Very smart thinking, dear."

"Thanks," Duster said, his feet up on a stool, his boots near the door. "And besides, this beats a tent any time."

Dawn had no argument on that statement at all.

"I also set up that we will have a load of supplies coming in from Boise every week until I shut it off before we leave," Duster said. "First load should arrive in two days."

"Perfect," Bonnie said.

"You really had this all thought through," Madison said. "Thank you."

"You are welcome," Duster said. "I came up with most of this while laid up in the hotel that first five-year attempt. I figured that if you two went back into the past often enough on research, you would have your rough times. This first one might as well be as comfortable and smooth as possible."

"You're not going to mind that we use the time travel device to do research?" Dawn asked, stunned.

"Of course not," Bonnie laughed. "That's what this is all about. Remember, even if you come back for fifty years, you are only using the machine in the cave for two minutes and fifteen seconds."

"Not going to be a traffic jam in the cavern," Duster said, smiling.

"And we'll teach you all the tricks," Duster said, "on how to get rich quickly while back in time, how to carry riches back with you, so most of the time you can live like this or better while you research."

"But not all trips will be smooth, and not all will end the way you want them

to," Bonnie said. "This is the west, after all, and if you go back to the 1878 period we like to start in, things are even rougher than they are now in 1902 for those of us used to modern ways of living."

"I don't know," Madison said. "This feels pretty darned modern to me."

"It does, doesn't it?" Duster said, smiling.

"Except for the fact that in less than seven years," Dawn said, "we know this valley will be mostly abandoned and forgotten and that town down there will be nothing but floating timber and lost dreams."

"Will this cabin be under water as well?" Bonnie asked.

"About five feet under here," Dawn said, nodding. She had used some landmarks from her trip earlier in 2014 to figure that out before dinner.

"That must be some landslide?" Duster said.

"It traveled two miles from the mine at the top of Mule Creek, moving about as fast as a man could walk," Dawn said. "It filled the entire valley just below the town to the level of one hundred and twenty-five feet. It took four days for the water to back up over Roosevelt and two weeks to fill the valley completely."

"What does it look like in 2014?" Madison asked.

"A huge meadow and marsh stretches for about a mile back up the valley, just about to where we stopped on the way in," Dawn said. "Monumental Creek has filled all that in over the hundred-plus years. The lake itself is now from right about where we are here to the landslide, and is slowly filling as well."

"The entire place will be a meadow in another hundred years," Bonnie said, nodding.

"And the landslide has one-hundred-year-old pine trees growing on it," Dawn said. "You can't even tell it was a slide unless you stand way back up the valley and look down at it."

"I can't believe I have never been in here before," Duster said, shaking his head and sipping his sherry.

"It is amazing," Bonnie said.

"Magical," Dawn said, smiling at Madison, the man she had fallen in love with.

# CHAPTER TWENTY-SEVEN

**THE NEXT TWO MONTHS** went so perfectly, Dawn had a hard time even believing on some days that she was experiencing it all.

Every nice morning, when the weather didn't look threatening, after a breakfast that one of them cooked, they dressed for a ride and went out into the valley. The first day, they decided that the ride would be through Roosevelt and up Mule Creek to the mine there, then back.

She was so excited, Dawn almost couldn't stay on the horse as she rode through the center of a town that in her lifetime had been submerged under water and completely forgotten for over a hundred years.

Even before the sun hit the valley floor, the pianos were going in the saloons. Through the wide open doors, Dawn could see a number of men in the saloons, some sitting at tables, some playing cards to one side. There were very, very few women in town and the few that were anywhere near the saloons were working girls.

Bonnie discretely pointed out the cribs to one side and against the rocks behind the saloons.

And since this was 1902, Duster made a comment after they got on the other side of town and started up Mule Creek how surprising it was to not have a Chinese section of town.

Dawn wasn't surprised by that at all. Not one mention of any Chinese miners was in any report about this area. And of course, by this time in history, the backlash against the Chinese had been so strong, laws had been passed not allowing them to own, or even work in mines. Dawn knew that in a few of the older placer mining towns in northern Idaho, most of the population at this point was still Chinese.

But not here, not in this new town.

They took many trips up the wagon road beside Mule Creek over the two months as well as many trips downstream along Monumental Creek as well. That was only a trail, since the valley was so narrow and rocky at times.

In fact, on nice days they often rode down the two miles to Thunder City, a small mining town below Roosevelt with two saloons.

If it were raining, they didn't go out at all.

Every night, after Bonnie and Duster retired to their bedroom, Dawn moved quietly down the carpeted hallway and crawled into the warm featherbed with Madison. Sometimes they made love silently, sometimes they just held each other and slept.

She felt like she had known Madison for a very long time, and he said the same thing about her. They fit perfectly together and she loved everything about him.

And as every day went by, she loved him even more. He was polite, generous, funny, and smarter than any man she had met. It was difficult in public to keep her hands off of him.

And he made love in a way that sent her spinning over the top every time. He was gentle, forceful, and knew exactly what to do and when.

She kept thinking that there had to be something wrong with him, but so far she hadn't found anything.

She was in love, plain and simple, and about a month in she told him that and he said he was also in love with her.

Madison spent a lot of time on his own, out talking with miners. And he always came back and shared every detail with Dawn, since she couldn't go out with him easily in the society in this place. He didn't mind sharing at all and actually enjoyed being her eyes and ears and asking questions she wanted him to ask, often about the people when he would have been more interested in the mining details.

A number of times over the months, Bonnie had warned her about never going out without Duster or Madison. There were so few women in this town, and from what they could tell, Dawn was the only single lady.

Duster had taken it on himself over the first two months in the valley to teach both her and Madison how to fire their saddle rifles. They often went down below Thunder City and after lunch had a session of target practice.

She had gotten pretty good, but not as good as Bonnie or Madison.

Bonnie told Dawn that Duster had made it clear to a few men that if Bonnie or Dawn had any problem from anyone, they would answer to him personally.

And even though Roosevelt didn't have any official law enforcement position, Duster sort of took over the job as Bonnie said he normally did, settling arguments between miners and one time having to run a man out of town by shooting at his feet a few times while a crowded saloon full of men laughed.

Then, almost two months into their stay, the valley had its first death.

Every time they had gone down the valley, Dawn had looked up the hill at where the Roosevelt Cemetery would be. But so far it was nothing more than an open hillside, the trees long cut down for building and firewood. Only stumps and brush remained.

The first man to die was William Armstrong. He looked to be in his mid-forties and owned a small supply store with his wife near the lower end of Main Street. Dawn and Bonnie had talked to both him and his wife, Grace.

Williams seemed to have died of a massive heart attack, simply keeling over in his store.

The day they buried him and placed a wooden cross on the hill, it was raining lightly. Dawn stood to one side and listened to the short ceremony with Bonnie, an umbrella keeping the rain from her black hat and dark dress.

Madison stood on the other side of her, his hat in his hands, the rain dripping off his handsome face as he stared ahead, not saying a word.

A large rock rested about five feet from Dawn and she knew that in over a hundred years that rock would have a metal plaque on it with William Armstrong's name at the top.

A month later they attended another funeral and then didn't attend yet another. The man who died was a miner working up Mule Creek. Dawn was told he died of some sort of infection. The next funeral

Duster would not allow them to attend and Bonnie agreed. It was for a working girl who went by the name de Faunte.

It was no wonder there was no first name on the plaque for her. No one knew her real name.

Dawn made a note to herself to try to research her more when they got back. There had to be a trail the woman left getting here. Chances are Dawn would find nothing, but she felt compelled to at least try when she got back to her modern computers.

The last week of August dawned perfect. The day was a beautiful, warm day with a sky up between the mountains that seemed to be a blue as any water. There was a slight breeze coming down the valley, cooling it slightly. Dawn and Bonnie had stayed back at the cabin instead of riding with Duster and Madison up to Colonel Dewey's mill. They weren't supposed to be back for at least another hour when Dawn heard stamping on the front porch and the door burst open.

Duster helped Madison through the door, almost carrying him as Madison hopped and leaned into Duster. They were both covered in dust and sweating. Madison's face was twisted up in pain in a way that made Dawn's stomach hurt. Feelings of panic swept over her, but she pushed them back.

Dawn and Bonnie had both been working on dinner and laughing about how perfect the weather had been the last month. They had bought fresh trout again that a supplier had brought up for them from near where Monumental Creek dumped into Big Creek.

They both immediately rushed to Madison as Duster helped him drop to the couch.

Blood coated Madison's right leg from his knee down, and he was clearly in extreme pain.

Dawn sat next to Madison, holding his hand while Duster held him on the other side and Bonnie carefully cut the leg of his pants away.

"Broke the stupid thing," Madison said, his teeth gritted.

"Big rock rolled down on him near the top of Mule Creek," Duster said. "Killed his horse and knocked Madison for a tumble down into the gulch about twenty feet."

"It could have killed you," Dawn said, her stomach twisting even more. She couldn't think of losing the man she had come to love so much. Just the idea of that scared her more than she wanted to think about.

"I'm tough," he said, trying to smile at her, but failing through the extreme pain.

Then Bonnie cut away the last of the pants and Dawn had no doubt that tough wasn't going to do it. A splintered bone stuck out of Madison's skin. It didn't look like it had broken any major blood vessels, or he would have been dead by now, but the wound was dirty and bleeding pretty hard.

"Bad, huh?" Madison asked, his head back, the pain clearly filling his face.

"Bad," Dawn said, squeezing his hand.

"You're supposed to tell me no problem," Madison said.

"I'm better in bed than beside it," Dawn said, brushing some hair from the dirt on Madison's face.

He laughed and then coughed, a cough that sounded like he might also have a few broken ribs and internal injuries.

Her panic almost overwhelmed her but somehow she managed to stay with him.

"We got to get this cleaned," Bonnie said, standing and heading for the water pitcher on the counter.

"I'll dig out the antibiotics and pain meds," Duster said, patting Madison on the shoulder and heading down the hall toward his bedroom.

"What a stupid way to end the summer," he said, shaking his head.

She brushed his hair back off his face and then kissed his cheek. "It's been a perfect summer and we'll have more."

He looked at her, the pain filling his eyes. "That a promise?"

"A promise," she said, squeezing his hand.

"Good," he said, laying his head back and closing his eyes. "Because I like it here."

# CHAPTER TWENTY-EIGHT

**THE MEDICINES** that Duster brought out of his stash knocked Madison completely out. Dawn was glad for that because of the pain Madison seemed to be dealing with.

He was strong, the strongest man she had ever met, but no one could deal with that kind of pain.

And Madison also had a nasty-sounding cough that made Duster frown and scared the hell out of Dawn.

Back in 2014, they would be rushing him to a hospital. But here, in the middle of the Idaho wilderness in 1902, there were no doctors or hospitals of any sort.

No help at all for the man she loved.

Dawn had learned over the summer that Bonnie and Duster had both picked up a lot of medical knowledge over the years, and were both experts in first aid in

situations like this.

As Bonnie had told her once, "You had to be. Trusting the medical in this time period often meant death."

They had left Madison stretched out on the couch, the leg wrapped and elevated slightly. Even though he was out cold, they moved over into the kitchen area to talk.

"It's as bad as I've seen a leg," Bonnie said, shaking her head. "I'm afraid we might sever an artery if we tried to set it."

"I agree," Duster said. "We need to just splint it completely so it can't move in the slightest."

Bonnie nodded and Dawn hated the silence that followed as they stood there and thought. Outside the sounds of the valley filled the air, from the hammering of people building to get ready for the coming winter to the pianos dueling from the saloons.

"The horse landed on top of him," Duster said, his hand on Dawn's shoulder as he looked across the room at Madison. "He more than likely has internal damage."

"We can't move him," Dawn said softly.

She felt like an entire truck of sand had been dumped on her and all she could do was stare at the injured man she loved laying on the couch. She couldn't think.

She didn't feel like she could even form words.

"No, we can't move him," Bonnie said, nodding.

She looked at her husband. "How much of the drugs do you have? We need to keep the pain down."

"A couple weeks worth," Duster said. "Different types, but they'll all do the job."

"I've got two or three weeks worth as

well," Bonnie said. "Maybe more."

"We have enough time," Duster said, nodding. "I'm going to go get Craig and Susan to help move Madison into the back room. I'll bring back some boards for the splint."

"What are you thinking?" Dawn asked, feeling as confused as she had felt in a long, long time.

"I'm going to make a ride tomorrow for Silver City, pull the plug on this wonderful summer."

He turned and left.

"We have no choice," Bonnie said. "We're done now for this trip."

Dawn stood there, finally understanding what Duster was thinking.

Of course, why hadn't she remembered?

Why hadn't she thought of that? Of course that was the answer.

After months living back here in 1902, feeling like she was part of this world and this valley, she had forgotten that in her real time, in 2014, if Duster could disconnect the machine from this time line, they would all be there again, standing in the crystal cavern, with only two minutes and fifteen seconds passed in their real time.

An entire summer in one hundred and thirty-five seconds.

And Madison would be whole and healthy, just as Duster had returned to normal after his accident when Bonnie forced him to reset.

How could Dawn have forgotten that in such a short amount of time?

Duster and Bonnie said they had spent up to fifty years in the past on some trips. How could they even remember the future after all that time?

She sighed, feeling the relief surge through her. They had enough drugs to keep Madison out of pain while Duster made it to Silver City.

He would be all right.

The relief flooded over her and she wanted to cry.

Bonnie put her hand on Dawn's shoulder. "Don't worry. It takes a number of trips to remember that we can go back to the future and just reset."

"Then he'll be fine?" Dawn asked, barely holding back the tears of relief.

Bonnie nodded. "No matter what happens here, he'll be fine when we go back. The rules of time and space won't allow anything else to happen it seems."

"Never thought I would be so happy to hear about science," Dawn said, looking over at Madison. Then she turned to the water pitcher and dampened a towel to go clean off the face of the man she loved.

If nothing else, she could keep him comfortable until Duster pulled the plug on this trip.

And then in real time, she and Madison would go from there.

# PART THREE

# CHAPTER TWENTY-NINE

**THE SUN WAS BARELY** coloring the tops of the hills the next morning as Dawn and Bonnie stood on the porch and watched as Duster rode up the trail with only a slight wave back. The valley was just coming awake and not even the pianos had started up yet. His long duster was blowing behind him and he had his head down and looked like he was getting ready to ride hard.

The day before they had managed to get Madison into the back room with the help of the Roosevelt General Store owners, Craig and Susan.

Dawn liked them both and both seemed to be very solid people.

Craig stood about as tall as Madison and had broader shoulders and a slightly balding head. Susan seemed to always wear an apron and have her brown hair pulled back up tight on the top of her head.

She had warm, caring eyes and Dawn had liked her the first time they had met.

After they helped Madison to the back room, Susan had patted Dawn's shoulder and said simply, "He'll make it. Honest."

That was very nice of her to say and Dawn only nodded.

Duster didn't mention to Craig and Susan that he was leaving, and they promised to keep Madison's injury a secret for now without a question as to why. More than likely Duster had paid them extra.

Duster figured that it was better in this mining community to not have the drunk single men thinking that there were two women alone in a cabin very close by.

Bonnie and Dawn both made sure the doors were blocked closed at night and they didn't venture outside at all during the day, not even out onto the porch. As far as anyone in the valley was concerned, all four of them were fine and still in the big house against the side of the hill.

Bonnie had rifles standing against walls in the hallway, both their bedrooms, and in the living room and kitchen, all within easy reach.

Dawn wasn't sure if she could use it, and said that to Bonnie at one point and Bonnie just shook her head. "Trust me," she said. "You got some drunk coming at you, you'll use it."

To Dawn that sounded like the voice of experience, but she didn't ask.

Together they managed to keep Madison sedated and as comfortable as his injuries would allow. Since Duster had given Madison that first dose, they hadn't allowed him to wake up fully.

As Bonnie said, just better to have him wake up in the crystal cavern and not remember much of any of this. "You can fill him in later."

Dawn spent most nights sleeping beside Madison's bed on a comfortable chair they had pulled in from the living room, her feet up on a footstool. If he did wake and need her, she wanted to be there.

They let him come close to being awake only to get water down him, and at one point Bonnie said that if Duster took too long she would set up an IV as long as no one came in and saw it.

At times Madison started coughing and twice it took both of them to calm him, even in his sleep.

On day three she and Bonnie were silently cooking themselves some dinner when Dawn finally asked Bonnie the question that she had been afraid to ask up until now.

"How long do you think it will take Duster to get back up to the mine in Silver City?"

"The weather's been good," Bonnie said. "Maybe four days at the earliest. He looked like he was going to ride hard. Five or six days if he runs into some sort of problem along the way."

Dawn nodded and they ate the salad and fresh venison steaks in silence.

Dawn just couldn't believe that this was all going to just reset like Bonnie and Duster thought it would. Granted, she had seen it with Duster, but now, after almost three months here in the past, that crystal cavern felt very, very far away.

In fact it felt like it had been a lifetime since she had been in her office on Campus, but in real time, it was less than a day.

Wow, that was hard to grasp after three months of living in this magical valley.

And a miracle that suddenly Madison would be healthy just didn't seem possible. She had to believe it was, because Bonnie didn't seem to be worried in the slightest.

And if Madison were going to live for them to have a life together, the miracle had to happen.

Dawn had to hold onto that belief. Somehow.

# CHAPTER THIRTY

**ON THE SEVENTH DAY** after Duster left the valley, Bonnie shook her head over breakfast of eggs and pancakes and said simply, "Something has happened to him."

Dawn had feared that was the case, but as the last two days had stretched into an eternity, she had been afraid to say anything as Bonnie got slightly more agitated and clearly worried.

Madison was in extreme pain, even though they kept him mostly knocked out. Dawn was worried Madison wouldn't even last until Duster reset things in the cavern and pulled them out. They did their best to get him water and some broth, but the pain was so extreme and the coughing

getting worse, there just wasn't much they could do for him.

And on top of that, his leg was starting to get infected.

It was September 2nd and the last two days it had been raining, cold and hard. The road outside was a constant stream of people packed and leaving the valley. This high in the mountains, snow was not unusual in September and often the valley was locked down by late September.

It wouldn't have surprised Dawn if there was already some snow over the top of Monumental Summit.

"So what do you think we should do?" Dawn asked.

Bonnie shrugged. "We bring in Craig and Susan to watch Madison and we make a run for Silver City."

Dawn was shocked that she had said that, even suggested it.

She pushed her plate of pancakes away. "If that were Duster in there, would you leave him?"

Bonnie nodded. "Now, I would, yes. When we first started coming back into the past, no, I would not have left him."

Bonnie stood and moved her plate over to the sink. "Let me go talk with Craig and Susan and see if they have any news from the valley that will give us an idea what happened to Duster."

Dawn nodded, staring into her food, not in the slightest interested in eating it.

Bonnie put on her dark rain slicker, tall boots over her shoes, a dark hood over her head, and then grabbed the rifle by the door. With the hood up and pulled forward over her face, Dawn was surprised that Bonnie looked more like a man than a woman.

She put on thin dark gloves, then said simply, "I'll be back as quick as I can and we'll figure out what we're going to do."

Then for the first time since Duster had left, one of them stepped outside.

Dawn blocked the door after she left and then with a rifle in one hand went to check on Madison and give him his drugs for the morning.

He was starting to smell really sour and Dawn had no doubt the leg was infected beyond saving. Neither her nor Bonnie had even opened the bandage and splints up to look at it. There was just no point.

How had such a fantastic summer turned so ugly so quickly?

But Dawn knew the answer. She studied history. She knew how rough life was in this time period, especially in the mining towns.

But knowing it from her comfortable office in 2014 and actually experiencing it in 1902 were different things completely.

She moved back out to the kitchen and with the rifle leaning against the counter beside her, she cleaned up the kitchen and then started the preparations on the venison roast they had planned to have that evening if they were still here.

Thirty minutes later Dawn heard steps on the front porch and then Bonnie said, "It's me."

Dawn unblocked the door and let in Bonnie, who was dripping wet and her boots were covered with mud.

She peeled off everything, hanging the hat and coat on the hook and slipping out of her boots.

Then she moved toward her bedroom to change her pants. As she did she tossed the Idaho Statesman newspaper on the table and pointed to it without a word. The Statesman was the major newspaper in the state out of Boise, and they usually got it up here about three days delayed.

Dawn opened the paper and on the front page read the headlines about the train wreck and the thirty dead. The train had been derailed and two passenger cars had dropped into the Payette River. There wasn't a list of the dead.

Her stomach twisted and feeling sick, Dawn quickly scanned for the date. It had happened the day after Duster left.

She sat at the table, just staring at the newspaper.

Bonnie came out of the back room in dry pants and wearing slippers.

"Would he have been on that train?" Dawn asked, pointing at the headline.

"Yup, a day's hard ride to the rail head, then another day to Caldwell on the train, then a day from there into the mountains and up to the mine on the fourth day. That's how he would have gone."

"Oh," Dawn said, staring at the paper. How could Duster be dead? How was that even possible?

"Now it's up to us to rescue both of them," Bonnie said, shaking her head and sitting across the table from Dawn. "Damn men."

"Resetting will bring him back to life?" Dawn asked, remembering the conversation with Bonnie about dying of consumption in another man's arms, but needing to ask anyway.

"Yup, as annoyingly handsome and alive as ever," Bonnie said. "Remember, only two minutes and fifteen seconds will have passed, no matter what happens back here. We are all still alive and healthy in our original time line."

"Wow, that is so damn hard to believe sometimes," Dawn said, shaking her head.

She wasn't really believing it, but she had to.

Somehow.

"Impossible early on," Bonnie said. "In one of our early trips back I died in a freak accident with a stagecoach and Duster damn near went crazy. When he finally got back to the mine and reset us, he wouldn't leave my side for the next three hundred years."

"Death makes you a little clingy, huh?" Dawn asked, actually trying to smile.

"For the first few times it sure does," Bonnie said, smiling in return.

Then she got very serious. "So Duster is more than likely dead and Madison is on death's door. Hell of a summer vacation to write home about huh?"

Dawn just shook her head. "Who would believe it?"

"Yeah, good point there," Bonnie said.

Dawn refused to think of the man she had fallen in love with dying on her. But she had no idea how to stop it.

"So," Bonnie said, "one or both of us needs to make a run for Silver City before the snow flies out there. It feels like it's getting colder by the minute."

Dawn looked at Bonnie. She couldn't leave Madison, she just couldn't.

Bonnie nodded without saying a word. "Let's get that roast in and have a nice dinner and get me packed for the ride. As soon as the weather clears some, I'll make the ride to the mine. And I won't take the train, I promise."

Dawn nodded. "Thanks."

Bonnie smiled. "It's amazing what we'll do for the men in our lives, that's for sure."

Dawn just hoped that Madison would continue to be the man in her life. She couldn't completely believe it, but she had to because she had no other choice but to believe.

# CHAPTER THIRTY-ONE

IT KEPT RAINING for the next three days and then finally it cleared, lifting Dawn's mood some. The towering peaks climbing up into clouds really made the valley seem closed in when it rained. The air was bitterly cold and even the sun hitting the valley floor didn't help.

And everything looked like it had turned to mud. Monumental Creek was running high and brown.

The valley itself felt almost empty now and the sounds of construction had mostly stopped. Even the piano music sounded distant and weak in the cold air.

Madison had seemed to stabilize some, and Bonnie had helped Dawn change his bedding and nightclothes on the day the rain finally stopped. There was still almost two weeks of pain medications left to keep him completely knocked out, but Bonnie said she didn't think he would last that long.

Dawn hadn't said anything to that. She knew Madison dying was more than likely right, but she wanted to stay in denial if she could for now.

Bonnie had said that once she got started toward Silver City, it would take her five or six days to get to the crystal cavern and pull the connection to this timeline. Then they would all be back healthy and together in 2014.

Over the three days of rain, they had talked about what would happen to the house when they left?

Dawn had been surprised that nothing would happen to it until Bonnie again explained the timeline. For some reason Dawn had thought that when they all went back to the future, everything they had done and everyone they met would just forget them.

Bonnie explained that they were actually here, in this timeline.

Living and dying as the case might be.

Duster had the house built here, in this timeline, and more than likely in millions of other timelines Duster had built the house for them as well.

The house will just remain, as will the record of Duster dying in that train wreck. And the record and memories of us being here and then just vanishing.

"It's like we will step through a window and just vanish to this timeline."

"Will Duster's body vanish as well?"

"Yes, it will," Bonnie said, nodding.

"But in our timeline we aren't back here?" Dawn asked, slowly starting to understand at a level a little deeper than she had before.

"That's right," Bonnie said. "Remember, in many timelines, millions and millions, you and Madison decided to not come with us. And in millions of timelines, Madison wasn't in that accident and Duster wasn't killed trying to get us out of here."

"And in our real time, we started this trip and it will only take a few minutes?" Dawn asked, doing her best to get everything clear in her mind before Bonnie left her alone.

"It's only about two in the afternoon that first day, the day we had breakfast in Murphy," Bonnie said, smiling. "It's hot outside the mine and the Cadillac is parked in the trees."

Dawn just shook her head and Bonnie laughed. "You come back into the past enough, you get used to the idea of all this."

Dawn wasn't sure about another trip. Right now she wanted Madison to survive this one. She just wanted to hug him again and make love to him again and enjoy his laugh.

The next morning, September 7th, Bonnie gave Dawn a hug just as the darkness of the valley started to fade with the rising sun, then with her rain slicker on and a cowboy hat with her hair pulled up under the hat, she got ready to ride.

Her breath was clear frosty white in front of her, and Dawn was stunned at how cold it felt.

Dressed the way she was, Bonnie just looked like any other man on the trail. Someone would have to get pretty close to her to know she was a woman.

"Good luck," Dawn said, as Bonnie turned and headed up the road toward Monumental Summit.

Dawn went inside, blocked the door closed, and then with a rifle across her lap, went and sat beside the man she loved.

Never in all her life had she felt so alone.

And so scared.

# CHAPTER THIRTY-TWO

**DAWN MUST HAVE DOZED** because the light was fading from the valley, the sun low behind the high ridges, when someone pounded on the door.

She leapt out of her chair, her heart pounding like it might explode from her dress. Madison hadn't moved, but he was still breathing.

She did a quick check of her clothing to make sure she looked appropriate for the year, and then with the rifle in her hand, she headed toward the front room.

"Dawn, it's me," Bonnie shouted from the front porch.

Dawn got the door unblocked and open and let Bonnie come staggering in. Her face was red and she was shaking from the cold. She seemed to be completely soaked.

Dawn closed the door and immediately worked to help Bonnie from her wet coat and the jacket under that, then went to warm up the stove and get water boiling for tea while Bonnie stoked the fire in the fireplace to warm the big room up.

Bonnie's teeth were chattering and she was shaking. Her nose had been running and had caked to her face.

Dawn got the water on and went over to help Bonnie with the fire, motioning for her to sit down and pull a blanket over herself. Then Dawn used a second blanket and covered Bonnie with that as well.

"What happened?" Dawn finally asked as the fire came roaring up.

"Pass is snowed in already," Bonnie said. "Two people died yesterday trying to go over it."

"Oh, no," Dawn said, standing to go get the hot water and make Bonnie some hot tea.

She felt stunned by that news.

Stunned.

Could they really be trapped in this valley she loved so much? Was that possible so soon in the year?

She made herself calm down and make both of them a cup of tea. Then she started water for soup to get it boiling for dinner.

Then she took Bonnie her cup and warned her to sip it because it was so hot.

Bonnie seemed to be looking a little better, but her face was almost burnt from the cold.

Dawn sat her cup on an end table and went to get a towel and washcloth.

Then she poured a little of the warming soup water over the washcloth and took it back for Bonnie to use.

Bonnie thanked her and pressed the warm towel to her face for a moment, before working to clean herself up a little.

"I haven't been that cold in a few hundred years," Bonnie said, her voice cracking slightly. "Not since I tried going over Lolo Pass in December. Froze to death that night. Literally."

Dawn started to open her mouth to ask a question, then realized what Bonnie had said and just stayed silent, letting Bonnie sip her tea.

Dawn had been amazed at how Bonnie was calm about Duster and Madison. Now she was starting to understand. When dying became something that happened and you ended up back completely healthy, then you could face death better.

But Dawn still couldn't believe it, no matter how hard she tried. She had lived her entire life just knowing death was the end of things.

Believing anything else, even intellectually, was going to take time.

"Is there another way out of here that's better?" Bonnie asked after a moment.

Dawn knew this valley and history better than anyone in 2014. It was her specialty. But that didn't mean she was an expert now, living here. It was one thing to read stories and diaries about how difficult the trip in and out was.

Another to sit here and plan a reality.

"Two other ways out," Dawn said. "Down Monumental Creek, then down Big Creek to the tail up and over Elk Creek Summit and into Warren. It is the most deadly of all the ways in and out of here because of snow and mud slides, so that's more than likely shut down to only snowshoes now. And mud makes that one really, really dangerous."

"And the third way?" Bonnie asked, her voice gaining strength.

"Up Mule Creek and past the Dewey mine and then down the other side on Marble Creek to the Middle Fork of the Salmon River."

"That would be passable, wouldn't it?" Bonnie asked.

Dawn was doing her best to remember all the history. "A rough ride down Marble Creek. At least twenty-some miles on mostly rock and side-hill and the mud would make it dangerous. The trail would be easy along the Middle Fork. But then the trail leaves the river after about ten miles and goes up and over two summits and drops down onto the Payette River. From there it's easy to get down into Boise."

Bonnie nodded and sipped her tea.

Dawn went on. "The Marble Creek route is the way most packers come into here if they attempt it in the winter, usually on snowshoes. Suppliers brought in goods and food that way last winter to cover the food shortages. A few tried it over Elk Creek Summit as well. But it takes snowshoes and traveling in the snow or even mud is dangerous in these mountains and only one made it last winter."

Bonnie just nodded again.

Then she set her empty tea mug down and pulled off the blankets. "Tomorrow, if the weather is clear, I'll try again. If that doesn't work, I'll go up to the Dewey Mine and try to hook up with a packtrain going out. That way will take longer. Can you hold on?"

"I can," Dawn said, now more scared for Bonnie than for herself.

This area was the last of the wild mining areas. Duster and Madison had

been right to always stay with Bonnie and Dawn when they went out. Bonnie riding alone might just be suicide. Civilization in these mountains at this point in history was only a surface illusion.

A very thin surface at that.

Bonnie stood and headed for her bedroom. "I've got to get out of these clothes, then get the horse bedded down for the night."

"I'll check on Madison and get dinner started," Dawn said. "Take your time."

Madison seemed fine for the moment, but he was wasting away and the infection smell was getting worse by the day.

Dawn then checked their supplies, both the ones in the kitchen and in hidden stash Duster had built on the way out to the outhouse in the back. From what she could tell, if she and Bonnie managed to get some basic supplies regularly from the general store, they could hold out easily until next May and go out then.

She didn't much like the idea of wintering here, basically trapped in this house, but that seemed to be the sensible thing to do unless the rest of this month really warmed up enough for the Monumental Summit pass to open.

So an hour later, over warm chicken soup and bread, Dawn brought up the idea to Bonnie.

"Don't go," she said simply.

Bonnie looked up at her.

"Unless the weather has a warm break over the next two weeks," Bonnie said, "I think we should just hole up and stay here until spring thaw."

Bonnie looked at her and then said simply, "We would bury Madison if we did that."

Dawn looked down into her soup, doing her best to not think about that, but she knew that was going to happen.

"We're all going to end up healthy back there in that crystal cavern, correct?" Dawn asked, twisting her spoon in her soup but not daring to lift it out of the broth for fear of her hand shaking.

"Yes," Bonnie said, staring at her with a very worried expression. "But that does not mean that burying a man you have come to love will be any easier."

"I know that," Dawn said, trying her best to sound brave.

"I don't think you really do," Bonnie said, shaking her head. "If the weather is clear tomorrow, I'll try Monumental Summit again. If that's still closed off, I'll go out Mule Creek the following day."

"Why?" Dawn asked. "Why risk your life like that?"

"Because," Bonnie said, "I know for a fact I can't be permanently killed. But mostly I want Madison and you back healthy in that cavern before he dies and you have to live with that memory for a very long time."

Dawn let the silence fill the room along with the faint crackling of the fire in the fireplace.

Then she looked at Bonnie who was working on her dinner, slowly, savoring each bite as if it were the best meal she had ever eaten.

"How many times?" Dawn asked.

"How many times what?" Bonnie asked, not looking up.

"How many times have you buried Duster?"

"Too many," Bonnie said, not looking up, her voice soft. "Too God-damned many times."

# CHAPTER THIRTY-THREE

**BEFORE SUNRISE** the next morning, Bonnie rode off up the valley toward Monumental Summit without so much as a look back. The day looked like it was going to break clear, but Dawn was stunned how cold it was.

And more than likely this would feel warm compared to temperatures later in the winter. This area of high mountains was known for its brutal weather and extreme cold temperatures.

Bonnie wore extra layers and had two layers of gloves on and a hat that pulled down over most of her face. She said if the pass wasn't open, but looked like it might tomorrow, she would camp at the base and try early in the morning.

If it looked like that pass would remain closed, she would come back and try going over and down Marble Creek the next day.

Dawn stood on the porch of the big log house and watched her ride away, trying to tamp down the fear she felt. She wasn't so much afraid for herself at the moment. She would be fine if she remained sensible in her actions over the next week.

Now she felt terrified for Bonnie.

She sat with Madison most of the day. He was stirring a little more and she worked to keep him sedated and comfortable. But the smell of the infection in his leg sometimes just forced her out of the room.

Bonnie did not return that evening, so Dawn decided to start a journal and make sure she was touching it at all times to record exactly what happened over the next seven or eight days while Bonnie made her way to the mine and the crystal cavern above Silver City.

It was like carrying their supplies through when they came back. If she had the journal on her, it would transport back to the future and her timeline with her.

Or at least that was what Bonnie had told her in one of their conversations.

She hadn't bothered with taking many notes this summer, figuring she would just get them all down when she got back.

But now she felt like she needed to really write it all down. Everything. The good times, and the bad of the last few weeks.

And all the emotions.

She was known for writing about the human element of the Old West. Now she was living it and she better get it right.

She put on an apron with two large pockets in the front and kept the journal in one pocket and a light pair of gloves in the other for minor tasks.

With the thin mountain air turning cold, her hands seemed to never want to warm up.

It turned out that now that she was alone, she had time to record everything.

The focus of that task helped her pass the time, make her feel like she was back at work.

Bonnie didn't return on the second day either, and the weather broke clear and sunny again.

It felt like the air was warming up, actually.

Numbers of people were leaving town, headed for the passes, which told Dawn that at the moment they were back open.

Only one saloon with one piano remained now, filling the night with its sound. If Dawn remembered her research

right, less than two hundred of the seven thousand people who had filled the valley this summer remained over the winter. And fifty of those were housed in the dorm up at the Dewey mine and would never come down into Roosevelt because of the snow.

Craig and Susan had said they would winter in the valley and try their best to keep the Roosevelt General Store open.

Grace, the wife of William Armstrong, the owner of the other general store on the other end of town had died few weeks before, right before Madison's accident. She was buried next to her husband up in the cemetery, something that Dawn found surprising that wasn't on the plaque in 2014. Fifty people had come to the gathering near the cemetery, so someone should have remembered that Mrs. Armstrong had died.

Unless in Dawn's timeline, she hadn't died.

On the third morning, it warmed up enough that Dawn opened the window in Madison's room to try to clear out the smell from the infection. He was getting feverish, so she increased his dose of antibiotics and kept cool towels on his forehead. All she had to do was nurse him through the next four or five days and all would be fine.

She had to believe that.

She just had to.

The alternative she refused to think about.

She spent most of days four and five working to keep Madison's fever under control and recording her thoughts in her journal, holding it on her lap while she wrote, and then putting it back in the pocket of her apron when finished.

She couldn't believe how much she loved that man in the other room. And how much she missed talking with him, hearing his laugh, hearing his thoughts.

Even as sick as he was, she still loved him and loved caring for him.

In the evenings, after a light dinner, she sat in his room just telling him about her fears, about how much she still loved this valley, and about how much she wanted to spend her future with him.

Any future. She didn't care, as long as there was a future.

On day six it rained again, but stayed fairly warm, as if the valley were having a late summer.

Bonnie clearly had made it out of the valley. Dawn felt with each passing hour the sense of anticipation that one moment she would be here, the next she would be standing in the crystal cave with Madison beside her.

Day seven the morning turned cold and she woke up to the first snow on the valley floor. She stepped out onto the front porch to look at it and was struck by the silence.

When they had arrived here in May, the place had been a beehive of activity. Noise of construction and the pianos and shouting from the saloons constantly rebounded off the high mountain slopes, giving the valley a sense of being alive.

Now it was completely silent through the light snow.

Not even Monumental Creek was running enough to make any noise, more than likely already frozen solid.

The weight of all the mountains around her came crushing down on her and suddenly she felt so alone.

More so than she could ever remember.

She tried to shake off the feeling, staring at the beautiful scene spread out in front of her. She took a couple of deep breaths of the crisp, fresh, cold air. Then she reminded herself that she liked being alone.

But this was very, very different.

Her wonderful office at the University seemed to be a long, long ways away, like she had dreamed it only.

She took an armful of firewood from the pile to the right of the porch and went back inside. She stoked up the fire, cooked herself a light breakfast, checked on Madison, checked on the two horses that remained with her, then sat on the couch, and worked on her journal.

Waiting.

Finally at dark she ate a cold dinner, set a damp towel on Madison's forehead, and retreated back to the couch in front of the big fireplace to keep warm.

Maybe tomorrow morning Bonnie would make it up to the mine and bring them all back.

With the journal in her pocket of her apron and two blankets over her, Dawn slept on the couch until sunrise.

Then she checked on Madison. He was still breathing.

She went back to waiting in front of the fire as outside the snow drifted down, slowly building up deeper and deeper in the silence.

# CHAPTER THIRTY-FOUR

**FOUR DAYS LATER** Dawn just had to admit to herself that something had happened to Bonnie.

Maybe the weather in Silver City had slowed her down, or she had had an accident and was resting for a short time.

But something had clearly happened.

Or the entire idea of her returning to the future was just a cruel joke that Duster and Bonnie had played on them.

Maybe time travel was just a one-way proposition for anyone but Duster and Bonnie.

Dawn didn't know what to believe any more.

Madison was barely breathing when she checked on him after a light and cold dinner of jerky and hard bread. It was amazing to Dawn that he had held on as long as he had. He clearly was a very strong man with a very strong constitution.

Something more for her to love about him.

That night she kissed him on the forehead as she always did and then moved out to the couch in front of the big fireplace.

The snow had stopped a few days before, leaving the valley coated with a beautiful layer of pure white. She had never expected to see this valley in the winter and had never even seen a picture of it.

She thought this place magical in the summer warmth, it was even more so in the winter snow and cold.

She wrote her thoughts about it in her journal, tucked the book back in her apron pocket, then curled up in the blankets to watch the fire in the huge stone fireplace.

When she awoke, the sun was starting to light the tops of the mountains, the fire was mostly out, and the big house was getting colder by the minute.

She built the fire back up until it was roaring, then went to check on Madison.

He was dead.

# CHAPTER THIRTY-FIVE

**DAWN MOVED OUT** to the couch and sat staring at the fire.

Somehow she had to think.

How could he be dead?

But he was. Of that there was no doubt. The man she had come to love more than anything in her life in just a few short months was now dead.

If she were going to survive just the next month, let alone the entire winter, she needed to think.

She was alone, but she needed help.

She forced herself to take a deep breath. She wanted to just lie on the couch and cry, but at the moment she didn't dare. There would be more than enough time for that.

She needed help.

She could not deal with Madison alone.

She didn't want to even go back into that bedroom, but she knew that when the time came she would.

Feeling like she was walking under a ton of blankets with gauze over her eyes, she dressed much like Bonnie had dressed to head out. She kept the journal in her heavy jacket pocket, put her hair up under one of Madison's cowboy hats, put on heavy gloves and then put Madison's long duster-like overcoat over everything.

Then looking like a fairly thick man, she stepped out of the cabin and down into the snow.

The air was biting cold, but the sun was going to shine on the valley floor at some point later in the afternoon. She went to the few wagon tracks showing in the road and walking in them, she headed down into the main part of town.

This was the first time she had gone this way alone.

At this point she was too numb to feel any fear or worry.

Madison was dead and she needed help.

Craig and Susan's general store was the third wooden building on the right as she reached the main part of town. Most of the buildings looked boarded up, but smoke curled from a rock chimney in the store.

She entered to the sound of a bell above the door and Craig glanced up from behind the counter, surprised.

"What can I do for you, sir?" he asked, moving forward.

Dawn pulled off the hat and Craig gasped. Then he turned and shouted to the back room. "Susan, I need you out here."

Dawn nodded her thanks and said nothing until Susan arrived.

Then facing both of them she said simply, "Madison died."

She had not imagined that she would ever have to say those words to anyone. "I'm going to need some help getting him up to the cemetery and getting him buried."

"Of course, of course," Susan said, coming around the counter and hugging Dawn.

Dawn didn't want to let herself cry. Not even for an instant.

Not yet.

"I can pay you for the help," she said. Duster had left her and Bonnie with a lot of extra money and gold stashed in various places in the cabin.

"There's no need," Craig said. "Duster has paid us more than enough already."

"Where is Bonnie?" Susan asked.

"She went out a few weeks ago to see if she could find out exactly what happened to Duster," Dawn said.

"So you are here for the winter," Craig said, nodding.

"We can't let anyone else know that," Susan said. "This has turned out horribly, that's for sure."

Craig nodded. "First things first," he said, looking at his wife. "We need to give Madison a proper burial."

"Thank you," Dawn said.

Somehow she managed to stay there, standing, leaning on the counter, as Craig and Susan both put on their coats and boots and hats.

"I'll get a couple men digging up in the cemetery," he said.

"Near the rock, if possible," Dawn asked.

"As close as possible," Craig said. "The ground shouldn't be too frozen too deep yet, thankfully."

"I'll go with you to get Madison ready and on a sled," Susan said.

The next two hours seemed like a nightmare that Dawn thought she would never wake up from.

They moved Madison with all the blankets from the bed out the back door to the cabin and into the snow. Dawn knew that the man they were working on wasn't the man she loved, just his body.

And if somehow, Bonnie was right, she would see him again when everything reset. But at the moment, this was very real and somehow she had to get through it.

Susan seemed incredibly strong and between the two of them, they got the splint off of Madison's infected leg and got him in a suit coat and a tie.

Then they wrapped him up completely in the blankets and managed to drag him up onto the sled right before Craig showed up.

Dawn had on her hat and Madison's heavy coat and she tried to keep her head down and her eyes on where she was walking as the three of them drug the sled over the snow down the side street next to Monumental Creek and up the trail toward the cemetery.

No one seemed to notice, since there were very few people left in the town and the three of them dragging the sled made almost no noise.

As they neared the cemetery, it was clear the two men digging had managed a pretty good distance down into the dirt.

Craig had them stop and he went ahead and paid the two men and thanked them.

Dawn kept her head down and stood next to Madison on the sled.

The two men walked by and Susan said, "Thank you, gentlemen."

Dawn didn't look up. She didn't want them knowing she was a woman.

Craig came back and the three of them got the sled up near the narrow and fairly deep grave. Then they rolled Madison into the hole, blankets and all.

Susan held Dawn's arm as Craig said something over Madison that puzzled Dawn, but she didn't think about it.

Craig said simply, "Here is a great man, a great writer, a man ahead of his time."

Dawn just stood there staring down at the pile of blankets in the bottom of the deep hole.

How could Madison be down there?

She looked over at the rock that held the plaque and suddenly realized, for the first time there would be a Rogers on it.

A Rogers with no first name.

How could that be if they really were in separate timelines?

Her knees felt like they wanted to give way. She felt like she wanted to tumble into that grave with the man she loved.

But instead she stood next to the rock that in over a hundred years would carry the name of Rogers on it. A plaque she would feel a strong attraction to, just as she felt a strong attraction to this cemetery in 2014.

How could any of this be happening?

Craig said he would take care of filling up the grave and Susan turned Dawn away and walked her arm-in-arm through the beautiful snow back to the big empty house.

# CHAPTER THIRTY-SIX

**THE NEXT WEEK** Dawn somehow managed to feed herself, keep the doors locked, take care of the horses, and keep the fire stoked. But past that it felt like she was walking underwater.

Duster was gone.

Bonnie was gone.

Madison was gone.

At times she wondered if they ever had existed, if her entire life in the future had ever existed.

Maybe she was just insane. She didn't have pictures of them, just her memory of them.

She really could be insane. That was very possible.

She had closed all the bedroom doors and taken to sleeping on the big couch facing the large stone fireplace in the living room. She only went into her bedroom to get a change of clothes. She refused to open either Madison's room or Duster and Bonnie's.

Her biggest chore of each day was to take care of the two remaining horses and make sure they had enough feed and fresh water. She had never been much of a horse person, but over the winter she would become one, she knew that. She didn't want her horses dying on her as well.

As each day went past, all the events seemed to be far away, distant, as if they had happened to her only in a bad dream.

Finally, the morning of the eighth day after Madison died dawned bright and sunny. She figured it was time she went to thank Craig and Susan and get some more basic supplies to hole up.

And pay them for their work and time and friendship. If she were going to make it through the coming winter, she was going to need that friendship at times.

And some supplies.

Next spring, after the passes cleared, she would make a ride for Silver City and the mine. She had to know if it were really there or if this were all just a bad dream and she had gone completely crazy.

Most of the last seven days she would have bet on crazy.

Only one small thing kept her somehow believing.

She had an old key that Duster had given her. Actually two, and they were supposed to open the mine door.

On the third day she started carrying the old skeleton key in a small pocket in the apron with her journal.

And no matter what, she kept the journal on her at all times just in case Bonnie actually did make it to the mine and pulled them all back to the future.

That journal had become her second touchstone to sanity.

Since Dawn was going out, she again dressed as a man, using Madison's hat and long coat over her own coat, and keeping the hat down low over her face and a scarf wrapped tight around her neck.

The day was stunning, the sun almost too bright on the pure white snow that coated everything. In the future she would have pulled out her sunglasses. Today, she just kept the brim of the hat low on her forehead.

The snow was still only about eight inches deep on the valley floor, so the walking was easy She knew it would get a lot deeper before the winter was through. It was still only early October.

She followed the trail around the center part of town and down the valley toward the cemetery. Madison's grave was still a fresh scar on the hillside, the dirt covered with only an inch or so of fresh snow.

She brushed the snow off the rock and sat down.

"I miss you," she said to the grave. "I didn't know you very long, but I miss you more than I can say."

Around her the beautiful mountains and the valley were silent.

"I sure hope Bonnie and Duster were right," she said to the grave. "Because more than anything I want to kiss you again."

Silence as her voice drifted off on the cool breeze.

She just sat there, thinking about all the good times she and Madison had had together, from the hot springs over the Snake River to the wonderful nights cuddling in his featherbed.

And the image that burned clearly in her mind was his handsome face turning to look at her in the parking lot that first morning.

And the surprised and stunned look when he saw her.

That memory made her smile.

That had been real.

She had felt the same way seeing him.

All of this had been real.

She had to believe that and hold that close over the coming winter months.

She always considered herself a survivor. Now she really had to prove that to herself in one of the most hostile places on the entire planet.

She sat for another ten minutes, then told Madison she would see him soon and headed back up the valley toward the town.

> *Madison's grave was still a fresh scar on the hillside, the dirt covered with only an inch or so of fresh snow.*

She again kept her eyes down and made it around the side of town and to Craig and Susan's general store without anyone even taking a second look at her.

As she walked in, Susan looked up and smiled. Craig turned and also smiled.

Susan had her brown hair down around her face and she looked beautiful and radiant. She had dark green eyes and seemed to be slightly taller than Dawn had remembered her.

Craig looked younger than she remembered as well, even though he was going slightly bald. His brown hair swept back long and his smile lit up his face and his dark eyes.

Their store felt wonderful, and even though it was winter, the shelves seemed to be packed with supplies. There was sawdust on the wooden floor to help soak up moisture and mud and two mats for customers to wipe their feet on.

Someone had just cooked fresh bread, so the air felt thick, warm and inviting.

"Great to see you up and around, Doctor Edwards," Craig said.

It took Dawn two more steps into the wonderful-smelling general store before she realized what Craig had said.

"Did Madison or Duster tell you something about me?" she asked, trying to act normal.

"Oh, heaven's no," Craig said, smiling.

"It's your book on this area and this town and this time that made us want to come back here and start this store."

Dawn was feeling the room spinning slightly and she took off her hat. "My book?"

Susan smiled. *"Thunder Mountain: The Brutal Magic of America's Last Gold Rush.* I did my thesis at Stanford last year real time on this area because of your book."

"I don't understand," Dawn said, leaning against the counter to try to catch her breath."

She hadn't written anything like that yet. But she had come up with the title the day after Madison died.

Craig poured Dawn a glass of water from a pitcher and handed it to her.

She took a drink of the ice-cold water and that cleared her head a little.

Then she looked up at Craig and Susan's smiling faces.

"Just because you and Madison were the first time travelers that Duster and Bonnie took with them," Craig said, "you don't think you will be the only ones, do you?"

"Even as bad as this first trip turned out for you and Madison," Susan said.

Craig stepped forward and extended his hand. "Doctor Steven Conklin, University of California, Berkley, history department."

Dawn pulled her glove off and shook the man's firm hand, not having any idea what to think.

He then indicated Susan. "Doctor Janice Franks, Stanford Cultural Studies Program."

"It is an honor to meet you, Doctor Edwards," Susan, or Janice said, extending her hand. "I've studied your work for years and then that last book about this area just stunned me. And from what Duster tells us, you were responsible for him thinking of telling us about that incredible cavern and the ability to come back here to do research."

"When exactly does he do that?" Dawn asked, then managed to take another drink of the cold water.

"2015," Janice/Susan said.

"And did he and Bonnie know you were here this time?"

"No, remember they don't know us yet in the future, and they can't until 2015," Craig/Steven said, smiling. "We're trusting that you can keep a secret until then. That's why we used fake names, just in case Duster remembered us here."

"This time travel stuff gives me a headache," Dawn said, trying to let herself believe that the cavern was real and that she wasn't alone here for the winter."

"It made us crazy as well," Janice said, "for the first few hundred years back in the past."

"Okay," Dawn said, shaking her head. "Now I really, really need to sit down."

Then, taking the glass with her, she just sat down on the floor of the general store, her back against the front counter.

Her hands were shaking so hard, she was spilling the water.

Both Steven and Janice came running around the counter to see if she were all right.

"So, you are telling me Madison isn't dead?" Dawn asked as they approached her.

Janice kneeled beside Dawn, took the glass away and handed it to Steven, then took Dawn's hand. Then she waited until Dawn looked her directly in her eyes.

"Madison is far, far from dead," Janice said.

"He will be there," Steven said, "standing beside you touching the machine in the crystal cavern, completely healthy, two minutes and fifteen seconds after you four left in 2014."

"I assume you have one of these?" Janice asked, smiling, as she pulled out a skeleton key.

Dawn nodded, stunned at the sight of that key.

And with that Dawn finally let herself feel it all, let it all come flooding in.

The worry, the grief, the uncertainty, and now the relief.

Madison was alive.

And somehow, in some future, in her future, she survived all this.

# PART FOUR

## CHAPTER THIRTY-SEVEN

**EVERY EVENING** for the entire winter, Dawn cooked for Susan and Craig, or as they are known in the future, Steven and Janice. She felt she owed them that much and so much more.

So much.

She missed Madison almost every second of every day, but Janice and Steven kept her sane and looking forward.

They spent every evening talking history, talking various aspects of how Steven and Janice used time travel, and how they met.

They were careful to not tell Dawn much about her own future. And about the future of the world between 2014 and 2015. But since the three of them had so much in common with their studies and with their love of history, they had more than enough to talk about every evening.

If the weather allowed, Steven and Janice made their way back to their own cabin about a quarter of a mile from Dawn's after dinner and conversation around the fire. But if the weather was rough, the snow blowing, they just crashed in Duster and Bonnie's bed.

Again, the house felt alive to Dawn.

And she felt far from alone.

There were very few people wintering in the valley around the town of Roosevelt. Most of them were either up at the Dewey Mine, working the mine, or scattered between Thunder City down the valley and eight miles up the valley to the headwaters of Monumental Creek.

Only one saloon stayed open over the winter and two working girls remained in town, staying in the back of the saloon. The saloon kept its doors closed so even if someone were playing the piano, it couldn't be heard.

The valley was silent except for the rumbling storms that seemed to come out of nowhere and shake everything.

Steven helped her with the horses, showing her how to brush them down and care for them in the extreme cold. The three of them built the horses a better shelter against the side of the cabin and on a few of the really cold nights she even brought the two horses in the back and put them in Madison's room, covering them with blankets.

She needed at least one of them to stay healthy until she headed back to Silver City next spring.

Besides, she was starting to like them and treat them like part of her family. She had named one John and the other Paul. She was going to miss them when she headed back to the future, especially Paul. He was a special horse to her.

On Christmas, the three of them put up a small tree and strung some popcorn as decorations. Janice had some Christmas decorations she had brought in with them on their first load to supply the store, and she surprised both Dawn and Steven by making the log cabin feel festive with the tin stars and colored paper decorations.

That Christmas Eve they sat in the living room around the fire just talking and feeling content with the world. Dawn had spent a lot of Christmas Eves alone. This one felt special.

She would rather have spent it with Madison, but she now believed that she would spend many Christmas Eves with him in the future.

And in other pasts.

At one point Steven raised a glass of bad eggnog they had tried to make and mostly failed. "To missing friends," he said. "And to our quick reunion."

Dawn drank to that, thinking how wonderful this evening would be if Madison were here sitting beside her.

Then she said, "And to learning how to make good eggnog in the past."

"Do we have to drink to that?" Janice asked. "This stuff really sucks."

And the wonderful Christmas Eve went on like that.

On a number of the conversations as the winter moved slowly past, Steven and Janice talked about how they had both died on different trips into the past.

"Always seems to be some freak accident or other," Steven said, shaking his head.

They said that if it were sudden, or like Madison died, it was simply like falling asleep and then suddenly finding yourself standing in the cavern with no idea how you got there from where you died.

But as Bonnie and Duster told us, and you have discovered, dying back here in the Old West is not often pleasant.

And something to be avoided.

Dawn had no disagreement with that.

"Madison might be a tad embarrassed when he arrives back in the crystal cave," Janice said.

"Why?" Dawn asked.

Janice smiled. "We didn't put any pants on him, remember?"

Dawn didn't think she would ever stop laughing at that.

A few evenings they also speculated about what had happened to Bonnie. It could have been anything. But nothing had appeared in the papers they had brought in before the valley shut down.

Dawn would find out the answer to that as well as soon as she disconnected the machine from the crystal wall.

The three of them spent one evening in early April talking about how Steven and Janice managed among the millions of timelines to hit the one Dawn was in.

"Well," Steven said, smiling at Janice. "We sort of aimed at it."

"And how do you do that?" Dawn asked. She wasn't sure she would understand the answer, but she needed to ask.

"We always move the crystal connections around some on the wall when we come back," Steven said. "So do Duster and Bonnie."

Dawn nodded at that.

"And since there are billions of timelines in those crystals on that cavern wall," Janice said, "we tried to figure out by watching the pattern Duster was using to move the connection about where he would have been on the wall a year before when you all took this trip."

"Now that was sneaky," Dawn said. "And you didn't tell him what you were doing, did you?"

"Of course not," Steven smiled.

"And since our decision to come back here was being made by us in millions of other timelines," Janice said, "and not made in millions of others, and you being here also existed in millions of timelines, we had a very small chance of cross-over."

"But a chance," Steven said. "Besides, this valley is so small and set in such a limited set amount of time in history, we figured we might have a little more of a chance to overlap your famous first trip."

"Took us ten tries here," Susan said, "before we saw this cabin being built and heard that four rich people were coming into the valley and knew we had finally overlapped and hit a common timeline."

"So what was the story of this trip here, with me living here without you two being here?"

Steven brushed that question away. "Other timelines now, for all of us. We are here in this timeline with you and in millions of others."

Dawn just shook her head. "Have I said how much this time travel stuff gives me a headache?"

Both of them laughed.

Susan patted her hand across the table. "A couple dozen times."

All of them laughed at that, something Dawn had not imagined she would be doing without Madison and Duster and Bonnie.

In fact, without Janice and Steven, she couldn't imagine surviving this winter.

She would have, she was sure of that.

But this form of survival was at least pleasant.

# CHAPTER THIRTY-EIGHT

**THE CLOSER THEY GOT** to the first of May, the more excited Dawn got. She knew that the passes started to really open in early May. So the long winter was almost over.

A few lone miners had made it in with snowshoes, but the passes were still too deep and covered to be safe for anything

else. But the excitement could almost be felt in the air.

Steven and Janice had decided to leave with her, go back to Silver City with her. And along the way they all planned on trying to figure out what happened to Bonnie as well.

"So you don't remember from the future what happened to her?" Dawn asked Janice at one point while they were doing dishes after dinner. Outside the light still filled the valley since the days were getting longer and longer.

"Never thought to ask her," Janice said. "Now we're just more curious than anything else."

"I'm real curious as well," Dawn said, laughing.

"Besides," Steven said from the table. "If three of the top historical researchers can't track down what happened to her while we are actually in the history we research, we need to worry."

"Real good point," Dawn said.

Over the months she and Janice had become very close friends. Both their interests in history centered on the human side, the lives of everyday people of all types. That was why she and Steven had come back and set up a general store, to get a chance to meet the most number of people.

Dawn really liked that idea.

Since they were planning on leaving with her when the passes opened, they had already sold the store to one of the saloon owners who had wintered in the valley.

They had also sold their cabin and Dawn had sold the house as well for a lot less than what it had cost Duster to build it. The terms of the sale allowed her to live in it until she left.

Steven and Janice had moved in with her, letting their cabin go with the store.

Dawn was really going to miss the house. With three of them living in here, the place felt wonderful again.

Dawn had maintained her journal, and now it was mostly full. She kept it tucked into an apron pocket still and always wore the apron over her clothes in the house and under her jacket when going out. No matter what happened, she was going to make sure that journal stayed with her into the future.

She had a great deal to tell Madison and she didn't want to miss any of it. And on top of that, she had already started writing her book and she needed to get that work back with her as well, since it was that book that would influence Janice and Steven to come here.

One afternoon, Janice showed her how she kept her research journal tucked into a slot in a girdle that fit the time period. "I've lost a few journals over all the trips, but not many."

Steven kept his small notebooks in a form of money belt, writing very small and in a form of shorthand that Janice said she didn't really understand at all. And then he kept them wrapped in a waterproof cloth that he had brought with him from the future.

"Toward the end of any trip back," Janice said, "when those books start getting full, we sleep with them on us."

Dawn understood that. She slept with her apron on at all times and kept a string from around it tied to her wrist when she took a bath.

Finally, on May 6th, 1903, the first real signs that the passes had opened appeared in the valley in the form of a large packtrain of horses and donkeys bringing in supplies for one of the saloons that had shut down all winter.

And as the weather stayed clear over the next few days, more and more people streamed into the valley until the silence of the long winter was pushed back by the sounds of construction again echoing off the high walls of the mountains.

They stayed for one more week, allowing all the trails to be completely open, then over dinner Steven looked at Janice and Dawn. "You two ready to head to Silver City?"

Dawn was surprised that she actually felt sad. She would have felt that after a long winter trapped in the snow and storms of a high mountain valley, she would have been ready to go.

But she really wasn't. Sure, she wanted to get back and see Madison again. And Bonnie and Duster.

But she had come to love this valley. Even after all the tragedy last fall, the place still felt magical to her.

But she loved Madison more.

It was clear that Janice didn't really want to leave either.

"We can come right back," Steven said, reaching over and touching his wife's hand. "I love it here as well."

"We leave tomorrow?" Dawn asked.

Steven nodded. "Tomorrow, at sunrise, if the weather breaks clear. We'll go up over Monumental and down the supply road into Stibnite and Yellow Pine. But we need to get up to the summit before the sun hits that trail and loosens the snow."

Janice and Dawn both nodded in agreement.

And the next morning the weather broke clear and as beautiful as Dawn could remember seeing.

# CHAPTER THIRTY-NINE

**DAWN HAD SPENT** most of April and the first part of May everyday riding her horse up and down in the valley. Often Janice and Craig came with her. With a long ride from central Idaho to southwestern Idaho ahead of them, it was better they all get used to riding again.

She often rode past Madison's grave where a white wooden cross marked the spot. It had a light covering of grass and weeds and a few small trees were trying to take root nearby.

She believed Madison would still be alive when she disconnected the crystal. So the grave seemed somehow off and now out of place.

Mostly, over the winter, she had just put away everything to do with his death, deciding that she would deal with it later, when she wasn't snowed into a valley with no place to go.

And with him holding her and telling her it was all right.

She had mostly packed the night before, and had cooked one last solid breakfast in the wonderful kitchen that morning in the dark.

Then, with only one look back at the cabin that had been her shelter all winter, they rode up the trail just as first light colored the sky.

"I'm going to get the plans from Duster and build that place again," she said to Janice who rode behind her.

"I don't blame you there," Janice said. "Amazingly comfortable."

"That it was," Dawn said.

The air was biting cold, but not as bad as it had been through most of the winter, so it actually felt fairly comfortable. Around them the sounds of men sawing logs and hammering and building echoed in the early morning.

The trail up the side of the mountain was cut down into the snow and at times she couldn't see over the edge of the drifts as the horses seemed to walk up through a trough.

That made that part of the climb so much better and less terror-filled.

Once they met a large packtrain, but they were close enough to the top that they managed to edge over into some deep snow uphill and let the twenty horses and mules go past with their heavy loads.

They rested in the trees on Monumental Summit and Dawn told Janice and Steven about the legend of the hotel up here.

"We've heard of it as well," Janice said, "but in all the timelines we've been back here, it's never been built."

"So information sometimes flows through timelines?" Dawn asked.

"Got to check with Bonnie and Duster about that," Steven said. "They are the mathematicians. I'm just a history professor."

"I asked them once about that," Janice said. "They said it did because history is always a fluid thing because of the nature of different timelines branching off of every decision."

"And nothing is determined," Dawn said. "Right?"

"That's right," Janice said. "I slipped on one trip and fell in Monumental Creek. Caught a nasty cold that turned into much worse and I died in our cabin."

"I'm very glad you went back," Dawn said.

"Didn't even think anything about not going back," Janice said.

"But she's awful careful around that creek," Steven said, smiling at his wife.

"Well, duh," Janice said.

They camped that night near Yellow Pine and the next day made it out and all the way to the railhead above Emmett where they asked about Bonnie.

No one there remembered seeing her, but when she came out the train was still not running because of the slide that had killed Duster.

The three of them decided that they would try to trace the path Bonnie would have taken instead of taking the train, since they were in no hurry.

In the small mill town of Emmett they checked out some of the local stores and a small hospital there, but no one had seen her and the papers had no record of anything happening to a woman last fall.

Dawn was glad that there were three of them doing the search. She was learning all sorts of tricks about researching in the past, tricks that they had already learned.

And along the way she kept adding more notes to her journal. In fact, around the campfire on a ridge above the Boise River that night, they all sat in silence scribbling in their journals.

Three historians traveling through history together.

She and Madison would most definitely need to travel with them at some point.

Then she realized what she had been thinking. She was making a lot of plans for her and Madison and he might not feel the same way.

She mentioned that to Janice and she just laughed. "Madison is going to remember going back to the cabin with Duster and the next thing is standing in the crystal cavern without pants. He's going to be in as much love with you as he was the day of his accident. You are the one who has had a year without him."

Steven nodded, glancing up from his journal. "The key is do you feel the same way after watching him die and burying him?"

"More so," Dawn said. "More so. When I see him I'm going to hug him so hard, I might break his ribs."

"Might want to let him put on some pants first," Steven said, laughing.

"Sure wish we could see that," Janice said.

Dawn was about to ask why not, then she realized why not. Janice and Steven didn't leave the crystal cavern until a year in the future real time.

Damn.

She had lost Madison for the winter. Now she was going to lose her two new friends for a year.

She didn't like that one bit.

# CHAPTER FORTY

**FOLLOWING THE TRAIL** they thought Bonnie would have followed, the next day they stopped and asked around in Caldwell, Idaho, a small farming and railroad town about thirty miles to the west of Boise.

No one in the hotels or stores remembered seeing anyone of her description come through. It wasn't until they checked with a blacksmith and described her horse that they found a lead.

The blacksmith remembered the horse because it had to be put down because it had shattered a leg. He seemed to remember something about the rider being taken to a hospital.

A hospital in 1903 wasn't a place anyone wanted to be. Dawn knew that.

The blacksmith gave them directions to it and where it sat up on a slight ridge above the town.

The hospital was a wide wooden building on the top of a ridge overlooking a nearby cemetery. It was painted white, but the paint had pealed and the sign was barely standing.

Just walking up toward the main door, Dawn could smell piss and human waste and death.

It was awful. So much so it gagged her before she even opened the front door.

Dawn could see through a window in the front door that the insides were one room with some curtains pulled to separate some of the patients.

Steven shook his head and declined to go inside.

"I'll watch the horses," he said and turned to move them a little more distance away from the building.

"Don't touch anything in there," Janice said, wrinkling her nose. "No wonder people thought for a long time that going to hospital meant you were going to die. You actually were."

Dawn could only agree to that.

Janice and Dawn opened the front door and Dawn felt like she was wading into the smell.

The found a woman in a stained white nurse's uniform sitting at a wooden desk to the right of the front door.

Dawn asked about Bonnie by name and the woman looked up surprised.

"You are her first visitors. Family or friends?"

"Family," Dawn said, glancing at Janice, who nodded. She was looking as green and sick with the smell as Dawn was feeling.

The nurse nodded and took Dawn's name, then pointed to the bed in the far back of the building near a window with curtains.

Both Dawn and Janice headed for the back of the room.

They had to pass at least thirty other patients along the way and Dawn refused to look at any of them. Luckily, it had been some time since she had eaten, or she might have thrown up right there from the smell.

Bonnie lay with her eyes closed, facing the light. Her long brown hair was brushed and she seemed moderately clean. But she was frighteningly thin.

Dawn knew at once that she was just wasting away.

"Remember, I'm Susan," Janice whispered as they approached and Dawn nodded.

"Bonnie?" Dawn asked, her voice almost shaking to see the strong woman she had known laying here like this.

Bonnie stirred and turned her head, opening her eyes slowly.

Then her face brightened as she saw Dawn.

"Oh, my, God," Bonnie said, her voice hoarse. "You made it?"

She reached out a frail hand, far, far too thin and Dawn took it carefully.

"I made it," Dawn said. "You remember Susan from the general store?"

It clearly took Bonnie a moment, then she nodded and smiled at Susan.

Then Bonnie looked back at Dawn. "Did Madison die?"

"He did," Dawn said, nodding. "About two weeks after you left. Susan and her husband helped me bury him."

"I am so sorry," Bonnie said.

"It's fine," Dawn said, lightly squeezing Bonnie's hand. "What happened to you?"

"Following a trail down through a gulley," Bonnie said. "Horse stumbled and next thing I know a farmer was hauling me in here. My back is broken they tell me."

Dawn nodded. Then she glanced at Janice before going on.

"Susan and her husband are going to help me get up to Silver City. They are thinking of trying a little mining there. As soon as I get things settled there, I'll come back for you."

"Thank you," Bonnie said, taking a deep breath. "I thought I was going to die in this bed."

Dawn smiled and squeezed her hand. "Not if I can help it. See you soon."

"Soon," Bonnie said, smiling.

Dawn smiled at Bonnie and then she and Janice almost ran for the door.

Outside the three of them mounted up.

"Isn't there a hot springs about ten miles from here?" Dawn asked, "If memory serves."

It had been the second hot springs she and Madison had spent time in, and they had made love in it just as they had in the first one.

"There is," Janice said.

"Good," Dawn said. "Because I got to get this smell off of me. And then we got to get to the mine and get Bonnie out of there."

"I second that," Janice said.

"That bad?" Steven asked.

"Worse," Janice said.

"Can I ride in the lead?" Steven asked, turning his horse. "I honestly don't want to be downwind from either of you."

With that they rode hard for the hot springs.

At the springs they stopped and had a late lunch while getting cleaned up. Then they rode hard until it was too dark to ride safely any more.

Then the next morning, as the sun was just starting to pretend to color the sky, they started off again.

In ten hours, if they rode hard, they would be in Silver City.

And then she would get Bonnie out of that nightmare. And bring back Duster and Madison.

And once again kiss the man of her dreams.

## CHAPTER FORTY-ONE

**THEY REACHED SILVER CITY** by three in the afternoon. The snow still covered the hills and it was cold. Clouds filled the sky, but it didn't look like it was going to storm hard. Dawn felt relieved at that. She was going to hate the idea that they would be stuck almost within sight of the mine by storms.

"We walk from here," Steven said, pulling up at the hotel. "Get your saddle bags and everything else off the horses."

For a moment Dawn was going to ask why, then she realized that they couldn't vanish and leave the horses roaming around the mine. That would draw too many suspicions and maybe get someone searching the area around the mine.

None of them wanted that.

Dawn patted Paul goodbye, feeling very sad that she was going to be without the animal she had taken such care of all winter long. She was going to miss that horse.

Janice and Dawn went in and checked into the hotel, paying cash for two days, while Steven took the horses down to a blacksmith and basically sold them cheaply, telling the Smithy that he needed the money to buy equipment to work a mine that he and his sister and wife had bought up on War Eagle and were going to try to reopen.

The crystal cave wasn't anywhere near War Eagle Mountain. It was across the valley on Florida Mountain, so if anyone actually noticed they were missing and started to search for them, they would be looking in the wrong place and on the wrong mountain.

Dawn was certain that Bonnie and Duster would have taught her and Madison these tricks if they were here. Thank heavens Janice and Steven were.

Dawn wasn't certain, after being alone all winter in that cabin, if she would have thought of any of it.

The old hotel felt rundown and smelled musty and damp, rotting wood. They stayed in their rooms until dark, then started up the trail when no one was looking, going out the back door of the hotel and around on some side streets.

Silver City this early in the year and this late in its history, had very few people around. Only two saloons were even open and they sounded tired from what Dawn could hear.

And they didn't even have pianos.

Roosevelt was at its peak. Silver City was twenty years past its top days and declining by the year.

They had to rest twice on the way up the hill carrying all their gear on a trail that thankfully had been packed down. They really didn't need to take all their gear back with them, but they didn't dare leave it in the hotel room either.

They needed to vanish without a trace. That was the key.

The trail turned on the ridge right about where the Cadillac would be parked in the future and went up the hill. The last hundred yards across that same open slope she had crossed in the heat was now covered in knee-deep snow. Dawn was afraid of it letting go, but somehow the snow held on the hillside and they made it across to the flat top of the mine tailing.

When they did finally reach the mine, it was snowing lightly. From the looks of it, the snow would cover their tracks easily in an hour or two. A large drift of snow had built up against one side of the old mining shack.

"Who gets to do the honors?" Steven asked as all three of them stood there in the dark and snow, panting from the climb.

Dawn held up the key that had been a major beacon over the winter for her.

"Let me," she said, her hands shaking in the cold.

Both Janice and Steven nodded that she should go ahead.

Dawn turned to face the mine and then, as Duster had showed her what to do a lifetime ago, she twisted the head of the key.

The rock moved back silently.

"God, it worked," Dawn said, her knees almost giving out from pure relief.

"That is does," Janice said, easing Dawn forward.

All three of them entered the dark cave.

Steven hit the button and the door slid closed, plunging them into complete darkness before the light came up and Dawn could see the mine tunnel stretching out in front of her.

"Holy mother, it's real," she said breathlessly.

She felt like she wanted to just sit and cry. A large part of her had just not believed this place actually existed.

"It really is," Janice said, holding Dawn's arm as the three of them headed down the mine tunnel.

This time Dawn just walked through the holograms without closing her eyes.

And then they all went through the outer cavern and into the crystal cavern, still carrying all their stuff.

The fantastic cavern was as amazing as Dawn remembered it. Actually more so. All the walls glowed with a light of their own and the crystal where Duster had hooked up the machine earlier had grown into a huge cluster of crystals.

Dawn just stood and stared, her mouth open, not really believing this.

The room was real.

The machine sitting on the table was real.

And that both excited and scared Dawn more than she wanted to think about.

In just a moment she would be back in the future, in her own time, with the man she had come to love and then watched die.

Janice had assured her that Madison would love her as well.

And be very much alive.

But now Dawn would find out for sure.

It had been a very long winter since he died.

# CHAPTER FORTY-TWO

"REMEMBER," STEVEN SAID, "to not tell Duster and Bonnie about us."

"Wow, that's going to be hard to do," Dawn said, frowning at her two new friends.

"At least not until we come back from this trip," Janice said. "In just over a year. You can't tell us that we know you either until we come back from this trip."

"So I'm going to meet you before you meet me?" Dawn asked.

"We can't say one way or the other," Janice said, smiling. "Just remember that as far as this trip for you went, Craig and Susan helped you. And you left them in Silver City. Duster and Bonnie will understand completely in just over a year."

"So when we unhook that wire, I'm going to go back to 2014," Dawn said, "and you two will end your trip in 2015. Right?

Steven and Janice both nodded.

"What day exactly, and at what time?" Dawn asked.

"Three-thirty in the afternoon," Janice said, "July 19th, 2015."

"And no time will have passed for you at all from this moment until then?" Dawn asked.

"True," Janice said. "But over a year of real time will have passed for you. I hope you remember us."

All Dawn could do was laugh at that.

There was no way ever she could forget them.

Ever.

They had saved her life, kept her sane, made the winter enjoyable, and kept the magic in her favorite place.

She hugged Steven, then gave Janice an extra long hug.

Then she stepped back. "Thank you both for your friendship and helping me survive."

They both nodded.

"Everyone got their notebooks?" Janice asked. "We all have books to write."

Dawn patted her apron she wore under her two coats. The notebook was still there.

Steven patted his notebook as well and smiled.

Dawn picked up all of her possessions, most of them tucked into her saddlebag.

She still had on her heavy coat and Madison's long coat and his hat.

"Have a great year," Janice said to Dawn, smiling.

Then Janice reached over and pulled the wire from the machine.

And the next moment Janice and Steven were gone.

And Dawn found herself standing, touching the machine, beside Madison.

Duster and Bonnie were on the other side, also touching the machine.

"Oh, my God," Bonnie said, lighting up. "You made it!"

Dawn dropped her saddlebags and turned and looked at the man of her dreams. He was staring at her, with a very puzzled look on his face.

He was as handsome and healthy as ever.

It had worked.

It really had worked.

She was back in her own time.

She hugged Madison and then kissed him hard.

Then she pushed him back and looked over at Bonnie, smiling.

"I did make it, didn't I?"

Bonnie had just kissed Duster just as long and as hard as Dawn had kissed Madison. She just laughed, her smile filling her face from ear-to-ear.

Duster was looking very confused, considering that his wife was wearing a very thin hospital gown that smelled awful.

Duster had on a suit coat, a tie, and no pants.

None at all.

And Dawn looked like a person who belonged in the Old West in her cowboy hat, long coat, and saddlebags.

And she did.

She knew without a doubt that she did.

# CHAPTER FORTY-THREE

**AFTER DAWN** kissed Madison again, long and even harder than the first time, she took off his coat and handed it to him.

He looked puzzled for a moment until Dawn pointed to the fact that he had no pants.

He turned a bright red and took the coat, slipping it on quickly.

"Oops," Bonnie said and then laughed.

"Just never thought about it," Dawn said, smiling at Bonnie and Duster.

"Someone's going to have to explain to me what exactly happened," Madison said, shaking his head as everyone laughed. "Last thing I remember was breaking my leg and Duster getting me back to the cabin."

"Explain what happened to me as well," Duster said. "Last thing I remember I was dozing off on a train."

"There's an entire winter I don't know about either," Bonnie said, smiling at her husband. "I was stuck all winter in a hospital in Caldwell."

"Oh, god," Duster said, a frown crossing his face as he gently touched his wife.

"I'm fine," she said. "Gave me time to do a lot of thinking all about the nature of the echoes through timelines. We'll talk about that later. What I need right now is a change of clothes and a long, hot shower."

"I think all of us would agree to that idea," Duster said, "Especially a shower. A very good idea."

Bonnie just took him and kissed him hard. "Next time, don't fall into a stupid river."

"Is that what happened?" Duster asked as the four of them headed for the big supply cavern.

Dawn could only smile and keep her arm firmly around Madison as they walked. She just kept staring up at the man of her dreams until he finally took his hat off her head and kissed her again long and hard.

She just let herself go into his arms and his kiss.

When they finally reached the kitchen area, they learned that the supply cavern was also decked out with a modern restroom and shower with water being pumped in from a well.

They let Bonnie go first while Madison and Dawn sat at the table, not even talking. He just kept starting at her and smiling and she kept smiling back and squeezing his hand.

Duster finally went to get a change of clothes from the other side of the cavern.

When Bonnie came out, dressed in 2014 clothing and drying her hair, she let Dawn go next.

The modern hot shower felt wonderful, and putting on her own modern clothes also felt great. More than likely she took

too long, but she didn't care. Time seemed to be relative anymore.

When she came out both Madison and Duster had put back on the clothes they were wearing when they got to the cavern earlier that same morning, yet a lifetime before. Madison was sitting at the kitchen table with a glass of iced tea in front of him.

Bonnie and Duster were both standing in the kitchen, their hips touching, working on some sort of lunch for all of them.

"Now that we're all back," Madison said, "someone want to start the story of what exactly happened?"

Dawn walked over to him and reached out her hand. "First, I've got to see what's outside."

"Me too now that you mention it," Madison said, standing.

"Good idea," Bonnie said, turning to smile at Dawn. "Lunch in fifteen minutes."

She and Madison walked in silence back down the mine tunnel, then after checking to make sure no one was out there, she opened the big metal door and stepped into the hot summer air.

After a winter of being cold, that felt fantastic, she had to admit.

And a little shocking.

She had forgotten how warn it had been on the day they came up here.

She walked to the edge of the mine tailings and looked down. Below her Silver City was only a few buildings of a ghost town. Trees again covered the once bare hills. And the Cadillac sat parked across the slope, the same slope she had just crossed in deep snow what seemed like just a moment before.

"Amazing," Madison said, squeezing her hand as they looked down. "We were only gone for a couple of minutes."

"And a lifetime," Dawn said.

Madison looked at her with real concern and worry. "Bonnie said you spent the entire winter in the valley alone. Are you all right?"

"Now that you are standing here beside me again, I'm perfect," Dawn said.

And she felt that way as well.

"Do you want to go back?" Madison asked, clearly worried.

"Are you asking me on a date, Professor Rogers?"

He laughed. "I suppose a little trip back into the past could be a date, Professor Edwards," he said. "But I was hoping for a little more."

"More?" she asked, smiling up into the handsome face that she had dreamed about every night all winter long.

"Not just a date," he said. "How about a lifetime?"

She kissed him long and hard. The hot air of the afternoon surrounded them with the silence of the mountain.

Then she finally pushed him back and said, "No, not for just a lifetime, because as I discovered, that can pass very fast."

"Then what?" he asked, smiling at her.

"A hundred lifetimes," she said. "Maybe a thousand. One here in the present, the rest in the past."

"I love the sounds of that," he said. "And I love you. When do we start?"

"How about after lunch?" she said as they turned and headed back into the old mine.

"As long as I'm with you, that sounds perfect," he said.

"As long as I'm with you, it does," she said. "But in the next lifetime, try to stay alive, would you?"

He laughed that wonderful laugh and then said as they headed deep into the mountain and toward the past and their future once again. "I'll do my best."

~

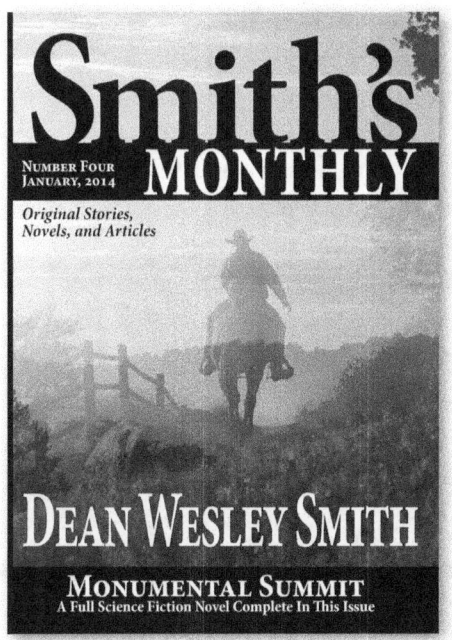

# The Story From THUNDER MOUNTAIN Continues....

**Dawn and Madison and Duster and Bonnie all continue on in the novel MONUMENTAL SUMMIT**

**And that's not counting Janice and Steven and new characters...**

Subscribe at www.smithsmonthly.com

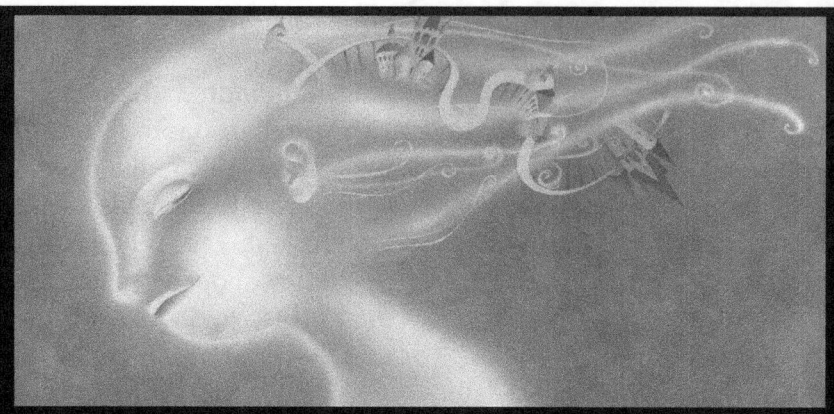

# Poems by DEAN WESLEY SMITH

## Nostalgia Factor

At twenty years of age, no one talks about the old days,
about ex-wives, bad jobs, missing friends,
fun trips, bad experiences, great meals,
or spending a night in an airport.

At thirty you look back ten times more than you used to,
remembering the single days, the wild college days,
remembering when your kid was in diapers,
remembering when you were still really skinny.

At forty, the drifting back through time uses up more words,
at least twenty-five percent of all conversations
with any friend, either old or new,
the stories far more interesting than the reality ever was.

At fifty, seventy-five-percent of all conversations
are about the past, either yours or your friend's.
The future is too known, too short, too scary
to think or talk about much.

At sixty and beyond the nostalgia factor drops,
due to bad memory, too-often-told stories,
and the reality of the fact you can't go back.
Stories about death and dying take up the slack.